TAKE-OUT CITY

TAKE-OUT CITY

Cynthia Lawrence

Carroll & Graf Publishers, Inc.
New York

FIC

First Carroll & Graf edition 1993

Carroll & Graf Publishers, Inc.
260 Fifth Avenue
New York, NY 10001

Library of Congress Cataloging-in-Publication Data

Lawrence, Cynthia.
   Take-out city / Cynthia Lawrence. — 1st Carroll & Graf ed.
     p.   cm.
   ISBN 0-88184-942-1 : $18.95
   1. Los Angeles (Calif.)—Fiction. I. Title.
PS3562.A9115T34   1993
813'.54—dc20   92-47583
                                                CIP

Manufactured in the United States of America

My gratitude to my mother
and to Anne Doyle, my friend and reader.
Thanks to you both for cheering me on
and for gasping in all the right places.

Prologue

*W*hat a giggle when she finds out. Maybe she'll faint. Maybe she'll tear her clothes and scratch her face with those long red claws of hers. She doesn't care how fat and sloppy she is as long as she can go to Teresa every week and get her claws sharpened and looking like she dipped them in blood. So what if I bite my nails, he doesn't mind, he says my eyes are the identical blue like Princess Di, he says, don't let her make you crazy. He says just smile and tell her you're thinking about Our Lady, and you don't go to Confession because you're working too hard to have anything to confess, and don't shout at her when she says everyone is sinful, and so what if Mrs. Doyle looks at me funny when she comes downstairs (who is she when her son has so few manners, he ducked his head again when I tried to say a friendly hello, wait till he finds out). He says I'm sleek like a racehorse, he always says that was the turn-on the first time he saw me, remember? I'll never look fat and old like her, I don't eat in front of her anymore, always shoveling it in. It's a fasting day I tell her and I don't care if she believes me, she believes anything if you sprinkle it with incense. Maybe I believe anything if he says it in that soft wheedly voice of his that sounds like the movies I watch*

when I'm pacing the floor at three in the morning and they've run out of American movies. And I wonder if he really loves me, and I think about how to make sure he loves me, please God, let him love me, Mother Mary let him love me, oh God, make him love me.

Chapter One

I tend to carry back unsavory food from foreign airports. A damp French pastry wrapped in a napkin, a slab of overripe Gorgonzola, anything to use up the shillings, pence, lira at the bottom of my purse. This time, I nibbled at a clammy Scotch egg as the plane from London broke through the cloud cover over Los Angeles. It was two in the morning, but the headlights and the freeways below glowed and looped like gold party ribbon, tying the darkened city into a homecoming present.

Some present. There was still the traveler's penance ahead: immigration, customs, the luggage scramble. Finally, there would be Aunt Sadie, ginger hair curled, lipstick impeccable even at that horrendous hour. Really heartwarming. There are times when even a woman of the '90s needs a welcoming, flag-waving, hugging '40s aunt.

I finished the Scotch egg. Maybe I needed that last taste of Europe to fortify myself for Aunt Sadie's usual questions: Did you meet someone? Is he American? Does he have a job? When will you see him again? Aunt Sadie, Aunt Sadie, Delphi was inspiring, I saw eternity in the digs in Crete, the

London theatre is brilliant this year. Well, yes, I went out a few times with this very nice schoolteacher from Duluth, but he was going on to Cairo. Etc., etc.

This time there was no quiz. I was relieved; she looked tired, I felt fuzzy. She kept to small talk for the small hours. The local weather (fair). The traffic (fierce as ever). I was just a little surprised when she suggested I stay at her house for what was left of the night.

"After all, Catherine, I promised your mother I would always look after you, and I keep my promises." She did, too, but I craved my own bed.

It was nearly dawn when I kissed her good night, with promises to call when I woke, no matter what time. I didn't even notice the urgency in her voice.

Home is a fifties Spanish-style apartment house, about a semiprecious stone's throw east of Beverly Hills. A no-name neighborhood of old wrought iron and green lawns, with a decent dry cleaners, a Volvo mechanic, a Chinese take-out, and two bistros trying to recoup heavy investments in raspberry vinegar and goat cheese.

That Sunday morning of my return, I slept late, pushed aside nearly a month of mail that my landlord had left on the kitchen table, and opened the fresh can of whole bean coffee I had left for my return. There was another open can of coffee, a dreary supermarket brand going stale, in the cupboard. Aunt Sadie had my key, maybe she had brought the can to stock my cupboard. That didn't make sense, but I dismissed the matter as a small mystery. Small? I had read enough damsel-in-distress thrillers; at this point, any heroine worth her smelling salts would have said: *Had I but known.* Poor coffee, to me, is almost a sign of poor character, and anyone who knows me well knows this.

The phone rang. It was Aunt Sadie, her voice slightly hushed, the way it is when delivering news of import or delicacy: a birth or death in the family, or the impending third marriage of a second cousin (junior in age to me).

"You're up" was all she said. "I'll be right over."

While I waited, I put the answering machine on rewind and played back weeks of phone messages. The personal calls were near the end of the tape: best buddy Marcy, among other friends, calling to welcome me home; Nick, my partner, saying, glad you're back, babe, get ready to hit the decks running on Monday morning; Gil, my ex-husband, hoping for my sake I hadn't spent too much money; Winston, who hadn't phoned in two months, explaining that he'd decided after all not to go back to Anita and that he'd call me again, which he had. Then there were the siren songs: VISA desired me, so did a time-sharing club; I could have my typewriter serviced, the vacuum cleaner fixed, the carpets cleaned, all at amazingly low prices (did they care that I had walked among the Olympian gods?). The ballet wanted my patronage as did three Equity-waver theaters; UCLA was pushing season tickets for football; and so on.

All comfortable and familiar, except for two messages. The first said, in a jovial male voice, "Katie? (*Nobody* calls me Katie. I'm Catherine or Cat.) This is Harv, remember me? You helped me toast the eighth race, we finished off a bottle of champagne. Yeah, that's me. Oh, well, you're not home. I'll try again next time I'm in town. I have a hunch you'll bring me luck. 'Bye, love!"

I would have thought Harv had misdialed, but there was a second caller. "Hi, Katie, Baxter here. The guy who does magic tricks—that's the one. It's Tuesday evening, you said you'd be home. This is (he repeated my phone number), isn't it? Or, hey, did you give me the wrong number? No, you were too hot to do that. I'll call again in a couple of weeks. Keep happy. Stay sexy."

I was still puzzling it out when Aunt Sadie arrived. She was a tropical delight in lime-green flowered chiffon and matching lime pumps, her hair firmly fixed with super-hold spray and looking as bright as if it had been buffed to a high gloss. She patted my cheek and then hugged me for good measure. I knew she missed me during the month I was gone, but she wasn't into implanting guilt so she'd never tell. Not that she's above scheming to ensure my happiness. Aunt Sadie is childless and, since Uncle Art died five years ago, I have become her closest kin and ongoing project.

She flits; I put one foot in front of the other and advance with caution. In looks and temperament, I take after my father's side of the family. I have his Scot's angularity: all simple lines and sturdiness. My hair is black, thick, and tends to look as if I'd forgotten my comb. I have hazel eyes and decent cheekbones. The light dusting of freckles across my cheeks is not enough, thank heaven, to make me look like Raggedy Ann. Since my career involves food—gorgeous food in big quantities—I do try to work out regularly. All considering, my body is okay, but Aunt Sadie has *curves*.

She said, "I wish I could stay with you all day today, honey."

"Why should you stay? I haven't unpacked. I'll have to do laundry, and Nick called, he expects me early. I vastly appreciate last night, but why don't we catch up at dinner this week?"

She shook her head. "No, we must talk now, for a few minutes, it's important. Mr. Kelsey, my new friend, is taking me to brunch. We're meeting at the restaurant, so I could stop here first."

A new friend, eh? After sad years of mourning Uncle Art, Aunt Sadie had discovered that she also missed companionship and male attention. Gradually, she found new gentlemen friends, *beaux* would be a more exact word. They paid court to her, took her to brunch or out dancing. Why, I'd seen morose widowers charmed into becoming nimble-toed gallants. More than once, I'd wished I could shimmy like my Aunt Sadie. Today, though, she was subdued.

"I don't know how to say this," she began.

"Just plunge in."

She hesitated, then plunged.

"While you were gone, there was a murder in the house next door. A young woman was strangled with her own pantyhose."

Oh.

"And—this is so dreadful—the police think the murderer may have stayed in your apartment."

I sat down.

"But the police wouldn't take fingerprints here until you came back. They said, most times it's someone you know, that you gave him the key. Did you give him your key?"

"Who?"

"I don't know."

"Neither do I."

This had echoes of Abbott and Costello. I took a breath.

"Aunt Sadie, why don't you start at the beginning?"

"He didn't seem like a murderer. He left chocolate ice cream all over your refrigerator."

I gasped. "You met him?"

"No, thank heaven! But I found the ice cream. It was a mess. It was all melting." Her voice wobbled. "I looked at that drippy chocolate and got chills up my spine. Because I had helped you clean out that refrigerator, and it was empty the day you left!"

"Auntie, please sit down. I'll get us coffee."

"The *coffee!* Yes, that was the other thing. There was a pot of fresh coffee on the counter."

Ah, the mystery coffee. I dropped a teaspoon and it clattered rat-a-tat on the floor.

"It happened just two days after you left. Remember, you asked me to come by and see who was taking in your mail while your landlord was on vacation. Well, Betty Hansen next door stopped me. That teen-age son of hers had hung around the police, and he knew all the gruesome details."

"About my apartment?"

"No, no, about the murder. But they both had heard someone in your apartment the night you left and the next night. This house is not as solid as you like to think it is." She raised one carefully penciled eyebrow in disapproval.

"The Hansens told me they can always hear your shower running. And those two nights they heard—it and *him!*"

"Did they call the police?"

"They assumed you gave your key to a friend. And with your landlord away, and Mrs. Cappelli in front—who's no help at all—looking after things, they didn't do anything. Until the murder."

"Who was she?"

"The poor thing. She was a waitress at that coffee shop on Sunset Boulevard. Fifties Flavor, that's the name."

I knew the place. The waitresses dress like 1950's car hops and serve five-dollar burgers and four-dollar malts. Mondays, they have James Dean lookalike nights. I give them six months. I said as much to my aunt.

"You're a food snob. It could be fun. But, anyway, the police think that someone followed her home from the res-taurant—or was waiting near her carport. And then stran-gled her."

The sun at the kitchen window was bright and reassur-ing. I walked over and looked out. It wasn't much of a view but I could see the carport belonging to the apartment house next door. The only thing that appeared sinister was Sylvester, the tough grey-striped tabby with the chewed ear. As usual, he was up to no good. He sat on the fence that separated the two buildings, flexing his claws at a squirrel climbing the bark of an ancient plum tree that shaded the carport.

That tree. A thick trunk, dense and leafy branches. It

would give shelter at night to anyone who lurked behind it. I had always thought the tree cast too many shadows, swallowed up too much light.

Turning away, I asked, "Did you talk to the police?"

"That same day. I called from this apartment and spoke to a nice Detective Velasquez. At least, he seemed very nice, even though he didn't *do* much. He came by, looked around, then gave me his card. He wants you to call."

The card said he was Detective David R. Valasquez of Homicide. I asked, "Did he really think the murderer stayed here?"

"Well, it was obvious that someone had."

Someone. Who'd taken over my living space. Someone. Who ate ice cream and fixed coffee in *my* kitchen. Who'd possibly followed my neighbor home and murdered her. Did he then hurry across the way and cleanse himself in my shower? Did he rest from his labors in my bed? And, how did he enter?

Aunt Sadie confirmed that it probably was a key. According to the police, there was no sign of forced entry. I promised myself to change the lock tomorrow.

It was time for Aunt Sadie to leave. She hugged me and got my promise to call her, day or night, if I was afraid. Then, trailing chiffon and the heady scent of Obsession, she was gone into the sunny morning.

I assured myself it was more jet lag than fear that made me feel as limp as a noodle on a steam table. I decided to use my small store of energy to unpack. Afterward—if I chose to give in to worry—I would think about this night intruder. Gathering my tattered wits, I headed for the bedroom. I was wearing the travel robe I'd pulled from my suitcase. I removed it, put it on the laundry pile, and reached in my closet for the robe I'd left, with usual forethought, washed and waiting for my return.

It was a champagne-colored robe, not enhanced at all by a chocolate-colored stain about the size of a pancake on the bodice. The stain was lighter at the edges, as if it had spread when someone tried to wash it out. *Someone.* Who came into my apartment and slopped chocolate ice cream on my robe.

The phone was ringing. I dropped the robe as if it had suddenly begun to bleed.

"Hello?"

"Katie, I'm at the airport. This is Warren, remember? I told you I'd come in a day early so we could *really* get acquainted."

"Um, Warren . . ."

"Listen, I'm on my way to pick up a rental car. Just give me your address . . ."

Warren was out of luck. He could have been Warren, Future King of Ruretania, but to me he was just one more stranger on the prowl. Without even saying, Welcome to L.A., I slammed down the receiver.

bus who stopped for coffee, then followed the girl home. They picked him up in West Hollywood, after he mugged a homosexual who invited him into an alley. The police found the waitress's inscribed gold locket on him. His name was Harley Brown, he was wanted in Oklahoma, and they hadn't asked him if he liked chocolate ice cream.

Detective Velasquez was older, stockier, with the wary eyes of a man who had edged into too many dark alleys. His smile was easy, though, and he showed a decent amount of concern.

"It doesn't seem as if anyone's out to harm you. Most likely, whoever it was needed a place to hang out, and knew you'd be gone. Take some time and think about it," he said. "And let us know if anything else happens out of the ordinary."

That's it? That's it! No investigation? No lining up of suspects?

"Well, okay, sure," I said.

"And get a better lock," offered Detective Wang.

"Oh, I will."

They left and I sat down and thought it over. I thought about friends, acquaintances, and strangers. I thought so hard and so unsuccessfully, I felt as if I was struggling with a blob of dough that refused to rise no matter how I punched and kneaded. That made me hungry, so I fixed breakfast while I waited for the locksmith, and finally went to work.

Angela

My red bra. He loved it. He said, ooh, it makes me want to grab you and never let go. He kept kissing and biting all over each cup until I started to scream. I never knew a red bra would be such a turn-on. Next day I bought some other colors, too, black, of course, and shiny sapphire blue that you could see through, and I thought the best was white with lace from Christian Dior, *very* French, like bridal but low cut and it pushed you up, but I wasn't nervous anymore because he said he loved my breasts, because he never knew what to do with big ones because you couldn't really get your hands around them and, I admit, I giggled when he said that because that was never my problem, I was practically flat, flat, but he said he could cup his hands around them and oh, he did, and I never knew I could feel hot and shiver at the same time. I bought two more red styles, one was so low cut you could see my nipples pushing up like half-moons and the other was lace and it hooked in front. I imagined his tanned hands unhooking it, and that was a turn-on, too, like the romance novels at the drugstore, his big-rough-but-tender hands against her white-delicate-flawless skin, well, maybe I'm not flawless but who ever thought it would happen to me? I told him, from now on call me at the office, my apartment is being painted. Why didn't he call today? Not that I'm worried, but I can't sleep, I can't sleep.

Chapter Three

As I drove into Westwood that sunny morning, I could almost imagine its 1930's village charm was intact: the low-rise, pastel Spanish-style buildings still cater to a college population with shops that offer chiliburgers and friendship rings, UCLA sweatshirts and book sales; sharing the tiled roofs are the boutiques, haughty as truffles in a stew, serving the pricey canyons of Bel-Air and, more recently, the million-dollar condos on Wilshire Boulevard. But the Village is under siege. Luxury hi-rise developers paw the ground and howl around the nervous boundaries of Westwood, while youth gangs surge into the town on weekend evenings, sometimes shooting at each other (or an out-of-luck passerby) on the sidewalks between the movie houses and the frozen yogurt shops. Nowadays, UCLA's Bruin bear mascot might well be sporting a Rolex watch and a Uzi. I could weep.

My office on the floor above Dellacasa's Trattoria is the shape of a lasagna pan, and not much bigger. But it's airy and efficient, and I love it. There's just enough space for my desk and chair, a couple of upholstered client chairs, a file cabinet and a bookcase stocked with party menus, wedding cake pictures, and portfolios of artistic appetizers for the rich and famished. Nick has donated an oversize oil painting of Sorrento for one wall. On the others are our credentials as successful Southern California restaurateurs: pictures of celebrities with inscriptions to Nick or to me. "Osso Bucco just like mama's," from Vance Cunningham, born Vito Calucci in the Bronx; "What an evening—my Oscar, your pasta!" from a screenwriter's postceremony party. And more.

A beaming Nick met me with a breath-defying hug. He is strong, solid, and though his curly black hair now has streaks of grey, he moves with the quickness learned on some tough Brooklyn streets.

Business was good, he said. We'd go over the schedule, then Rosie would join us for lunch. My aunt Sadie had called; she was worried that I hadn't arrived yet. Was anything wrong?

Over fettucine and salad, I gave them my little gifts from Italy and Greece and then, though I hadn't planned to, told them about the mysterious food in my kitchen, the phone calls, the detectives's visit this morning.

"Catherine," said Rosie, concern making lines on her smooth olive skin, "you shouldn't be in that place alone. It's spooky. You come stay with us until you find another apartment." Nick agreed, but I said no, I felt safe with the new lock installed.

Before I dug into the pile on my desk, I returned Aunt Sadie's call. It was more of the same: Were there any problems last night? Shouldn't you move? She was worried about me. And so on.

I was glad to turn to the matter of the TinyToddlerTogs annual picnic. Half of the employees in the factory were now Latino; about another third were from Asia and the Pacific. The owners were two rounded, balding identical twins named Nat and Art, the Lewis brothers. We had our annual serious discussion about the new ethnicity in Los Angeles cuisine, and how it impacted workers in the garment industry. Nat argued for tacos, refried beans, and chow mein. Art defended the All-American picnic and its role in bringing newcomers into the cultural mainstream. We settled (once more) on hot dogs, barbecued chicken, all the trimmings and, as a trial balloon: enchiladas.

It was late afternoon by the time we decided how to make the seamstresses's stomachs safe for democracy. I returned a few phone calls, looked over the list of prospects I was to contact this week, and left to meet my friend Marcy for dinner. Actually, I stopped at the supermarket salad bar, heaped up two plastic containers, and headed for home. Marcy had offered to bring over the wine. I was glad for the company, even more so when I checked my phone machine to find that luckless Warren had called again.

"You're a bitch," said Warren. He sounded slightly drunk.

"Remember, you came on to me. I didn't even look at you at first, you're not that much to look at. Am I supposed to crawl because I couldn't get back to L.A. last weekend? Uh, uh.

"If I had your address I'd tell you in person, bitch. S'okay, I'm leaving town tomorrow. Maybe I'll see you again sometime at the Paddock. You'll be sitting at the bar, in that tight black leather skirt. Just don't forget. You owe me one." End of message.

Chapter Four

I rewound the tape and played it for Marcy.

"He hardly sounds like your type," she deadpanned.

Marcy is tall, slender, and will probably never have to cope with cellulite. It's okay. She's also wise and funny, and I'm glad she's my friend.

I said, "I don't even know the gent."

"And that tight black leather skirt! Congratulations, you're finally on the Victoria's Secret mailing list."

I sighed, and told my story one more time, ending with:

"I don't intend to move, but I wish I could figure this out. My aunt calls to make sure I'm not stretched out dead on the kitchen floor. Nick and Rosie want me to phone them every evening. And I'll admit, I didn't sleep well last night."

Marcy had brought a classy North Coast Chardonnay, and now she refilled our wineglasses.

"Then let's think about it," she said.

Some two hours later, I was sure I had the answer.

We had written down the names of just about everyone

who knew I'd be out of the country for nearly a month.
Everyone, from the sweet Pakistani family who own the dry
cleaners to the Hansens's son next door. Even Gil, who says
our divorce was a mistake. It wasn't. Finally, we had
twenty-six names on the list.

"The perp," said Marcy (she is a Kojak fan), "knew exactly when you left—the Hansens heard your shower the
very first night."

"I'm scratching out Jimmy Hansen. He was next door
with his mother." I drew a line through his name.

"You're probably right," said Marcy, "but he was a good
candidate. Remember, that detective—"

"Velasquez."

"—thought it was someone who just needed a place to
hang out. A teenager with a girlfriend, raging glands, and
no apartment of his own—doesn't that fit?"

I was firm. "It's not Jimmy. He's a nice kid."

Marcy held up one, two, three fingers.

"Motive. Knowledge of when you left and when you'd
return. Opportunity, when his mother wasn't looking. Why
not?"

"No key. The detectives thought my visitor used a key."

"You can't be sure," said Marcy, "but let's assume it is
someone with a key to this apartment. Who has your key?"

I groaned. "Et tu, Marcy. Just who you'd expect. That
notorious chocolate ice cream eater, my aunt Sadie. And, of
course, my landlord has a master key."

"Aha!"

"Calm down. Mr. Moskowitz is about seventy-five years
old, and has arthritic knees. I can't imagine him dashing up
the back staircase while Mrs. Moskowitz is folding the laundry."

"How about Mrs. Moskowitz? Maybe she has a friend
who's just, ahem, a bit livelier than Mr. M.?"

I laughed. Mrs. Moskowitz loves her husband, her poodle Nathan, and the mineral springs at Palm Desert, in that order. Wait a second!

"They were away that first weekend. They were in Palm Desert. That's why Mrs. Cappelli in the front apartment was taking in my mail."

"I've seen her. She's the hefty grey-haired woman who always carries a Bible, even when she's dumping her trash. Why would she want to use your apartment?"

I was excited. "No, no," I said, "not Mrs. Cappelli. She has a *daughter!*"

"And you think it's the daughter?"

"Listen, Angela is *weird!* Her mother is proud that she works for an attorney, but he must keep her busy typing briefs. I can't imagine her dealing with clients.

"I mean, this girl never looks directly at anyone. She has to be pushing thirty, but she dresses like a convent school-girl, starched white shirts and pleated skirts, for heaven's sake."

Marcy shook her head. "You can't accuse her of breaking and entering because she doesn't subscribe to *Cosmopolitan.*"

"Don't you see?" I said. "It all makes sense. Even Warren's phone call, and the others."

I could almost see the lightbulb go on. "Of course," said Marcy, "she posed as you! She went down to the Paddock and said she was you, because she knew she could use your apartment for a month." She paused, and chewed her lip.

"Are you sure?"

"I'm sure," I said. "Mrs. Cappelli goes to church every day. Angela could borrow the master key for the building, and make her own copy before mama came home. Who knows how long she's had the key? Maybe she got the idea when she heard that the Moskowitzes would be away while I was on vacation. Then all she had to do was wait for me to leave for the airport.

"Any evening she could call mama and say 'That nasty boss is making me work late.'"

"It figures," said Marcy. "Then she could change at the office, put on her Cinderella slippers and her tight leather skirt, and head for the Paddock."

"Where she gave her phone number—*my* number—to Harv and Baxter and Warren. Maybe even a few others."

About the Paddock. It's a steakhouse and bar on the Sunset Strip. The name tells you that it caters to the horse-playing crowd. The lights are subdued, the drinks are honest, and the barstools are real wood and leather. Evenings at the bar, you can get the latest odds, see replays of that day's races around the country, have a chat with your favorite bookie, and get any other action you'd like.

Although it started as a chummy extension of a track clubhouse, the Paddock has become one of L.A.'s better known singles bars. How could it miss? All those winners and losers looking for a good time or a sympathetic shoulder, it's not a bad place. If you like singles bars. Obviously, Angela did. It's just one of the ways we're different.

Angela

I t's lucky that I met him before everything hit the fan. And that he's not afraid of anything. He laughed like a wild man when I confessed what I'd been doing. He laughed so hard he rolled off the couch and onto the floor. Then he pulled me down on top of him and I put my hands on his face and kissed him frantically to stop his laughing. We made love right there on that ratty carpet in his apartment, but I didn't dare to go back to her place. He kept saying we're two of a kind, con artists he said, and I'll admit I was offended, but he was in such a good mood that night (sometimes, I've learned, he can be rough and nasty but that's exciting, too) I hid my negative feelings. She always tells me I'm negative. She also tells me I'm lost because I stopped saying the Rosary every morning, but that's her thing and not mine, and I finally got up enough nerve to tell her. He says, leave it alone, don't let her get to you, keep up appearances for now. It's easy for him to say, but it's me who has to get dressed and go home before she suspects (I told her my boss is being audited by the IRS, but

23

she's a shrewd old bag, who knows when she could catch
on). I've never spent the whole night with him, my insides
ache thinking about it, but he doesn't seem to mind. It
makes me wonder if anyone else goes to his apartment after
I leave. I get so scared.

Chapter Five

Crime in Los Angeles has become so anonymous, what with riots and looters, freeway shootings, muggings and crazed movie star fans, there's a jolt of nostalgia when it turns out your neighbors can also do terribly nasty things.

I was feeling as smug as if I'd found the real Maltese Falcon. A couple of visits would tie up the loose ends, and put the case behind me.

No unfinished business, sweetheart, says gutsy private eye Catherine Spade-Marlowe.

The next evening I talked with the Moskowitzes about their tenant in the front apartment. My story was met with shock and disbelief. Even Nathan, the poodle, squeaked, although I'm sure it was because Mrs. M. clutched him so tightly.

"But such quiet, reliable people," Mr. M. protested. His wife nodded agreement. They are both small, plump, and white-haired; they even walk and talk alike, as some couples do when they have been married almost forever. "Otherwise," he said, "I would never have trusted Mrs. Cappelli to take care of things while we were away."

"I'm sure Angela didn't involve her mother," I said. "And I have no intention of filing charges. Even though I'm convinced it's true, I have no actual proof. And, there was no real harm done. Nothing's missing or broken."

Mr. Moskowitz patted down the few stray hairs that covered his bald spot, as if to reassure himself that all was not lost.

"I wanted you to be aware of what went on, though," I continued, "so it never happens again."

"It won't," he assured me. "Impossible. They moved just before you came back from vacation.

"Probably a coincidence," he added hastily. "Angela said she wanted to be nearer her office."

"I didn't think she was telling the real reason," volunteered Mrs. Moskowitz. "She works on Wilshire Boulevard. That's not far."

There was heavy silence. I could tell that this was even more embarrassing than the time Nathan peed on the Avon lady's sample case. Ah, well, no problem now, no fuss. Angela was gone and everything was cosy again. I looked at my watch, made my excuses and left, to their relief and mine.

Finally, I had dinner with Aunt Sadie and she helped confirm my theory.

"Your *neighbor?*" She thought it over and decided it was possible. "When I came to see Mrs. Cappelli after I saw the mess in your kitchen, her daughter answered the door. I told her who I was, and she seemed flustered. She called her mother and then she backed into their living room and stood listening.

"At one point, I remember, she started to giggle. But I'd seen her before when I visited, and I'd always thought she'd bolt and run if I said hello, so I wasn't surprised. An awkward girl. Mrs. Cappelli said she didn't know about anyone staying in your apartment. She seemed sincere so I left." She paused for breath. "It was her daughter. Imagine! Why would she do that?"

"Angela might be ashamed to bring a male friend home to mother. He'd be more likely to get a Bible than a cup of coffee."

"I feel rather sorry for Angela," said Aunt Sadie, rearranging her leopard-print chiffon scarf so it lay dramatically over one shoulder. "That young woman must be very repressed."

I shrugged. "Maybe in her mother's apartment. I think she would have used my place the entire time I was gone, but the murder next door scared her off. That's why whoever she picked up at the Paddock never found her at home."

"But she did bring someone home that first night."

"Beginner's luck," I sneered.

"I'm not excusing Angela," said my aunt. "What she did was so unfair to you. But at least she made an effort to meet men."

I didn't dignify this with an answer. "Auntie," I said, "this is probably the last restaurant in Los Angeles that doesn't know that Cajun is finished, but you like blackened redfish, so let's order."

Chapter Six

few weeks passed. I was in Chinatown buying rice noodles when I met Detective Wang, he of the manicured mustache. It may seem a long way to drive for a rice noodle, but a Westside ad agency had ordered our Chinese Chicken Salad for a client luncheon in their conference room. To give the salad its soul, you must use the noodles that sizzle and puff up into a crisp and weightless white cloud when you drop them into hot oil. And you should add slivers of pickled red ginger. Otherwise, it's just another stir-fry. When Mario, our catering chef, is busy I'm happy to volunteer to go to Chinatown to buy his fail-safe imported brands, and I usually manage to arrive near lunchtime for the dim sum.

About dim sum: If your idea of a Chinese banquet is ordering the No. 5 Dinner with Almond Duck instead of the No. 3 with Sweet and Sour Pork, let me introduce you to the best export from the Orient since Marco Polo brought spaghetti home to Italy.

This rolling feast of Chinese teacakes and dumplings, of wondrous variety, is usually served at brunch or lunch.

Waitresses whose command of English is often limited to "One ordah oow two?" roll serving carts through the aisles between tables, offering small plates of barbecue, meatballs, chicken feet, sausage, as well as dumplings, buns, pancakes, wontons, noodles, rolls, pastries, and puddings that may be filled with chopped, minced, sliced beef, chicken, duck, shrimp, crab, lobster, vegetables, tofu, taro, winter melon or coconut and then pan-fried, boiled, steamed, barbecued or baked.

It helps to bring along some ravenous friends to sample and share, but dim sum for one is preferable to no dumplings at all. I was waiting for a solitary table when Detective Wang arrived. It was easy to see him: that mustache, for one thing, and then he's taller than most Chinese, with the shoulders of a quarterback, which it turns out he was when he played in the Rose Bowl for UCLA. What with one thing and another, and because he was also alone, we ended up sharing a table.

Neither one of us was a novice at this. True, he had been born to chopsticks, but I became dexterous at an early age. We made small talk over the pumpkin dumplings. He had come downtown today for a meeting at Parker Center, the main police headquarters at the edge of Chinatown. We discussed traffic over a double order of char sui bao, the fat steamed white buns stuffed with barbecued pork. We divided a dish of scallion pancakes and talked about apartments and spiraling rental costs. He told me he lived alone in a one-room, kitchenette and bath guesthouse in Santa Monica, on a bluff overlooking the Pacific. It featured noisy, pre-World War II plumbing and fantastic sunsets. He was terrified that the property might be rezoned for multiple units and sold. I joined him in sympathetic silence as we split an order of lemon custard tarts. Finally, he asked whether there was anything more to tell about the break-in. I hesitated, wanting to bury the matter for all times. But when he speared the last turnip cake, and then generously offered to share it with me, I felt I had to offer something in return. I told him my theory about Angela.

"Not bad," he said. "You built a good case."

"Paul," I said hastily (we were now on a first-name basis), "I don't intend to do anything about it."

"No," he said, "just leave it alone. But I'll keep it in the back of my mind. I have a mental folder there called 'Information that's maybe useless, maybe not.' That's where I'll file Angela."

There was something more on my mind. "It almost seems like too much coincidence," I said. "I mean, that woman next door was murdered the same night Angela took over my apartment."

Detective Wang shrugged. "Except for the gang wars, which tend to be predictable, crime in Los Angeles doesn't follow any rules. And it isn't tidy, the way it is in detective stories."

I smiled. "No Hercule Poirot?"

He sipped his tea and thought. "Poirot would have to adapt to the random element in big-city life. I doubt if he could stand around among the imported chintzes in a Hancock Park study, and tie everything up in the last chapter. Not in L.A. There are too many rootless people coming here to escape something in their pasts. And too many others on the make. You might have a banker plotting to murder his nagging wife, and he gets lucky because some addict looking for drug money breaks in through the French windows and beats him to it."

"Then it *is* coincidence," I said.

He smiled sadly. "It's the odds."

"Does all this make you a cynic?"

"No, just careful."

He insisted on picking up the check, so I said thanks and invited him for lunch at Nick's next time he was in Westwood. For some reason I didn't feel like taking the freeway back to the office. It was a balmy day in early September and I headed west on Sunset, driving through the old neighborhoods where the tall spindly palm trees, if they don't shade the taco stands and peeling, graffiti-covered buildings, at least soften them. They remind me of those souvenir postcards of Los Angeles, printed in primary colors and cropped to show just red tile rooftops and the silhouettes of palm trees, as if the city floated skyward under a dazzling, optimistic sun. Once upon a time.

I hadn't called in, so Nick had to hold his excitement. He rushed to meet me. "You'll love this one, Cat." Nick, when he's enthusiastic, flings about his arms as if he were conducting Italian opera. It's what gives his pizza such clout.

"We got a call from Ronald Wesley's assistant. They want us to do a supper party at Wesley's house in the Canyon."

Ronald Wesley probably has more Academy Awards than any other director working in films today. His last drama, *The Fool and his Money,* not only took Best Director, but Best Picture, as well.

"Nick, that's wonderful. How did he hear about us?"

"I suppose at the Harrington dinner party last month. He was a guest."

I'd planned the menu just before I left on vacation. I said, "I heard it went smoothly. He must have been on the wagon."

Ronald Wesley not only has gargantuan talent, he has a thirst to match. And his exploits make headlines in the scuzzier tabloids.

"Who do we work with?" I asked.

"His personal assistant, a fellow named Bob Crosswaithe. He'd like to come in tomorrow morning. How's your time?"

"Oh, I'll be in early. Whatever time is convenient for him."

Nick left to call Crosswaithe. I cleaned up my desk,

booked the clown and the magician for the TinyToddlerTogs picnic, and went home. Gil, my ex-husband,
wanted to stop by for a drink. It was a guaranteed early
evening.

Chapter Seven

Why I married Gil.
I was in love with him. At least, I think I
was. For a short time anyway. Among other
possible reasons: 1) Biological. Thenight-
sgetcoldersuddenlyyoureolder. I was twenty-eight. 2) Dubious. You have bought so many shower and wedding gifts
for your friends, they owe you. 3) L.A. reality. Rental
agents will accept your spouse more easily than your dog or
cat.

Gil is as sensible as nonfat yogurt. He is medium height
and medium build; his light brown hair is (to his despair)
thinning. He jogs at 5:30 A.M. He picks up his clothes. He
designs computer programs for engineers. Even now, he
buys my aunt Sadie flowers on Mother's Day. Gil is okay.
But after five years, on a glorious Saturday morning, I eyed
him as he ate his oatmeal and realized I did not want to
hurry up breakfast so we could recap our six-month budget. I did not want to prepare his usual baked potato for
dinner (never shredded, or sauteed, or gratinée or pan-

cake-style, always baked). I did not want him to father my child.

I'm sure he was hurt, but he coped by splurging on an advanced laser printer. There was as little pain in our divorce as passion in our marriage. We have remained friends.

I'd brought Gil something noncommittal from Greece, cufflinks that looked like ancient gold coins. He assured me they were just what he'd always needed, and didn't even add that souvenirs were frivolous and a waste of money. He wanted to see my photos of the trip, so I poured a Pilsener for him, and sherry for me, and it was pleasant and companionable sharing an evening, now that the tension of the divorce was over.

The sharp *brrring, brrring* of the doorbell startled us. I went to the door.

"Who is it?"

The man on the other side answered in a nasal cockney twang.

"We've come to talk to Bobby," he said. "We're his pals from London. Open up."

I put the chain on its latch and opened the door a few inches. Two men crowded close to the doorway. I say *crowded* because they were both large and muscular. One had florid, pudgy cheeks and a stomach that strained the buttons on his Hawaiian shirt; the other showed a torso as sculptured as that of a Ninja Turtle, under a tight shirt that read: My Mom Went To Hollywood And All I Got Was This Lousy T-shirt. Both sported straw fedoras over what I suspected were rather small heads. Just your typical sun-seeking tourists from the cold northern lands.

It was reassuring to feel Gil standing close behind me.

"There's no Bobby here," he said evenly. "You must have the wrong address."

"We don't think so, chum," said the cheeky one, in a tone

as polite as Gil's, but somehow more menacing. "Bobby doesn't make mistakes."

The Turtle spoke up. "Bobby wrote that your name was Catherine Deean, just like it says on your mailbox. But he said *we* could call you Katie." The Turtle beamed, showing a bright-gold front tooth. I had the feeling that his mouth had once met a fistful of brass knuckles.

Gil whispered into my ear, "Cat, do you know what these clowns are talking about?" I had an inkling.

"Fellows," I said, without opening the door any wider, "Bobby really isn't here. He hasn't been here in over a month. There's been a change in plans. When was the last time you heard from him?"

Cheeks and the Turtle exchanged glances. "There was a letter from him," said Cheeks, "at my sister's flat in London. It was waiting for us when we got out—uh, got back."

The Turtle continued. "He wrote for us to come in September. He said he didn't have a real address yet, but he'd likely be here, with you. We've been in the States over a week, we rented a car and drove from New York—for the sightseeing, you know. Today we went to Universal Studios. It was smashing, the way they shot it out on *Miami Vice.* Those fellows know a thing or two about explosives."

It was a long recitation for the Turtle, and he would have continued, but Cheeks glared him into silence. I don't know why, but at that moment I felt like laughing and laughing. Probably a touch of hysteria, but it was difficult to keep my face straight.

"Look, chaps," I said, with the sincerest smile I could muster. "I have no idea where to find Bobby. My best suggestion is to try the Paddock, it's a bar and restaurant on Sunset Boulevard. I think he might hang out there."

Cheeks thought it over. "The Paddock, you said? That sounds like Bobby. He never could leave the nags—or the ladies—alone." He sighed. "Well, we'll try it. If he's not there, I'll ring up my sister from the motel. There may be another letter."

The Turtle looked anxious. "He didn't leave any number?"

Damn, I could feel the laughter bubbling up again, but I managed a few more seconds of sincerity.

"Truthfully, not with me."

They were convinced. We said our friendly good-byes, and I could hear them lumbering down the stairs. I slumped against the door and I didn't feel like laughing anymore. Gil was aghast.

"What was *that* all about?"

"You wouldn't believe."

"How did you get involved with those hoods?"

I took his hand and led him back to his chair and drink.

"Sit down," I said, "and let me tell you about Angela. If Bobby is anything like those two, I really wonder about her taste in men."

Angela

He wants to own a horse. I can see his eyes turn brighter blue when he says it, and he wets his lips and smiles, then he takes my hands and holds them so tight they begin to tingle. I can feel the power in him when he says it will be *our* horse and it will bring us a beautiful, glamorous future. It's a dream he's always had, he says. He'll buy a thoroughbred and he'll train it to be a champion. Then we can travel on the racecourse circuit, that's what he calls it. And we'll enter the Derby and we'll be at Ascot, maybe when the Queen is there, and then here at Santa Anita, of course, and even down to Argentina.

Argentina. That's probably far enough from *her*. I still go home nights, although it hurts, it hurts, when he's sprawled there in bed and his skin is warm and shiny with sweat after we've made love, and he doesn't even pull the covers over him, he props his head up on his arms and smiles that naughty smile when I look at him. Right then, I want him again, so much I start to shake and I have to turn away. But he says, go home to her, you have to do this now

37

while we work out a plan. So I get dressed and I go, with the smell of his body still on my skin as I drive home, and I feel so restless I can't sleep. I know I could if we were holding each other close, that's the way I always thought sex would be, like in the novels, you'd sleep wonderfully after. It will happen, he says, but I want it to be *soon,* I need him like crazy.

Chapter Eight

P romptly at nine A.M. the next day, new client Bob Crosswaithe knocked on my open office door, inclined his head inside the door and said, "Catherine?"

I stood and invited him in. I was impressed. At something over six feet and broad-shouldered, he almost filled the small room. He had curly golden hair worn slightly long and eyes the color and intensity of blue flame. The combination gave him a look of, what shall I say? *purity*, like a Botticelli angel grown up. Do I sound too rhapsodic?

He was dressed in show-business casual: white shirt, jeans, and boots. His accent was English, his manner alert and self-contained. I had the impression he shunned the attention that his startling good looks would attract. I wondered how he came to be in the entourage of someone as off-the-wall as Ronald Wesley. I didn't find out then, because the conversation was all business: menus, prices, date, number of guests, etc., etc.

Usually, three weeks is impossibly short notice to any of the in-demand caterers in this town. An alternative is to

entertain your fifty best friends at a restaurant where the
celebrity chef is another best friend. That's quite accept-
able. However, at a certain level of power and influence, an
invitation to dine at your home is the local equivalent for
your guests to moving up from the House of Representa-
tives to the Cabinet. Especially when your home is a show-
place in the grand Hollywood style.

Ronald Wesley dwelled (when he was not making movies
in Louisiana or Mozambique) in a mansion built in the
same era as the Pickfair and Harold Lloyd estates. I'd never
seen Wesley's home, but it was famous, even notorious, as
the setting for a Hollywood tragedy of the late thirties.
Nothing too baroque. A matinee idol came home one evening after a publicity tour to find his movie star wife in
their pool, cavorting nude with her Hungarian director.
The matinee idol, distraught, it was said, from overwork
and slipping box office receipts, shot the director and
drowned his gorgeous wife. He then committed suicide by
gulping sleeping pills and chasing them down with Napo-
leon brandy. For a long time the mansion stood empty.
But, what with time passing and Benedict Canyon real estate being what it is, the tragedy became a romantic legend
and the house increased its value on the market.

Ronald Wesley is the most recent owner, buying from
one of the Iranian royal family who lost some of his assets
and a former Miss USA after his country's revolution. I'd
seen pictures of the interior and its hotel-size kitchen, and I
looked forward to taking command there for an evening.
Nick was willing to supervise the Taubman-Osaki garden
wedding and reception that same evening, so I was free to
be a working movie fan.

I arranged with Bob Crosswaithe to visit the mansion the
following Monday, same time, bringing a suggested menu
and taking a tour of the kitchen and the areas where we'd
be serving. He seemed quite enthusiastic about my tenta-
tive ideas. As he left, he said, "I'm looking forward to this,

Catherine. I like to learn from people who are tops in their professions."

This was endearing. We said our goodbyes and shook hands, like proper colleagues. His look was direct and his blue eyes were approving. Did he hold my hand a second longer than courtesy demanded? Nah. Probably not.

I pulled out my file of chocolate recipes for the Friends of the Beach Cities Homeless fund-raiser. They wanted all desserts, all chocolate. A very popular theme menu. I would feed them brownies. And miniature chocolate cream puffs. Chocolate raspberry walnut torte. Chocolate-dipped giant strawberries. Maybe a parfait or two. I set to work, humming "You Ought To Be in Pictures."

Chapter Nine

Italian weddings are to most other weddings like wine is to water. Champagne is to Perrier. They both have bubbles, but I'll take the champagne. Preparing for that weekend's Bonfiglio-Polizzi gala made me wistful for the gaiety I missed in my minimalist wedding to Gil: a brief ceremony at City Hall, followed by luncheon for a dozen of us at the restaurant, thanks to Nick and Rosie's generosity. I suppose I should have been more insistent on romance and merriment. As a party planner, I ought to have fired myself. But Gil had convinced me that since neither of us had much family, we should preserve our savings toward a down payment on a house.

It was a logical point of view—but since when are weddings a matter of logic? Ah, well, a girl gets married for the first time only once. Next time—if there is a next time—I want to dance at my wedding and, yes, there should be an accordian playing "La Vie en Rose." Why am I rambling? Oh, yes, Italian weddings . . .

This one was a beauty. Jack and Marie Bonfiglio's youngest daughter, Nina, would be wed to Mark Polizzi, a distant relation who, if he did not prove to be a complete nincompoop, would someday take over management of his future father-in-law's construction company. Jack Bonfiglio had made his first fortune after World War II, building tidy ranch-style tract homes for ex-G.I.'s in the raw outer reaches of the San Fernando Valley.

He prospered again as the Valley populations pushed out to the foothills of the Angeles National Forest, replacing sagebrush and jack rabbits with pools and PTA's. About twenty years ago, Jack built his own home on a mountaintop in the Hollywood Hills. No ranch-style here. The Bonfiglio gated estate was a Mediterranean villa, complete with marble entrance, gazebo, fountains, reflecting pools, and Olympic-size swimming pool. I'd guess Jack also bought up the artworks, silver, and porcelain from half of Palermo's decaying aristocracy. The cost of the cherub-bedecked sterling punchbowl alone could have financed a small feudal war, and possibly did. Not bad for a kid from a modest neighborhood in Brooklyn. Jack and Nick grew up together on the same street. Their families are interrelated all the way back to a town near Messina noted for its oranges and its poverty. I'm always amazed at Nick's connections, how many people he knows and how far back the ties go. The Bonfiglio connection is how I came to be serving two hundred wedding guests at a sit-down luncheon on a gently rolling green lawn high above the city smog.

It was a warm sunny Sunday afternoon and it didn't help my wedding-best peach crepe dress that we were shorthanded by one waitress and an assistant bartender. It is every caterer's nightmare. I'd planned to stay in the background, like a one-woman command post, but then Lupe called to say her ten-year-old had just broken out with chicken pox spots; Philip decided he was sampling too much of his supplies (I could see that coming), and was going to his first AA meeting that morning. I'd called the temporary agency and my own stand-by list, but no luck.

What I saw of the festivities was lovely, but I was too busy setting out trays of crabmeat tartlets and duck breast *glacé* to get teary-eyed.

To me, the excitement of the afternoon was meeting the Webers, Walter and Sally Ruth. Walter Weber is Establishment, Power Elite, the man to meet across a polished table in at least a dozen of the boardrooms in downtown's glass-walled financial district. Sally Ruth is smart, buoyant, and twenty years younger than her husband. She gave up her own successful public relations firm to help steer the fortunes of the Music Center, the historic downtown library, and both the County and the Contemporary art museums. They are not the entertainment industry Movers and Shakers; they are Old Money.

I was leaning against a marble balustrade that prevented the guests on the patio from tumbling into the canyon below. The tiered rum-and-whipped-cream wedding cake had been cut, champagne toasts given, the first waltz danced, and now the orchestra was launched into an irresistible Sicilian tarantella. I straightened up and tucked in a stray wisp of hair as a beaming Nick led the Webers toward me. Nick, through Jack Bonfiglio's introduction, already had brought in the Weber's charities cocktail party for five hundred guests, on the Saturday evening before Christmas. For caterers and their clients, the holiday season for private parties starts early. We'd signed up the Webers last February. Today, Sally Ruth was a blond vision in swirling pink chiffon and understated afternoon diamonds as she implored me to take on another assignment.

"You and your staff are just *wonderful*," she asserted. "I'm *thrilled* that you're doing our very own Christmas party." Walter Weber's craggy face smiled in agreement.

The flattery was nice, but I knew it was a prelude.

"Now I'm going to ask you a very special favor," said Sally Ruth. "You know how we all want to help the homeless."

"Of course," I said.

"Well, the very next evening after our party, *my* close-to-my-heart group," Sally put her hand over her heart, "the Downtown League, is having its first Christmas party to bring cheer and food to the homeless. I don't know yet where it will be, somewhere near Skid Row, but not so close that everyone gets nervous—and we don't want to be in competition with the missions on Main Street—but there are more than enough needy people at that time of year." She paused for breath. "Will you do it? I know it's short notice. The League members planned to bring the refreshments, but we've finally realized that's not practical. And Walter and I will be in Europe on a museum project early in December, so I can't help much. So will you do it? Nick said he would leave it up to you."

Christmas was over three months away. Of course, my staff and I could do it, ho, ho, ho. I'd just celebrate my own Christmas sometime in January. It had happened before.

"We'd be honored to help," I said, and I mostly meant it. Sally Ruth hugged me, Walter shook hands, and we parted in a glow of good feelings.

"Thank you, Cat," said Nick. "This has been a great afternoon."

I thought so, too. Now, if I could only stand on my high heels for another couple of hours, till we packed up. It's impossible to feel self-worth when your shoes pinch and your arches feel as flat as yesterday's soufflé.

Chapter Ten

I was racing through Benedict Canyon like a coyote in
heat. In spite of Bob Crosswaithe's good map, I'd
headed my car up a steep, windy road that ended in a
cul-de-sac, doubled back, and finally at 8:58 A.M.,
cursing at men who wanted to live like eagles, ascended the
curving driveway that led to Ronald Wesley's double front
doors. It was Monday morning.

The house was Tudor Gothic with a twist of Medieval, a
half-timbered, dormered, mullioned, brooding pile better
fitted to a dank English moor than to a hillside basking in
California's morning sun. I could believe that two murders
and a suicide happened here. I was glad I didn't believe in
ghosts.

The uniformed maid led me through an oak-paneled
entrance area, down a corridor, then through a series of
rooms with the look of Early Movie Mogul: dark woods,
straight-back armchairs with brocaded seats, overstuffed
sofas, handsome Oriental rugs on hardwood floors, a
grand piano. I was sure at least two of the lamps were origi-
nal Tiffany. I would have liked to linger with them, and
with the collection of contemporary art on the walls. We

kept walking toward the light, as if approaching some heavenly reception room. Just past the post-Tudor sliding-glass doors, there was a wide modern patio that overlooked the city and, a few steps down, a sunken pool. Its water was so pristine that from above I could see every detail of the white, gold, and turquoise tiles forming a mural on the pool bottom. The theme was mermaids, bare-bosomed and frisky, playing as if they were marking time until some sea change transformed them into starlets. I wondered which owner had commissioned the pool decor; odds are it was the royal Iranian.

Bob Crosswaithe was asleep. Even now, when I think of him, I see him in sunlight on that patio, stretched to the full length of a blue-and-white striped chaise, bright hair, lean body, taut runner's legs, fair English skin tanned to a pale gold. He woke as I entered. He was wearing damp khaki swim trunks, but he slipped a polo shirt over his head and, graceful for all his height, rose quickly to meet me.

"Catherine," he said. "Sorry I was napping. We had a late night." He paused and raised a hand in inquiry.

"Are we at a stage," he said, "when I can ask what your friends call you? Is is Katie, Kate—or strictly Catherine?"

"None of the above," I advised. " 'Cat' is the name. Everyone comes around to that, sooner or later."

"Cat." Stroking my name as if I was Siamese and pedigreed.

He gestured to a poolside table shaded by a blue canvas umbrella, and pulled out a chair for me. I set down my briefcase, pulled out papers, and we got to work.

It would be a small late supper on a Friday night, for twenty-six friends, colleagues and potential backers of Ronald Wesley's next film. It would follow a studio preview in a Westwood movie house of Wesley's latest production, scheduled to open during the holiday season. Most guests would come to the preview, and later the supper, directly from their offices or studios. If Wesley stayed sober, Bob

Crosswaithe informed me, the evening would end fairly early after the long business day.

I'd prepared a suggested supper menu taking into account the hour and the nature of the guests: Broiled shrimp kabobs for the dieters. Finger sandwiches of Emmenthal melted over roast beef and roasted red peppers for the meat-eaters. Goat cheese flan with grilled leeks to tempt the vegetarians. Two salads. Fresh melons. Beverages. And hot apple pie, because everyone loves All-American food. Bob okayed every course. He said he would buy the wines and liquor, tend bar, and supply valet parking. We toured the kitchen and decided that, if the weather continued this fine, supper would be served on the patio. My company would order the flowers and bring hurricane lamps to light the tables; the dazzling night lights of the city below were the only decorations needed.

All this decision-making proceeded so agreeably, we had the plans wrapped up in little more than an hour. It was very pleasant there on the patio, sitting in the shade of the big blue umbrella. Bob said, stay a while, so I did. Janine, the maid, brought coffee and croissants and left us.

"Is Mr. Wesley home?" I asked. "Should I meet him?"

There was a slight chuckle. "He's here," said Bob, "but I'm not sure you'll meet him today. He's probably nursing a hangover *this* big. I wouldn't dare knock at his door."

"You said you had a late evening."

The golden head nodded. "Oh, we made the rounds of just about every bar, private club, and pub from Santa Monica to Spring Street downtown."

"Is that your job?"

Bob threw back his head and laughed, a rich, hearty laugh, as if I'd just come up with a giant joke. He leaned forward and patted my hand, as if in appreciation.

"That's just part of my job, love. Mostly, I stop him from jumping into strange swimming pools."

I waited.

"I'll tell you how I met the right honorable Ronald Wesley," said Bob. "I was just off the plane from Blighty, and I thought I'd stop in at the Polo Lounge, have a drink and gawk at the rich and beautiful people.

"There I am in the lobby of the Beverly Hills Hotel, when I see two bellmen struggling with a small, red-faced bloke, and they're saying, 'Please, Mr. Wesley, don't try it, you'll disturb the other guests,' and so on. I gather that this Wesley chap is on his way to jump into the pool, Armani jacket, Gucci loafers, and all. Oh, and he's shouting something about saving the mermaids from drowning.

"Well, he's pushing past me with the two bellmen yanking at his jacket. So without thinking of the consequences, I decide to put out my foot and trip him!"

He was buttering a croissant, and he held out the knife in a musketeer's thrust.

"Was he furious?" I asked.

"No, Ronald Wesley gets happy when he drinks. At least in the early stages of a bender. As I've found out in the past few weeks."

"You've worked for him just a short time? You seem very much in charge."

"That's what Ronald needs. My rude gesture in the lobby did clear his head. He picks himself up, insists on buying me a drink, and then, after some chitchat—there in the Polo Lounge, he offers me a job. My title is personal assistant, but I do try to keep him out of strange pools. You see, every time he makes the tabloids, it becomes harder to get financing for his films."

He smiled. "Acapulco is my only failure. We've just got back. He'd finished postproduction on his new film, and he wanted to celebrate. His maid, Janine, tells me he goes to Mexico after every film. They know him quite well there."

Bob carefully spread thick black currant jam on his croissant. "Ronald doesn't like flying, so when we arrive in Acapulco, he's already had all the champagne and cognac that

Mexicana will give him in first class. Plus emptying his own flask. We get off the plane, hire a cab, and head for his hotel. Very posh, discreet and expensive. Upon arriving, Ronald leaves me in the lobby signing us in, and dashes for the pool. I rush after him with the hotel manager running alongside telling me, 'Please, Senor Crosswaithe, it is expected. It is Senor Wesley's greeting to Acapulco.'

"By the time we reach the pool, Ronald is halfway across, wearing everything but his shoes. And he's laughing his head off!"

"But he *did* want you along."

"Oh, I kept him out of fights, and stopped him from getting stiffed. You know, rich Yankee, big wad of dollars, deserted late-night streets. I got him home safe, and reasonably solvent."

I couldn't help looking him over: handsome, smart, lots of easy charm. He noticed.

"You're wondering what's in this for me. Well, a house, a pool, some ready change, Ronald's circle of pretty women and important men."

He took my silence for disapproval. I shrugged; his life was none of my business. "You should know," he said, "I knock around quite a bit, and I'm probably no better than I should be. So, if you're wondering whether I'll ever make the Queen's Honors List, don't. I'm not the type."

He said it in a lighthearted way, but there was confrontation in the words. I don't know where this would have led, because the sound of suffering came from the direction of the kitchen.

"Crosswaithe, where are you? I'm about to die."

"He's awake," said Bob. "I don't think it's a good time to meet him. I'll ask Janine to see you out while I fix him his Bloody Mary. He has amazing powers of recuperation for a man with such a slight build. Years of practice, I imagine."

He hastened toward the kitchen as I gathered my briefcase and made my way back through Gothicland.

Angela

I truly respect his privacy but sometimes in the darkest, loneliest part of the night when I'm staring at the ceiling until I think I see it move and it's going to fall and suffocate me, then I wonder: he knows every-thing about *me*, like where I work, what I do, about my boss Mr. Hastings and how he depends on me. He knows about my mother and her praying all the time and her lousy per-sonal habits, like stuffing her face all the time with gooey Italian pastries that drip rum and make the furniture sticky, but when I talk too much about her, he yawns and looks bored (I understand that—if she didn't make me crazy I'd be bored with her, too—and she doesn't get un-der my skin so much since I met Bobby). He knows every bump and hollow of me, one of the first times we were making love, he turned me over and ran his fingers up and down and around my body, exploring every inch, like he was taking this fascinating class and I was the subject and he was determined to get an A—and I hardly breathed because I didn't want him to stop, ever.

So he knows me every which way, but he holds back

when I want to know more about him. He laughs off my questions and says I'm just pouting, and that it makes my face ugly, so I laugh, too, as if sharing his life is really not important, maybe it isn't, I do trust him, but I wonder where he goes when he's not in that seedy little apartment of his, he says he works nights a lot at a very important job that requires all sorts of overtime, but he won't give me a hint of what it is, he says it's better I don't know, maybe he works for the FBI or the CIA?

I wouldn't want to hurt National Security but it's only natural to be a teeny bit curious. That's why one evening when I was staying late at the office after a stomach-churning day—Mr. Hastings was in court and he kept calling in with more rush changes to the brief I was working on, and the phone kept ringing, and Doris the receptionist was out sick so I had to take over the switchboard during lunch—from six o'clock on I kept calling his apartment, and calling and calling, and he wasn't home—I'd hang up after the third ring so I wouldn't get his answering machine, I didn't want him mad at me for annoying him—and I began to get frantic so I said, why not look for him? If he's at the Paddock we can have a drink and a laugh and go to his place after, and he'll make me feel calm and beautiful, the way he knows how to do. That's not spying, is it? So I called *her* and I said I had to work late again, she didn't care she never does.

I didn't have my sexy clothes at the office so I could change, but it didn't matter this one time. I wasn't trying to pick up anybody, and Bobby would understand when I told him about my awful day, even though I love to look, well, *provocative* for him like the models in the fashion magazines in those clinging jersey blouses and skirts that ride up when you sit down like by accident, ha ha. *She* would say I look like a whore and maybe one day I'll walk in dressed like that and maybe she'll faint or even have a heart attack. I get the giggles just thinking about it.

So I went to the Paddock wearing my striped blue-and-white shirt with my grey flannel blazer and pleated skirt and I knew no guy there would look at me twice, and what was great was, I didn't care. When you've got a man who wants you, you feel like you're strutting inside, even when the guys at the bar look past you like you don't exist. I had enough of that before I met Bobby, but he makes up for all the negative feelings, does he ever!

I hadn't been back to the Paddock since the night I met him, but it hadn't changed, singles bars never do. Everyone's cool and they're all trying to connect so maybe tonight they won't go home alone. That's okay if you have a positive attitude, though when too many eyes look past you, it can make you a little crazy.

I sat at a table in the back, by myself, looking over the crowd. I saw some faces I recognized—the regulars—but not Bobby, even though I waited for three hours, nursing the glasses of white wine and frowning if some loser came near my table. After a while I felt calmer. I was kind of relieved that he didn't show up. Maybe he doesn't go to the Paddock since he met me. Truthfully, I don't know what I would have done if he'd been there with another woman. My heart pounds when I think about it. But he never appeared so, finally, I went home and I slept pretty good.

Chapter Eleven

Halloween is the last major holiday of the year
without any pressure to spend it with a date, a
lover, a live-in, any significant other. Halloween is for fun, not memories. I like it a lot.

On a balmy day in late September I sat in my office, the
ghosts of Halloween future on my mind. I'd be working
this year; we were catering the food and a cocktail party for
the Interfacets annual sales meeting at their Westside offices.

Interfacets creates and manufactures computer software
from a plant somewhere in the hi-tech heart of the Silicon
Valley. Their marketing department is in L.A., and either
their MBA's lead healthy lives—or no one is hired past the
age of twenty-two. Our planning meeting was as gee-whiz
as Mickey and Judy putting on a show in the school gym
(ours would adjoin their small, cerebrally grey auditorium).
What with the meeting falling on Halloween, they'd chor-
tled, whistled, made spooky sounds and planned the day
around Sales Ghouls, Chip Thrills, and the theme: "We're
Taking A Byte Out of the Competition!" At their request,

I'd promised them a cake in the shape of a computer diskette. I was reaching for my Rolodex to find Charismatic Custom Cakes when the phone rang.

It was Aunt Sadie, sounding bright as the shine on a copper tea kettle.

"Have I caught you before lunch?" she asked, rushing on to add, "I hope so, because I'm just ten minutes away at the mall in Century City, and I hate to eat alone."

I'd planned to carry up a salad from the restaurant and eat while I worked. One of my less admirable habits. I said, "Good, I can use a break. Drive over to Dellacasa's and I'll treat."

I was downstairs when she arrived. She wore a simple beige knit dress with beige-and-tan spectator pumps. Pearly Beige eyeshadow was meticulously paired with Champagne Pearl nail polish. She entered with her usual effervescent air, as if she were on a cruise ship, invited for lunch with the captain. She has that knack of suggesting that time spent with you will be unique, special, the highlight of her day. I don't; while I am not exactly dour, *bubbly* is a family trait that has escaped me.

We hugged, settled down and looked over the menu. Nick's special of the day was Spaghetti alla Puttanesca, meaning, literally: spaghetti as a prostitute would prepare it. This is one of Nick's best dishes, the sauce being a nervy blend of capers, tomatoes, hot red pepper, and anchovies. I promised myself another evening at the gym and ordered it; Aunt Sadie was Spartan, with a cup of minestrone and a small green salad.

She sighed. "I have my friend Peggy's daughter's bridal shower this Saturday, and the wedding a week from Sunday. I'll never get into my jade chiffon if I eat spaghetti."

I had a hunch that Sadie was here for more than a salad. I munched my way through a crusty Italian roll and butter while she free-associated about the wedding, Peggy's daughter Robin's sweet fiancé, the first-year intern, and how they'd planned a brief but romantic honeymoon in Monterey. I had just plunged my fork into the spaghetti when she paused for breath and then came out with it.

"Gil called me," she said lightly.

"Oh?" I looked down; I had jabbed at a sliver of anchovy and splashed sauce on my cream silk blouse.

"About Thanksgiving, you know," she added.

I knew. Aunt Sadie always prepared Thanksgiving dinner—it was too much of a busman's holiday to ask me to cook, she insisted. Except for last year, after we'd separated, Gil was always a part of the holiday, carving the turkey, enjoying man-of-the-house duties from the head of the table. Last year, Gil went on a Thanksgiving weekend cruise to Ensenada. I turned down Sadie's offer to invite the veterinarian she'd met as a volunteer for F.O.O.F.F. (Friends Of Our Furry Friends)—"He's a widower and a very young fifty-two, dear"—and enjoyed the fun of sitting next to Sadie's beau Charles, debating Sarah Vaughn versus Ella Fitzgerald in between heavenly bites of pumpkin cheesecake. A lovely day.

"Gil was very lonely going to Ensenada by himself," said Aunt Sadie, with the merest hint of reproach in her voice. I shrugged.

"I still think of him as family," she asserted, "and I don't see that you've met a man that's any nicer."

I dabbed at the spot on my blouse, probably rubbing it deeper into the fibers of the silk. Finally, I put down my napkin, looked Sadie in the eye, and said evenly, "I like Gil. I just don't want to marry him again. Don't you think he should break away and not depend on us to make him feel warm and fuzzy on the holidays?"

"He only wanted to know," she persisted. "If he's not invited, there's a ski package to Vancouver he could take, but he'd have to sign up now."

Jeering at myself for my weak spine, I gave in.

"All right," I said. "I like Gil as a friend. Invite him."

She smiled, openly pleased. "After all, Catherine," she said, "it's just a holiday dinner, not a lifetime."

"Let's all of us remember that," I said.

We ate in silence for a few moments, then Aunt Sadie sat straight up and exclaimed, "Oh! I almost forgot to tell you. I just saw your ex-neighbor, Angela."

"Where?"

"It was at that Cherchez La Lingerie shop in Century City. I was looking for a shower gift for Robin—it's a personal shower and finally I did pick out a lovely white satin camisole and half slip—anyway, there was Angela buying some *very* expensive lingerie. On her salary!"

"How do you know it was so expensive?"

"Well, these were designer things. The most beautiful peach silk, with black lace insets. I'd looked at the collection while I was browsing but I didn't want to spend that kind of money."

"Hmmn," I said. "That's interesting. But, after all, she's a legal secretary. They're paid well."

"Not that well," said my practical aunt. "She bought just two pieces—a bra and a bikini—and I saw her hand the salesclerk a hundred-dollar bill." Sadie paused for dramatic effect. "She got two dollars and some change back!"

I don't walk around with hundred-dollar bills, but they *are* legal tender. And, besides, if silk lingerie is Angela's idea of luxury, who can fault her? Most of us have our private indulgences. For example, for a long time I've had my eye on a complete set of French white enameled cast-iron casseroles. One day I'll treat myself. I can understand Angela wanting to wear something pretty under those severe tailored suits of hers. She must lead a drab life, what with that awful mother of hers. I said as much to Aunt Sadie.

"Don't forget that man she took to your apartment," said Sadie. She looked straight at me, her manner as smooth as a good Hollandaise: "*Some* women have more than one reason for buying sexy underwear."

It was best to take a light approach with Sadie. If I seemed the least bit reflective, she'd assume I was wracked with yearnings and regrets.

"I'll take it under advisement, Auntie dear. Maybe after the holiday season I'll go skiing. I bought some devastating pink silk longies in London, and I haven't had any chance to wear them."

Aunt Sadie looked as if she wanted to launch into her "Don't put off till tomorrow . . ." speech, but to her credit she bit down hard on her lettuce instead.

Chapter Twelve

G ather round the campfire, kiddies, while I tell you the Greek myth of Adonis, mortal man beloved of the goddess Aphrodite. As one version goes, Adonis was so beautiful that when he died in a hunting accident, Aphrodite refused to let him go to Persephone's underworld. The two goddesses had such an Olympian fight over Adonis's fate that Zeus himself began to grumble. Finally, Zeus decreed that Adonis would spend part of the year in the upper world with Aphrodite and another part of the year with Persephone in the land of the dead.

I could discuss how the myth is interpreted: birth, death, and regeneration; fertility; the harvest cycle, etc. But I'd rather look at the human side of the story. After all, here's a man splitting his time between two very different environments. How did he react? Was he raring to go to the harvest festival with Aphrodite and did he shudder at the thought of another skull ritual with Persephone? Was he joyous in one place, depressed in the other? Did he shift from noble—to depraved? And did he worry that his life had gotten out of control? When he met other (mortal) women, did they wonder what was behind that handsome face?

Relevant questions, all of them. But I wasn't thinking of them the day Bob Crosswaithe stopped by my office to leave a signed approval of my estimate. I was too busy trying to find a replacement for Philip, who'd decided at AA that he couldn't handle both sobriety and unlimited access to alcohol.

Bob sat down, crossed his long legs, and smiled a greeting as I finished my phone call to the employment agency. He had been spending more time at poolside: the halo of curls shone over his lean, deeply tanned face.

I must have looked perplexed as I put down the phone, because he asked, "Some problems?"

"Nothing that can't be handled." I was reassuring, the way one wants to be with a client. "One of the bartenders I use has resigned—personal reasons—and I'm looking for a replacement."

"Was he regular staff?"

"No, bartenders like Philip are mostly free lance. Either they're moonlighting from their regular jobs, or they're struggling students or actors or writers." I spread my arms to show the broad universe of the bartending fraternity.

"It's just that the timing is off," I added. "I'm doing a big company picnic this Sunday, and my regulars are booked up or busy. It's not complicated. We're just serving beer and soft drinks, but my clients want to keep the beer drinking under control."

"You've given me an idea." He leaned forward, blue eyes direct. "Anything I could handle for you?"

"Oh, no," I said, reacting in surprise.

He raised an inquiring eyebrow. "Why not? You'll find, as you get to know me, that tending bar is another of my talents."

"For one thing, you're a *client!*" I have this unrewarding tendency to put my life into neat little boxes.

He could change moods in seconds. Now he was diffident. "Dear girl, I'm certain I can juggle two things at the same time . . ." The rest of that unfinished sentence was: unless *you* don't believe I'm capable or don't want me around.

I was thinking it over, still surprised, when he added, with a touch of embarrassment: "You know, working for a famous director, the glamour rubs off but not the money. My sensible, drab London wardrobe doesn't really make any points with the peacocks I meet around Beverly Hills. Since I don't do well at robbing banks," we both smiled lightly at this, "I'm ready for the odd job or two. I assume you pay reasonably well?"

I nodded, but asked, "What about Mr. Wesley? Are you available this Sunday?" This was odd: suddenly, I was interviewing *him.*

"No problem. Ronald is invited as a house guest at Palm Springs this weekend." He mentioned the famous actor who would be driving them to the Springs, then added, "I'm at loose ends until late Sunday evening."

Well, why not? What was wrong with having an attractive man helping out at the TinyToddlerTogs picnic? Ordinarily, I'm quite cautious. I use a qualified employment agency; my employees are bonded. But there was no money changing hands here, no Bonfiglio house with its valuable silver and portable, expensive bibelots.

Perhaps I didn't quite trust his incandescent good looks. I'm not sure why. In a city where physical beauty supports an industry, he was not unique. Maybe he reminded me of Andy Whatshisname, the high school quarterback with the dimpled chin: I'd suffered agonies because I knew he admired me only for my coaching skill in English comp. Was I still that unlovable grind?

Oh, nonsense, Cat! Your teenage inadequacies have

nothing to do with this. More likely, it's that you know so little about him, except that he claims he's no better than he should be. (What does *that* mean?) It might shake you out of your rut to know a little more.

Besides, if Bob could handle as notorious a drinker as Ronald Wesley—and get paid for it—he could certainly turn off the beer keg spigots if there was any unruliness from the TinyToddlerTogs Packing, Loading, and Shipping guys let loose on a Sunday.

I looked over at him as he sat relaxed in a stray beam of morning sun.

"I'm glad you thought of it," I said. "I do this picnic every year, and it's a long day but it's always fun."

I had some instinct—probably the thought that I'd be working for his boss the following Friday—that told me to keep this businesslike.

"It's a helpful arrangement for both of us," I added.

"I'm sure of it," he said solemnly.

Hollywood quiz: What do a Western about Montana, a TV cops-and-robbers chase, and a dog food commercial all have in common? *Answer:* All were filmed off Topanga Canyon in the Santa Monica Mountains, at a private compound with the outworn name of Lost Canyon Ranch.

I believe Lost Canyon has always been more of a dude ranch for vacationers and Sunday cowboys than a working spread. There are a neatly fenced paddock and a barn for the horses that take guests along chapparel-edged trails for a view of the Pacific or a peek into rugged interior canyons. A few chickens peck around like so many movie extras looking for their chalk marks. In addition to dudes and films, the Ranch thrives on renting out its grassy fields, its winsome stream, and a well-kept softball diamond for private picnics.

We arrive every year for the TinyToddlerTogs outing in an untidy caravan. Some company employees drive their own cars, piled with spouses and kids. The single women who work in the office and factory, and the recent immigrants whose vision of Los Angeles is bounded by downtown's bus lines, are transported in private buses from the company's headquarters.

I hitch a ride in one of Dellacasa's two catering vans, along with my crew of five cooks and servers. I'd sketched a rough map for Bob Crosswaithe of the turnoff and road from Pacific Coast Highway. He drove up for a sweaty day's work in, I noted, a silver Jaguar XKE.

The company's picnic committee plans the annual potato sack races, three-legged races, male-female marathon runs, and signs up the baseball teams. We book a clown and a magician who entertain the children in a clearing shaded by spreading oak trees.

Meanwhile, we set up a serving table with snacks and large galvanized tin tubs holding ice and cans of soft drinks. From experience, and by request of the Lewis brothers, we hold back the beer until the picnic meal is served, around two in the afternoon.

I wouldn't go so far as to call it an incident, but three years ago, late in a hot, thirsty day, there was a scuffle between a Vietnamese factory foreman and a Filipino warehouse worker. I don't remember why. The garment industry in Los Angeles nowadays is like an egg that's become a Western omelette: you add a handful of this ethnic group and a handful of that, stir well until set, flip, and hope it doesn't break apart. One day a year, at the annual picnic, the minor rivalries get worked out with games, laughter, and handshakes. It's our job to help keep it all friendly, as I explained to Bob while we set up the tables.

"A mixed lot like that?" he protested. "Short fuses walking around. Your recent, what was it called, civil unrest? is proof."

I handed him a stack of paper cups.

"I'm oversimplifying the problems, but people who feel part of a society don't try to destroy it."

A shrug, a skeptical laugh. I'd noticed that Bob was in high spirits today. It wasn't just the modest sum he'd earn from Dellacasa's, I guessed. He was seeing a perfect California day: blue skies, green meadows, clear, breathable air.

Bob lined up three cups before him, dug into his pocket for a coin. He slipped the coin under one cup.

"Laydees and gents," he said, brash as a cockney barker, "watch me 'ands." The cups moved, switched, twirled.

"The coin's under the middle one," I said.

Cautiously, Bob lifted the middle cup. Nothing. I pointed to the far cup. He sneaked a worried peek, then lifted it. Empty.

I sighed. "You got me!"

With a flourish, Bob lifted the last cup to reveal the dime. I clapped my hands.

"The old shell game," he said wistfully. "This picnic would be perfect for it." He resumed stacking cups.

"You do it very well. So sleight-of-hand is another talent."

"I ran the most popular booth at the church's Annual Jumble Sale and Charity Bazaar."

"You? Doing good works for the poor?"

Solemnly, he assured me. "By personal request of the vicar."

"Really?"

The blue eyes looked into mine. "Really."

The sun rose higher, but an ocean breeze helped keep the open fields comfortable. At two o'clock we began to serve the All-American feast: hot dogs, barbecued chicken, cole slaw and potato salad, corn on the cob, and, yes, enchiladas. Soon the bar was crowded. I could see Bob Crosswaithe, forehead shiny, white shirt damp, filling plastic glasses from the kegs.

I was helping the servers, now also including my clients. Nat Lewis hovered around the trays of Mexican food.

"Eat. Try it. *Mucho* good," he hawked, urging crimson-sauced enchiladas on wary Chinese pattern cutters and Korean finishers.

Art Lewis personally took over the hot dog tray for a while, beaming as he married each dog and bun. I saw him explaining in gestures the essential finishing touches of mustard and relish to an audience of two giggly Hispanic women. Yes, they said in hesitant English, they saw hot dogs on the food wagons that stopped at TinyToddlerTogs every day, they enjoyed hot dogs every year at the picnic. They did not understand mustard and relish. Next year, asked the younger woman shyly, maybe chile for the hot dogs?

"Of course!" said Art Lewis, smiting his forehead. *"That's how to assimilate the cultures!"* And he rushed off to tell me about next year's bridge to understanding.

Finally, I seated myself at a picnic table in the shade of a handsome oak tree, to enjoy my own late meal of excellent barbecued chicken. I was pleased. I had managed to avoid splashes on my Levi's and plaid cotton shirt. My hair was tied back with a ribbon, so I could feel the cooling breeze on my overheated neck. (I used to sport a bandanna but no more since the gangs have adopted bandanna colors as insignia. You never know who you'll offend.)

Nat Lewis came over to chat. "Everyone's having a great time, Cat. What about the enchiladas? Did they go?"

"Just about all gone, Nat." I didn't have the heart to add that the Hispanics chose them over the Asians about five to one. California's eclectic table doesn't extend to the first generation.

The shouts from the crowd watching softball seemed to be getting louder. And, I realized, the noise was coming from the wrong direction. I turned toward the clearing where serving tables were lined up in an irregular row. A crowd had gathered. There were cheers, but they sounded angry.

Nat Lewis looked alarmed. "Something's wrong," he said as he rose and walked quickly toward the area. I followed.

At first I thought it was a game of tug-of-war. I could see two factions, separated by a space but surrounding the players on each side. Nat Lewis pushed into the crowd with me close behind.

"What's happening?" he asked urgently. "What's going on?"

Some watchers stepped back and froze as their employer rushed in. The two men scuffling on the dusty ground ignored him. At first sight they seemed grossly mismatched.

I recognized both. Henry Vau is one of the Samoans who work the loading dock, a huge young man with tawny skin and ham-size fists. Small, sinewy Freddy Garcia from shipping is one of my picnic committee regulars. I knew he was an ex-boxer.

The fighters broke and staggered to their feet. Henry's nose was bleeding and he wiped it with a dirt-caked hand. Freddy breathed heavily, right fist clenched, left arm holding his rib cage. The crowd was silent now.

"You and your pals ain't taking over *nothing*," said Henry, panting. His heavy brows looked like black wings as he scowled.

"You're too stupid to live, man," grunted Freddy. "Why are you and your asshole friends always making trouble?"

"The word's all over the plant."

Freddy looked tired, as if he'd had too much of this. He began to brush off his clothes, wary eyes still on Henry. "You're crazy," said Freddy, his voice calmer but still defiant. "Go put on your sarong and climb a tree."

It was not the language of diplomacy. With a strangled

cry, Henry leaped and clutched both hands around Freddy's neck.

Art Lewis arrived and pushed to his brother's side. Art listened, brow furrowed, hands to his face. Now he cried, "My God, what is this craziness? Stop it! Stop it!"

Nat Lewis grabbed his brother's arm. "Don't get upset, Art. Remember your blood pressure. I'll handle it." Nat Lewis, overweight and sixtyish, stepped up to the combatants. Freddy, gasping, was trying to break Henry's fingers.

"You quit this, boys," said Nat with authority. "Monday we'll talk it over. Now stop fighting and go home."

Nat put his arms in front of him, like a swimmer about to part the waves. I held my breath. If either fighter swung wide, Nat would be pounded into mincemeat.

To this point the picnickers had made no effort to stop the fight. Perhaps they saw Henry and Freddy as gladiators, champions of some cause unknown to me. Now, however, I saw several of the men, Bob Crosswaithe among them, rush forward to pull the fighters apart. Henry and Freddy were jostled to neutral corners. The field of combat was left to the two Lewis brothers, surrounded by the employees of TinyToddlerTogs and their families.

After a quiet, worried discussion, Art Lewis turned to the uneasy assemblage and smiled.

"It's okay, folks," said Art, clapping his hands for emphasis. "Just a little misunderstanding. There's still plenty to eat and drink, so let's go back to having fun. Right, Nat?"

"Right!" said his brother. "And we still have to give out the prizes to the best teams. So let's go to the grandstand now."

Straggling and whispering, the picnickers made their way to the softball field. The breeze from the sea had come up. Soon, I could hear shouts of laughter as the prize-giving began. I wandered over to visit Bob Crosswaithe at the beverage table.

"Thank you for helping stop the fight," I said.

"I was afraid Mr. Lewis would get slaughtered."

"What started it? Did you hear? They were near this table."

"Some argument, it seems, between the Samoans on the loading dock and Freddy Garcia's group in the shipping department."

I was concerned. "I hope there's no trouble in the factory. As far as I know," I added, "TinyToddlerTogs has never had any serious labor trouble."

"We chatted about this before," Bob noted, "about this ethnic paradise you have in L.A. The ragtag hordes inevitably will fight each other into bloody pulps. You see, the loot is so much better than what they left at home." He moved a towel in brisk circles, polishing away beer spills.

"Good Lord, even Anglo-Saxons like me. Now that we're becoming politically incorrect, I may have to push harder."

Bob's broad smile showed white, even teeth. "You can't tame the beast, dear Catherine, by feeding it hot dogs once a year."

I thought it over, wasn't sure I agreed. I'd had enough conflict for one afternoon, so I said lightly, "But they're such good hot dogs!" I smiled, and went in search of the Lewis brothers.

Art was seated in the bottom row of the small grandstand, enjoying the sight of his brother handing out prizes for the children's potato sack races. I sat down beside him.

"All quiet?" I asked. "No more hard feelings?"

Art shrugged. "It ended okay."

"What will happen to Henry and Freddy?"

"Not much. They're both good employees, but a little hotheaded. I'm more interested in stopping the rumor."

"What was it?"

"The Samoans have handled the loading docks for years. Henry and his friends heard this lousy rumor that they were going to be pushed out because the Hispanics wanted in. Absolutely untrue!"

"You don't know how it started?"

Art Lewis shook his head. "No, but it was here, today. If I ever catch the SOB, I'll strangle him with my own bare hands." He added, "We try very hard to give everybody a chance, no matter where they came from. It's only right."

His face brightened. "But it was one heck of a good picnic, Catherine. More excitement than I need, still everything can't be perfect. Maybe this is our version of ants at a picnic."

I thanked him and went off to help my crew make things tidy. Crosswaithe was working hard at clean-up, heaping empty soda cans into large green trash bags. I looked at him thoughtfully. Bob was quick and efficient at his labors. Sweat had turned his blond curls into masses of shiny ringlets. Like an angel.

Angela

O h, God, I didn't want to kill him! He was always a good boss. Why did he come back to the office? Did he suspect me? I don't think so. He had this surprised look on his face when he found me. I'd left the overhead light off, and I was sitting on the floor in front of the safe, in this little pool of light from his desk lamp. He was going—as usual—to his Monday-night racquetball game, he told me when he left the office, he was always trying to lose ten pounds and get fit. He was wearing grey sweats and those high-top court shoes when he came in, that's why I didn't hear him, those shoes don't make noise. I could have carried it off if I'd had even a minute to hide the briefcase, because he was used to me being there alone at night, after all where else did I have to go—home to *her*? I'd always said, Yes, Mr. Hastings, No, Mr. Hastings, I'll finish it before I go home tonight, Mr. Hastings. For five years I didn't mind, I really didn't—until I met Bobby. I'll admit, I changed after that, I couldn't wait to leave and drive to his apartment on the nights he let me come over. I don't mean he *let* me, but he's very busy nowa-

days and I understand, I do, I can't always monopolize his
time, not right now.

But Bobby always says, listen to me, he says, you have to
look for opportunity, and then you grab and run with it. I
knew tonight was it, the main chance, the big one. It was
scary. Bobby wasn't home, and he didn't answer the message I left on his machine, but I had to do it *tonight!*

Late this afternoon, Mr. Hastings came in with a briefcase stuffed with negotiable bearer bonds, maybe three
hundred thousand dollars worth he'd talked that crazy old
Mrs. Sherman into letting him take from her big Victorian
eyesore in Pasadena, because her nephew called him from
Paris this morning and said she was trying to give everything away to her gardener, even though he's half her age
and only speaks Spanish. Some of her jewelry was probably
already gone, but Mr. Hastings showed me a diamond
necklace in an old-fashioned platinum setting and a dia-
mond-and-ruby circle pin, he'd brought those back in his
briefcase, too.

I had to do it before he put everything in the bank in the
morning. Because even though I'd been writing small
checks to Cash and bigger ones on the trust accounts, hoping it wouldn't catch up with me until the accountant came
next month, and by then we'd be gone—and Bobby
needed new clothes, he was so affectionate when I bought
them for him, a cashmere jacket and silk ties and underwear—but I knew it couldn't last forever. So I told the others in the office I was working late—they'd expect it, I've
always worked hard, never socialized with anyone there,
even the other secretaries. I've never even hinted about
Bobby—why should I share him with silly, gossipy girls?
They'd want to know where I met him. So I planned to do
this tonight, then I'd have gone home, waited till she was
asleep, packed a bag and left for Bobby's place.

But Mr. Hastings came in and said, Angela, what are you
doing there, and then he saw that I was putting the bonds

in his briefcase. He pulled me to my feet and he was so upset he shook my shoulders and said, I can't believe this, I've always trusted you. And that really hurt me, because he always did, even with the key to his safe. He said, Just tell me why. And I couldn't say a word. He still held me tight by the shoulders as if he wanted to squeeze the truth out of me, and his nice round face was all screwed up as if he didn't know whether to be angry or cry. Finally, he dropped his hands and said in a sad voice, You know I'll have to call the police, this is too serious. So I thought about it for just a split second. I thought, if I go to jail Bobby will never have his horse and we won't go to Argentina, and I knew what I had to do. When Mr. Hastings turned his back to pick up the phone on his desk (he trusted me so much, he turned his back!), I picked up one of the heavy bookends that looks like three lawbooks stuck together, only in brass, and I hit him as hard as I could on the back of the head. He kind of cried out, like in surprise, then he crumpled and fell, face down, right at my feet. Then I hit him again, just to be sure. He looked like a big grey rag doll except for the spurts of blood that ran across the little bald spot at the top of his head and dripped down on the beige carpet. I was very calm, but there was a picture of Mrs. Hastings and their three kids on his desk, and they were waving from the deck of their sailboat and looking down at whoever was taking the picture, probably him, but now I felt they were looking at him lying on the floor and their eyes upset me, even though I knew I *had* to kill him, what choice did I have? so I turned the picture facedown. Then I took the briefcase and finished filling it with the jewelry and the bonds. I put a folder with a couple of hundred dollars in petty cash into it, too. I had to step over him to get to the desk, and when my foot accidentally touched his leg I jumped, but I opened the drawer where he kept his business checkbook, and I took that. At the last minute, because I remembered how it went in some TV mystery, I figured I should wipe off my fingerprints—not that doing it would save me, but it could buy me time. So I got some Kleenex out of my desk drawer and wiped the bookend where it wasn't bloody, and put it back next to him. I turned off all the lights and I knew, because the cleaning people had already been there earlier in the evening, that I was safe until morning when the other two law partners and the staff came in. I drove to Bobby's apartment, and waited for him. But he didn't come home all night. I knew no one would see me there. He lives on the top floor, and the other apartment is vacant. I was too tired to think, or even stand up, so I sat in front of his door until morning.

Chapter Thirteen

"Would you consider doing me a favor, Catherine?" I recognized the forthright tone, the clipped accent. It was Bob Crosswaithe on the phone, the Tuesday after the picnic. "In return, I'll take you to lunch. You name the place."

"If I can," I said, pleasant but evasive. Solid, careful, noncommittal Catherine. "What's the favor?"

He was reassuring. (I had the fleeting thought that he understood me rather too well.) He said, "Nothing major. Remember I told you I'd pick up the wine and liquor for Ronald's party?"

"That's right."

"My problem is, I'm still a stranger in town and I'm not sure what he'd expect me to buy."

"Mr. Wesley must have charge accounts in some liquor stores," I suggested.

"He does, of course. I have a couple of places. And I've gone through his liquor cabinet, so I know what brands to stock up on." He paused. "To be absolutely honest, I'm not much of a wine connoisseur—and he is. I know he thinks highly of California wines and I'm completely ignorant about them. I'd be awfully grateful if you'd point me to the right bottles."

I was tempted to tell him that the gourmet shops Ronald Wesley patronized would have a better fix on his tastes than I could. On the other hand, I was free for lunch. Why settle for yet another Salade Niçoise from the kitchen, carried up to my desk? Even with a Mediterranean tang, tuna fish is tuna fish. I arranged to meet Bob in Beverly Hills, at one of the grander purveyors of hothouse tomatoes, pâtés by the pound, and wines chosen by a buyer with the most exquisite palate this side of the Côte d'Or. There are worse ways to work up an appetite.

I'm more of a happy friend of wine than a lover, a devotee. I admire the experts who can sip, taste, and tell, eyes closed, whether the Beaujolais came from the Brouilly or the Moulin-à-Vent vineyards. I knew only that the light, young wines would be delicious with my Friday-night supper. We chose a few bottles and then, with a nod to Ronald Wesley's admiration for California's own, added some bottles of Napa Valley Blanc de Blancs, wines the color of pale gold.

"Tell me why you chose what you did," he said.

"Are you that interested?"

"I've said it before, I like to learn from people who are good at what they do."

"I'm hardly an authority on fine wines," I said, overplaying the modesty just a touch.

Lightly, he put one hand on my shoulder, and said, "But your eyes sparkle when you talk about them. I like looking at you."

Oh, well, in that case . . .

We strolled along the aisles, in turn serious and giddy, as if just the presence of the wine had its effect on our moods. I couldn't help thinking guiltily of how I'd avoid going to

markets with Gil. He is always sensible. He reads nutri-
tional information and compares per unit prices. I don't
know why I should remember only the boredom of those
trips. After all, by profession I'm a careful shopper. It's just
that Gil is so earnest. I wondered idly if Bob had ever
clipped double savings coupons, and the thought made me
giggle.

He looked at me inquiringly, and then smiled, a nothing-
held-back smile. We were standing there among the shelves
of Blush Zinfandel, grinning like two country simpletons,
when the interruption came.

"Bob?" said a startled female voice. "Bob Crosswaithe?"
The woman was at one end of our aisle. My back was to
her; I turned. One of her hands clutched a small store
shopping cart; the other was suspended in midair, as if she
were a comic strip figure, zapped by an alien ray gun as she
reached for a wine bottle.

Bob stared at her. For an instant his face flushed; I
thought I saw a split second of anger. Then the bright, easy
smile emerged, and he walked toward her, arms open to
take her hands and press them tightly, warmly.

"Elaine!" he said. "What a surprise."

She'd reached, I'd say, the wistful side of forty. Her hair
was blond (Clairol), she wore square, horn-rimmed glasses;
her figure wasn't bad, but she never should have bought
the low-cut clinging jersey print she wore: you could tell by
her hips she'd never met a Jane Fonda tape she liked.

As Bob held her hands, she squirmed like a pat of butter
in a hot frying pan. What I thought at first was pleasure, I
could see now was outrage.

"What happened to you?" she demanded. "Where did
you go?"

I'd stopped a discreet distance behind him. He glanced
back at me and shrugged in apology.

Elaine became louder, more shrill. "I looked for you,"
she said. "I tried every place I could think of."

He talked to her quietly, softly. I couldn't hear the words, but I could tell they weren't having much effect. He was still holding her hands. I thought: if he lets her hands go, she'll hit him. At this point, he tried to appeal to her sense of propriety.

"Oh, you two haven't been introduced," he said, as if he were standing in a receiving line next to the Queen Mother.

"Catherine, I'd like you to meet my good friend Elaine. Um, Elaine Stedman, this is a new colleague, Catherine Deean."

"How do you do?" I said with full gravity, and wondered: I'm a *colleague?* So formal.

She gave me a quick, hard look and then ignored me. But she stopped talking—just stared at him wildly.

It was the first opening she'd given him. Now he spoke to her in firm but kind tones, the way you do to Fido on Puppy Training Graduation Day.

"Stay there for a minute, Elaine. Just stay!"

He took my elbow and led me to the other end of the aisle.

"I'm so sorry about this, Cat. I can't imagine what you think."

I didn't *know* what I thought, so I shrugged and said, "Look, it's all right."

"I met her on the plane from London. We were seatmates. We got cosy, you know, but it was simply the way one kills time on a long flight. I'm upset that she thinks it was more than that."

"You don't owe me an explanation," I said. I glanced at my watch and said with a smile, "I've been gone from my office nearly two hours. Would you mind if I took a raincheck on lunch?"

He was obviously relieved. "If you don't mind . . . ?"

"Of course not. We'll talk on the phone about the party."

"You are such a good sport, Cat."

I looked down the aisle at Elaine, who was glaring at both of us. I waved a friendly goodbye and departed. On the drive back I lectured myself to be careful with him. Although, being a good sport has never been one of my life goals.

Angela

I t was cold before the sun came up, but I huddled against Bobby's door, using my navy suit jacket as a blanket and propping up Mr. Hastings's briefcase as a hard pillow. I tried to make plans and even though I didn't doze off more than fifteen minutes or so in that endless Monday night, my mind was clear. To tell the truth, I was excited like—how can I explain it—the first time Bobby made love to me and my body shook and I cried out until he laughed and gently put his hand over my mouth and then I felt, yes, purified and reborn. That is how I felt sitting in his doorway, like I was a new person now and I could do anything. And having to kill Mr. Hastings was unfortunate, but I felt it was the start of this greater destiny.

I was certain that Bobby would be home Tuesday night, because it was my usual time to visit him. I tried to imagine how I would tell him. Maybe start off, like, Sweetheart, I have a surprise for you. And then spread out the three hundred thousand in bonds. He'd be so happy, maybe he wouldn't care about what I had to do to Mr. Hastings. My

legs were getting cramped from the night on the cold concrete landing, so I decided to do my errands. I combed my
hair and put on lipstick, straightened my navy skirt and
tucked in my white shirt, although it wasn't crisp and
starched by now. There was just a drop of Mr. Hastings's
blood on one cuff, from when I hit him the second time. I
rolled up both cuffs until I could find a ladies' room and
wash out the spot.

It wasn't even seven A.M. yet, but there was a Denny's all-
night coffee shop in the neighborhood. I locked the briefcase in my car trunk and while I drove to the coffee shop I
listened to the radio. It was too early for anyone to find the
body, but I listened anyway, you never know. I bought the
Times on the way, just to give me something to keep in front
of my face until nine A.M., when the banks opened.

Before I ate breakfast, I washed up and scrubbed the
bloodstain until nothing was left of it but a light-pink tint.
Then I sat at a small table and ordered one of their breakfast specials and black coffee. I was too keyed up to be
hungry, but I needed something to push around on the
plate so I could sit there for an hour or so.

I thought about calling home, but I didn't know what to
say to her. She'd be a little crazy because I didn't come
home all night. Maybe I should phone her, I decided. I
didn't want her going off her rocker and reporting me as a
missing person. So I used the phone near the ladies' room,
and she told me she'd been up all night praying for me—
she sounded worn out and weepy, like she does after she's
been on a crying jag in front of her little shrine in the living
room. I didn't need her prayers—they never did me any
good before, why should they help now? But I told her I
was calling from San Francisco, Mr. Hastings had sent me
there to deliver some papers to the IRS first thing this
morning, I said, it was very important. I said I had flown to
San Francisco last night and got to my hotel too late to call
her. I didn't really care if she believed me, but I tried to

make it good because the story might give me a few hours delay when the police came to see her. I knew they would.

I made one more call, to Swissair, to find out the first class fare to Zurich, and if they had a flight out that night. I was afraid to touch the bearer bonds here, in Los Angeles. I didn't think any brokerage house would just give me cash on the spot, and I didn't think it was smart to wait around and have to come back for the money. I don't know why I thought of Switzerland. I suppose I figured they were used to handling money for strangers.

Meanwhile, we would need cash and I had to get my passport. Not that I'm a great traveler, but I went with her three years ago when our church had a group flight to spend Christmas in Rome. She even paid for my ticket, although that isn't as generous as it sounds, because the money came from my old man's insurance policy after he died. All he did was work day and night in his shoe shop, even after the old neighborhood got lousy and the gangs took over, and one night he was closing up and two punk kids from the block came in with knives and took twenty-three dollars and seventy-six cents—all he'd made that day —from the register and stabbed him to death. They got caught and went to jail—and I went to Rome with her on the insurance money. Did I miss him? I suppose. He was a sad, stooped little man who always wore brown suits and a brown felt hat, like the whole earth was brown and barren. He stayed away from the house because she drove him nuts with the praying, and I guess I resented that he didn't make more of an effort to be a father to me, but who could blame him?

We went to Rome and St. Peter's was cold and drafty with those marble floors and high, echoing ceilings. And the church group was put up in this cheap *pensione* where they didn't give any heat until your fingers and nose turned blue, and I remember the hard rolls and the watery pasta, because breakfast and dinner at the *pensione* were included in our economy tour. I was the only one single and under sixty-five, and maybe the others kept warm by praying, but I was cold all over, even my heart. I promised myself then, if I ever went back I would go first class, but I didn't have much hope.

That's why, exactly at nine A.M. when I went to Mr. Hastings's bank, where they knew and accepted me, I took out as much cash as I dared from his checking account. I wrote a check for a thousand dollars, and they didn't question it, because he'd given me the power to sign on his account and sometimes I did take out a pretty large amount of cash for him to take on a business trip. The teller smiled at me, and I gave him a flirty little smile back, which I never would have tried even two months ago. Then I walked out as casual as if it was a normal business day.

By half past nine I was at my own bank, a few blocks away. First, I went to my safe-deposit box and got the passport. Then I made out a withdrawal slip for my money market savings account and took out five thousand dollars. I had money left in the account, I have a payroll savings account and I've hardly ever touched it—what did I have to spend money on? but I didn't want to make anyone suspicious, so I said I was buying a used car and the seller wanted cash. The teller was nice and concerned that I'd be giving all that money to a stranger, so I said it was a cousin, it was funny how easy it was becoming to lie.

When I finished with both banks, it was only ten-thirty in the morning, and I still had most of the day to get through. I thought, get away from the Wilshire district and our apartment. I decided to head for the north end of the Valley. I had plenty of time, so I went west on Wilshire to Beverly Glen, drove over the canyon to the Valley side, took a long ride up Ventura Boulevard, and then, at the far west end of the Valley, headed north to the Topanga shopping mall. I found a drugstore and bought a toothbrush and such. Because I didn't want to be conspicuous, I went to two different department stores. In one, I found a red nightgown and negligee. In another, I bought some underwear, a couple of soft, pretty blouses, and the heaviest trench coat they carried in this hottest part of the Valley. At a luggage store, I added a little suitcase to carry everything in. It was still only two o'clock when my shopping was done, so I found one of those multiplex movie houses nearby. I just wasn't in the mood for a serious drama. I bought a big, buttered popcorn and saw a comedy about kids and parents, and I thought: wouldn't it be nice if Bobby and I settled down in Argentina (when we weren't traveling with our champion thoroughbreds) and had a few kids. I'd never asked Bobby if he was religious, but I didn't think he was, and it certainly didn't matter to me.

It was only four-thirty when the movie ended, such a long day. I sat in my car and listened to the radio and I finally heard a news bulletin that this prominent attorney had been slain in his Wilshire Boulevard offices, and the police suspected robbery. That was all they said. I took the longest way I could back to the city, and what with the homebound traffic and all, it was dark by the time I got back to Bobby's place. But I was still early, so I sat on the landing again and waited for him.

Chapter Fourteen

Tuesday evening, although I'd planned to work late, I called Marcy and told her I'd meet her at the gym. I was too restless to take a class. I wrapped myself in a giant towel, mummy-style, grabbed a bench in the sauna all to myself, and lay down and skulked in steam as thick as a London fog. Marcy finally joined me, glowing with vigor and self-approval after her hour in advanced aerobics.

She looked at me pityingly and said, "What's the matter? Poor truffle crop this year?"

"Poor judgment, more likely."

"Tell Marcy."

"I've been spending a few hours here and there with a possible cad and bounder. I find him very attractive, and that makes me nervous."

I told her about the afternoon's episode with Bob and Elaine. "I know it's a long plane ride from London to L.A.," I concluded, "but she was so possessive, I felt there was more between them."

"There could have been," said my friend, "but that doesn't necessarily make him a cad."

"You don't think so?" Hope rose in my sweaty bosom.

"Suppose this Elaine drank up her whole bottle of duty-free gin on the flight. Or cracked her knuckles during the movie. Maybe he cooled off by the time they got to customs. So he gave her a phony address and kissed her goodbye at the baggage claim."

"You think so?" I said.

"On the other hand," Marcy said, "it's possible he is a cad."

"You think so," I moaned, and pulled my clammy towel tighter around me.

"The problem is," said Marcy judiciously, "you don't know anything about him. Where does he come from?"

"London, I think."

"That's not what I mean. Does he have parents, brothers, sisters?" She paused. "A wife."

"A wife? No, I don't think so. No. He's not the type."

"Did you ever ask him?"

I defended myself. "We're not on personal terms."

"I've never seen you so passive," said Marcy. "You even look like that girl in *St. James Infirmary.*" She sang in a growly blues voice, ". . . *saw muh baby lyin' there, stretched out on a long white table, so young, so cold, so bare* . . . Next time you see him, ask him about himself. Get some answers. Then decide whether you believe him."

"I'll be working Friday night. I doubt if there'll be time."

"Then just make time—if you feel you'd want to see him again. He's obviously interested in you." More kindly, she added, "Better get along to the showers. I think you're melting."

Angela

He came home finally about eight P.M. I was getting jittery, waiting on the landing. I saw from his face that he'd heard about the murder. Maybe it was even on TV by now. As far as I knew, they hadn't mentioned my name, so he couldn't be sure I was involved, but he was so smart he'd guess. When he saw me in front of his door, he scowled and then looked in back of him, I suppose to make sure no one was watching, but I'd been careful.

His place is in one of those two-story buildings with only two apartments on the bottom of the stairwell, and two at the top. Actually, that plan is very common around here. They must have built thousands of them. Catherine's apartment was the same layout, on top of the stairs. Only, Bobby's place is a tiny bachelor apartment: one crummy room, a bathroom, a curtained alcove with a smelly refrigerator, a sink, and a hot plate. I'd been thinking about it all day, because I wanted to stay with him until we could catch a plane and leave the country, but I knew deep in my heart he wouldn't let me move in. He always tells me he needs his

86

space. Sometimes he has a night job, so he isn't even home every night—he won't tell me where it is because I might want to come and see him and he'd be fired. I tell him I wouldn't but he laughs and says I'm so passionate he doesn't want to take chances, and maybe he's right, I don't know. He's become my whole life. It's hard to be apart, like yesterday and today when I really *needed* him.

So he practically pushed me into his apartment, shut the door, and said, What happened? That's when I tried to go according to the script I'd written in my head this morning. Sweetheart, I started to say (trying to sound very up and happy), I have a surprise for you. I reached for the brief-case and started to open it so I could show him the three hundred thousand in bearer bonds. All of a sudden, he grabbed my wrist. He was staring at the gold-stamped initials on the leather. My God, he said, is that Hastings's briefcase? I nodded yes. You brought it *here?* He picked up his hand and slapped me, real hard, across the face.

I was surprised at first, but then I thought, he has a right to be angry, I shouldn't put him in danger like that. But he brushed past me and picked up the briefcase. He opened it, put in his hands, and pulled out a handful of the bonds along with the diamond-and-platinum necklace. Well! he said very softly, sitting down on the bed and dumping everything in the briefcase out on the blanket. He shuffled through the bonds and counted them. I held my breath and didn't say a word, I wanted so bad for him to be pleased and happy. He said, I heard about Hastings on my car radio this afternoon. I guessed it was you. The police are saying it was probably robbery, but they didn't tell what was taken. He looked me up and down, and I sat very still, waiting. Then he grinned and said, You're full of surprises.

I told him, I was scared but I had to do it. I wanted to reassure him so I added: We were in luck, dear. The other two partners were in court all day yesterday, so no one in the office but me knew about the bonds. No one? he said, looking cheerful. How nice.

I'd been thinking during the day, maybe I should have tried to cover it up better, come back the next morning and act innocent—as if it was a real robbery. Maybe, but I was scared they'd suspect me anyway. How could I take the chance that I'd never see him again?

Just the idea made me shiver. I said, I love you. And even though I had never begged him before, now I said, *Please* make love to me. He laughed and said, have I ever turned you down? Then he grabbed me so hard I could feel his fingers making red marks on my shoulders. He shoved me down on the blanket. I was still wearing my good navy jacket and skirt, but he didn't care and neither did I. He pulled off my shoes and pantyhose and he thrust himself into me without even a word or a kiss. We didn't even push aside the bonds, it all happened so fast.

Chapter Fifteen

Pizza, said a fan, is "bread, love, and fantasy." You may have your own melting mozzarella dreams. For me—who could predict? It was during my pursuit of basic cheese pizza that I nearly got sent to that big take-out window in the sky. But that happens later. I mention pizza here because of its importance in L.A. life. Imagine the long commute home, we are crawling along in glare and haze composed of tail-pipe emissions and twilight. But nestled at the end of the freeway off-ramp are the staples of the food chain—the *fast* food chain—McDonald's, Kentucky Fried, Domino's, any or all of them. Why fuss with forks and knives? We order take-out that's mouth-pleasing. Portable. Belly-filling. And mundane.

No wonder, after this diet of finger-lickin', artery-cloggin' fast mass foods, designer pizza has become the California culinary hope. Our visionary pizza makers are the true fantasts, the new mystics of the possible and portable.

I imagine that Nick, who is ardent about pizza, dreams of the good old days in Brooklyn when pizza was sausage or pepperoni, and fantasy was adding two handfuls of anchovies instead of one.

Dellacasa's pizza today is something else. Forget the mozzarella. We'll make you a BLT, hold the cheese; Brie with fresh blueberries; Gruyere with fennel; Thai-style with shredded chicken, chiles, and fresh mint—in individual, appetizer, and mob-size pizzas.

These and more are on our catering menu, mostly prepared by Mario, our catering chef. If Nick provides the love to Dellacasa's pizzas, Mario creates the fantasies.

Mario, I should explain, despite his name is not Italian. Actually, he's black. He's tall, narrow, skinny, and looks like a walking licorice whip. Mario is from the large Belize community in Los Angeles and speaks with a charming Caribbean lilt. His mother, who sings in her church choir, named him after her Mario Lanza records, hoping he'd also sing opera in the movies. Instead, he's a graduate of the culinary arts program at a downtown trade school and, at age twenty-four, he aspires to be a great chef. He's saving for a year in Lyon, studies French at night, and writes letters applying to the top restaurants in France but, so far, no nibbles.

Nick has trained Mario in Italian cuisine, encourages him, and realizes that someday soon, Mario will surpass him. Last year at Christmas, I ordered a Gastronomique Larousse for Mario, from the French bookstore in Westwood, and my gift has helped him forgive my lapses in taste.

Mario and I argue over menus and recipes. I am too timid to take gastronomic leaps, he tells me. He shakes his head in reproach. How could I possibly suggest *roast beef finger sandwiches!* yawn, yawn, for the Wesley supper party, while he was away taking a few well-earned vacation days? I humbly agree his individual pizzas topped with duck sausage, peppers and shiitake mushrooms have much more style and intensity. It is one of our typical exchanges. At the end, I agree to call Bob Crosswaithe and suggest the change. I hadn't talked to him since his stormy encounter with Elaine Stedman earlier in the week. Not that I was concerned. Crosswaithe, it seemed to me, would eventually sweeten up that lady like warm honeyed syrup on a simple poached pear.

As I reached for the phone, it rang. Mr. Moskowitz, my landlord, was calling. This was a rare event. Mr. M., despite my many reassurances, believes that I will be fired if I accept personal calls. He rushes through messages about sending the plumber, the roofer, or the electrician to my apartment. Sometimes the words get garbled.

Today he hesitated, sounding worried. "Catherine?" he said. "Is that you, Catherine?" I assured him it was.

"Somebody came to the door asking about you today. I didn't know what to tell him."

"What did he want?"

"Well, he kind of told me what you looked like, and wanted to know if it was you. He described you pretty good."

"Did he have an English accent? Was there a friend with him?"

"No, nothing like that," said Mr. Moskowitz. "He was just an ordinary guy, very friendly. He said he was looking for a Catherine Deean who has a sister in Baton Rouge, Louisiana. Do you have a sister?"

"No, I don't. What did you tell him?"

Mr. M. was reassuring. "Oh, I told him I never give out information about my tenants. You know, after that pretty young actress was killed by that nutty fan, not far from here, I wouldn't take chances."

I thanked him and added, "Did he say anything else?"

"No, like I said, he was very pleasant. He said he understood and thanked me for my trouble, then he walked away. But I saw he stopped at the mailbox, maybe to check on your apartment number."

"Well, I can't imagine who it is, Mr. Moskowitz. But if you see him again, I'd appreciate it if you let me know."

"Sure thing, Catherine."

"There could be another Catherine Deean who has a sister in Louisiana."

"That's probably it," he said. "Mrs. Moskowitz says hello."

He hung up and I frowned. Mario was waiting, listening idly.

"Anything wrong, *chérie?*" Mario likes to sprinkle his conversations with French words of endearment or, as he learns them, the more pungent Gallic phrases.

I shrugged it off. "No. Mistaken identity."

I called and left a message for Bob Crosswaithe, who was helping Ronald Wesley scout locations, that English roast beef was to be superseded by our magnificent California duck sausage pizzas.

Angela

He let me stay all night. Just before dawn we woke and made love again, this time slower, sweeter. After he fell asleep, I pressed against the warm length of him, making myself as quiet and boneless as a cat, so I could memorize how it felt being so close I was almost part of him. Then the light shone through the worn spots in the drapes. He got out of bed, and I could tell he was tense and excited. He let me make breakfast for him. Not much, bread, jam, and coffee was all there was in the cupboard, but it was our first breakfast together. I was wearing my new red negligee and I felt like this was our honeymoon, even though I knew in my heart that he would make me leave before tonight.

Switzerland was out, he said, you're making this too complicated. Besides, there was more chance they'd be looking for you at the airports. (He said *you*, not *us*, but I kept quiet, because he was right, the police would only be looking for me.) He said, first step, if the bonds are as simple to cash in as you think, we need to find out just how to do it.

At breakfast I'd explained municipal bonds to Bobby just

the way Mr. Hastings explained them to me: some investors like them because they're tax-free, easy to hide, and
easy to sell. They're like having cash—if the bonds are in
your hands, they're yours.

Now Bobby handed me the L.A. Yellow Pages and told
me to find some stockbrokers. I'm very quick at looking
things up—Mr. Hastings always said so—and I found the
listings right away, under "Investment Securities."

Bobby grabbed away the phone book, sat down on the
bed, took the phone, and dialed one of the big brokerage
houses. It was around eight in the morning, and they were
already at work.

I had to giggle when Bobby asked to speak to a broker.
He was putting on that high-class English accent he does
sometimes for fun, like Prince Charles only snobbier. They
gave his call to a Mr. Azir, and Bobby was so smart at fool-
ing him, I had to cover my mouth to keep from laughing.
(Bobby frowned at me, but then he winked, so I knew he
was having a good time playing at being a lord or an earl or
someone fancy.) He said to Mr. Azir that he had come from
his country home in Shropshire to settle his uncle's affairs,
being his sole heir; that he had found this rather large
amount of California municipal bonds in Uncle Neville's
wall safe, and that since most of his inheritance was in real
estate, and would take some time to sell off, he was anxious
to cash in the bonds now. He told this Mr. Azir: I must
return to Shropshire almost immediately—my cows are
calving and they need me.

This was so funny, I nearly choked. Then Mr. Azir talked
for a long time, and when Bobby hung up, he said he knew
how it worked.

Listen, love, here's how to do it, he said. We'll pick a
brokerage house, and I'll open an account in my name. He
took my hands and pulled me down, so I was sitting on the
bed, facing him. He said, looking deep into my eyes, you'll
trust me to put the bonds in my name, won't you? It's really

too chancy for you to open the account. I said, my eyes meeting his, you *know* I trust you, and I did. (It was like in the movies when the lovers swear undying devotion.) Even when I didn't know we'd have this much money—I thought it would only be about a hundred thousand, that's what I figured I could take from the trust accounts Mr. Hastings managed—Bobby had a plan, he's planned our whole wonderful future. Now he leaned forward and kissed me, it was just a fond little kiss. He could tell I wanted more, but he smiled and shook his head and said, every hour counts—we must move fast.

He said, once I have the account, I simply hand over the bonds, get a receipt, then give them an order to sell. It takes five working days, and it's all terribly discreet, according to Azir. Then Bobby said, if I open the account today I can pick up the check, less the broker's commission, a week from today. We'll have to hide you meanwhile. We'll drive south—near San Diego.

You'll stay with me? I asked. He said, darling Angela, I can't do that. Too many plans to make here in L.A.

I started to cry, I told him I was afraid, I didn't want to leave him. He didn't yell at me, he was so tender. He hugged me, and put his lips close to my ear—his warm breath made me feel weak—and whispered: you were so brave until now, just keep up your courage a little longer.

I said, why can't we be together now? Although I knew. I was in too much trouble in L.A.

He gently stroked my arms, and said: Here's why. You need to disappear. You told your mother you were in San Francisco, so you'd better head in the other direction. For now, I'll park your car next to mine in the empty space in my carport, I'll put a tarp over it, and I'll see if I can find this chap who replaces license plates—for a price.

I asked, do you think the police are after me already?

He said, you've been such a perfect employee, they may even suspect foul play—that you've been kidnapped or done in, too. I imagine you have a day or two before there's any warrant.

Then why can't you come with me? I pleaded. I have nearly six thousand dollars in cash—what I took from Mr. Hastings's account and from my savings. We could go to Mexico together while we're waiting out the week. We'd have such a good time.

Six thousand? he said, I could use a couple of thousand for expenses. The cash was in an envelope in my purse. I immediately took out two thousand and gave it to him, gladly, and asked, do you want the jewelry from the brief-case, too? Uh, uh, he said, wouldn't want to touch it. Even if Hastings's office doesn't know about the bonds, they've possibly contacted the old lady's nephew. You said he told Hastings there was jewelry. The police may figure he took some of it for safekeeping. We'll wrap it and hide it in your suitcase, until I can think about it.

He was thinking hard about other things, because he sat on the bed and whistled "Imagine" off-key, his eyes half closed. I sat very close to him, so our thighs touched.

I asked, my eyes getting teary again, you won't change your mind about Mexico? He didn't move away, but he looked at me reproachfully and said, you're not thinking clearly. (He was right, he knew me. I get so emotional.) He said, I'll have to figure what to do once I get the money. I can't do that in Mexico, looking over my shoulder to see if we're being followed. Besides, I'm a British citizen. I'd have to show my papers at the border, and I might be remembered.

He said, I know about a small health spa this side of the border near a backwater place called Jacumba, it's about an hour from San Diego. I met a woman who'd stayed there. She was getting over surgery to remove bad breast implants. (I wondered, how did he meet her? but I didn't dare ask.) We'll call from here, and you'll make a reservation. When you check in, tell them you're having a nervous breakdown or some such story and need lots of solitude, then relax for a week. He said, in a cheerful way, have some mud baths, they hide everything. I tried to smile.

He looked at his watch. If you get dressed now, he said, we could be on the freeway by nine. We'll stop in Santa Monica, and find a brokerage house there. With all those rich, retired people living near the ocean, they'll be used to big sums.

He said, after I finish with the bonds, we can pick up the 405 South, eventually cut over to the 8 and reach the spa by midafternoon. Once I get you settled, I'll have to turn right around and start back to L.A. I have to be at work this evening.

I didn't ask why. I was thinking: A week. A whole week without him. I wasn't sure I could bear that. But what else could I do, except trust him? I never, never before had anyone to love. I felt so empty until I met him. I swear, I never want to feel that way again.

Call me here tomorrow night, said Bobby, I'll be here. Let me know how everything's going. Oh, and on the way to San Diego, he added, we'll get off the freeway—find a small town—you'll go to a hairdresser and change the color of your hair. He smiled that sweet teasing smile. Deep down, didn't you ever want to be a blonde? he said. Bobby, I said, sometimes it scares me that you know me so well.

Chapter Sixteen

The Santa Ana winds chased away the mild autumn weather and stirred up mischief. It was so hot and dry in the Southland, the brushfire season began early, in the first days of October. On the evening news, the national and international crises took second place to vivid pictures of blazing shingle roofs and charred hillsides.

I called it nosebleed season; the dryness cracked the lining of my nose and parched my brain. I walked around with nasal sprays and vague feelings of irritation. Some afternoons the air was gritty with blowing dust and it carried the faraway smell of smoke uncomfortably close to home.

Possibly I was restless because vacation was over and there would be little free time for me until January. I wasn't a hermit, I saw friends and family. One Wednesday evening, I went to a Thai restaurant and the movies with Marcy. Thursdays, I renounced guilt and returned to my aerobics class. I took an afternoon off on a Friday, and did lunch and the Impressionist exhibit at the County Art Museum with Aunt Sadie. She apologized for not staying on for dinner, but she had her standing Friday evening date with Charles, who liked to make the rounds of jazz clubs. Charles has white hair and his hands are slightly palsied, but from the time he'd discovered Bunny Berigan and Artie Shaw, jazz had kept his ears young. I didn't *exactly* envy them. I could have gone with Gil to the computer software show at the Convention Center, and later we'd bump along the torn-up downtown streets (new subways and glass towers, and who's afraid of the big bad quakes?) to Chinatown for Hot and Sour soup. Gil has called quite a bit since my return from Greece. Warily I declined, rented a Mad Max movie, and spent an enchanted evening with Mel Gibson and a skin-purifying facial mask.

It was Monday when Detectives Velasquez and Wang paid me a visit. I had spent Sunday presiding over the cheeses, pâtés, and desserts donated by a wealthy Brentwood bachelor, along with his house and patio, to a garden party sponsored by Single Executives with Political Consciences. It was an afternoon wine-tasting, campaign debt-reducing, mingling fund-raiser. I make no judgments about the guests; I'm sure they help protect our besieged constitutional processes. However, having an astute conscience must make singles hungry or, having donated fifty dollars to enter, they are reacting to the high cost of democracy. Both our tables and the winery's were crowded all that hot, windy afternoon. So Monday morning, when Paul Wang phoned, I was seated at my desk with spray and moisturizer, nursing a stuffy nose and a sunburn. He said, "It's about your ex-neighbor, Angela." Serious. No small talk.

I was only mildly curious, even a bit annoyed. Angela again. She was about as welcome as lumps in the gravy. She had nothing to do with the predictable, let's face it, dull, yes, sometimes dull course of my life. She was an unpleasant incident, now closed.

An hour later, the two homicide detectives arrived and climbed the stairs to my small office. I fetched coffee for us. Detective Velasquez took out a small pad and cut straight to the chase.

"We're following up on persons who may have been in contact with Angela Cappelli. Would you have any idea of her whereabouts?"

"No," I said. "My landlord told me she's been gone for a while. I don't know where and, truthfully"—my distaste was showing—"I don't care."

"I understand that, Miss Deean, but this is important."

Paul Wang broke in. "Catherine," he said, "I told Detective Velasquez about meeting you in Chinatown, and why you'd decided that Angela did the break-in."

"It was over a month ago," I said. "Why this sudden interest now?"

Detective Velasquez's weathered face looked apologetic. "This has no relationship to what happened in your apartment. Homicide wants to question Miss Cappelli about a murder that took place last week." He paused. "Her employer was killed."

I was startled. "She worked for an attorney. That must have been the Wilshire district murder and robbery. I read about it in the newspapers. And you think Angela did it?"

The detective was noncommittal. "There is evidence that she may be involved. We'd like to talk to her."

There is something about two homicide detectives giving you their full attention that makes you remember everything antisocial you've ever done, back to the time you were five and socked your rotten four-year-old cousin when your mother wasn't looking.

I furrowed my brow and said, "She moved. My landlord told me that Angela and her mother moved while I was still away. Doesn't her office have her new address?"

"That's the problem," said Paul Wang. "We have her address, we've talked to Mrs. Cappelli. But she says that Angela hasn't been home since the night of the murder. She may be staying with friends. That's why we hoped you could help.

"Remember," he continued, "I told you I'd file Angela away in my mind under 'maybe useless, maybe not'? I remembered the phone calls you—or Angela—had, the different men. We wondered if you could tell us anything about them. Names, maybe phone numbers . . ."

"Let's see," I said, "There was Harv, and Baxter. And Warren. But first names only, and no return phone numbers. These guys were pretty casual. Possibly one or two of them were married. It happens."

Paul smiled and patted his remarkable mustache. "A cynic, hey?"

"Just life in the big city," I said, then added, "Have you checked out the Paddock? I'm sure that's where she met them."

"We have," said Detective Velasquez. "The name was in my notes from our first interview."

Paul was more communicative. "Mrs. Cappelli gave us a snapshot of Angela taken last Christmas. The bartender said she looked, well, mousy, compared to the girl he remembered, but he thinks Angela did hang out there a few nights in August."

Vindicated. I'd been a first-class detective. No question: Catherine Spade-Marlowe had cracked the case.

"None of the men ever called again?"

Ohmigosh! I'd forgotten Cheeks and the Turtle. I told the detectives about them, and about Bobby. I gave them a description of my visitors, and noted that possibly all three were English. That was it. There was nothing else I knew.

The two men thanked me and rose to leave. "Please contact us if you think of anything else," said Detective David R. Velasquez, leaving another card.

Detective Wang shook my hand. "I've been meaning to

get down to Westwood and take you up on that lunch. We've been very busy."

"Oh, whenever," I said airily, in parting. "We don't have steamed dumplings, but the ravioli is good."

An accurate statement, but insipid.

Angela

So now I'm a blonde, but I'm sure not having more fun. Just imagine spending a week in a jerktown spa where the whoop-dee-do entertainment is counting the scars on other people's bellies! I mean, this place is creepy. I told Bobby when he called last night I should get my appendix operated on just so I can fit in with this crowd. He laughed as if I was being funny, but it was a nervous laugh, I thought. He said, don't get impatient, I'm picking up the, ahem, gift, tomorrow. I giggled when he said that, I knew he didn't want to say *bonds* on the phone.

When are you coming for me? I asked, I've had it with watching Oprah and Sally Jessy Raphael and going to bed at nine o'clock. Why don't you relax? he said, it's a vacation. Well, I answered, this "resort" is a sick joke, and I don't have a car and the town is miles from anywhere, and I'm afraid to go into the whirlpool bath because maybe I'll catch whatever these repulsive people are here to recover from. So when are you picking me up?

It's not that simple, he said, I have to take care of our "gift" after they give it to me and that could take time. Just

take it easy, he said in that caressing way that makes me feel
like his legs are wrapped around me, you know I miss you
like crazy but this is best for now. I was shameless, I was
almost begging him: when will I see you? I *want* you. He
said, Monday, I'll come down and stay over on Monday.
We can go into San Diego and get the bridal suite in some
posh hotel. Y'know, with a king-size bed and satin sheets.
Wouldn't you like that? Can we have room service send up
some champagne? I asked. The best French champagne in
the oh-my-God size, he said, laughing. And caviar, he
added, I'll feed you shiny black caviar on little pieces of
toast with the crusts cut off. And then, very bold I said,
before or after we make love? Even during, he said, you tell
me what you want. He chuckled softly and said, I'll see you
Monday in time for lunch, then he hung up. For a few
minutes I sat by the phone, really happy. Then I thought: I
trust him, I do. But Monday is such a long ways away. I
wonder if there's anyone else he'd want to spend some of
that money on, before Monday.

Chapter Seventeen

Along with a muddy picture of me simpering over a dish of fajitas, I was quoted once in the Thursday Food Section of the *Los Angeles Times* as saying my professional secret is: I like to go to parties. Nick, Mario, and the others at Dellacasa's took the revelation in stride. The only other comment this raised was an anonymous phone call inviting me to an orgy.

It's true, though. I do like parties. By Friday, I was charged up and ready for an evening with Hollywood's fair, famous, and well fixed. I made one late-morning trip up Benedict Canyon to be sure the flowers, our buffet tables, and three round dining tables with blue-and-cream linens were delivered and set up. Bob and I had decided earlier to ignore the dining room with its long dark mahogany table, hanging tapestries, dim wall sconces, and lurking spirits. Instead, we'd have supper served on the heated patio, in full view of the sparkling night city below.

I didn't see Bob. The maid let me in; Mr. Crosswaithe, she told me, had been sent on an errand by Mr. Wesley to the preview theater in Westwood. I suppose I was relieved;

105

it was easier without him to concentrate on the business of the party.

I did meet Ronald Wesley. As I fussed with the location of the tables, I caught a blur of action on the terrace below. There was a splash, and I realized that Mr. Wesley had entered his pool. I heard a jovial yell, "Hello, there!" and turned to see him wave at me, hardly interrupting a clean backstroke that took him to one end of the pool and back again.

"You must be the caterer. Why don't you come down here and introduce yourself?"

I walked down the steps to the pool level. Mr. Wesley ascended from the water, leaving the eternal tile mermaids frolicking in the clear blue depths of the pool. Soaking wet, he was no more than a hundred twenty pounds, maybe five feet three, with thinning orange hair now flattened like that of some impish water sprite. The voice, however, was deep and sonorous, as if Orson Welles had taken over the body of Peter Pan.

"You are . . . ?"

"Catherine Deean of Dellacasa's Catering, Mr. Wesley."

He looked me over quickly and shrewdly. He was quite sober, genial but businesslike. It was obvious that he was used to taking charge.

He put out a damp hand and I shook it. "Bob has told me," he said, "that your firm does good work. I'm looking forward to enjoying my dinner."

"Thank you. We appreciate the opportunity."

"Are you getting cooperation from my staff? Do you have everything you need? Want to give me a quick run-down?"

Obviously he paid attention to details. I felt that with Ronald Wesley, all the world was a movie set; he wanted to know how I planned to set the stage for his supper party.

He drew on a thick terry-cloth robe, nodding his head

attentively as I reported on menu, seating, table settings, time we'd serve.

"Right. Right. Right."

Good. One professional to another.

"Are you using some of my silver service and those incredibly ostentatious serving pieces on the sideboard in the dining hall?"

I explained that we planned to bring our own silver and crystal. Many households do not own service for twenty-six.

"No, no," he said impatiently. "Didn't Bob call? I told him to discuss it with you. All those antiquated eyesores came with the house when I bought it." He grinned, making it an open secret that he enjoyed this baronial life.

"Look through the cupboards," he said. "A lot of Hollywood legends made drinking fools of themselves with those wineglasses. Ask Janine, my maid, to show you. Use whatever you can. She'll polish up anything you need for tonight." Poor Janine.

He wished me luck and strode off on bantam legs. I found Janine, who unlocked the serving pantry off the kitchen. The double pantry doors swung open slowly as if they were heavily weighted. I could see why. Inside the pantry and lining the doors custom-fitted shelves held a museum-quality collection of gold-and-cobalt-rimmed Art Deco china, Lalique crystal, silver service plates, and Tiffany sterling flatware to easily serve one hundred, in an exquisite fluted pattern. I felt as if I were wearing a pith helmet and this was the dining area of King Solomon's Mines. It was definitely a cut above Arnie's Restaurant Supply Company.

I enlisted Janine's help and we carried out what would be needed for tonight, carefully setting the pieces on a worktable in the great yellow-and-black tiled kitchen. Meanwhile, we chatted. Janine was pretty, plump, and Gallic. She was also gracious about the extra washing up and polishing she would need to do in the next few hours. She and her husband Maurice adored Mr. Wesley. He had brought them from France ten years ago, hiring them away from a villa he had rented in Deauville while filming his World War II epic, *The Devil's Beaches.*

Maurice, *hélas!* was currently in France, visiting his ailing mother near Nantes. He would return next week. Mr. Wesley had provided the airline ticket. Although I felt cheaper than Woolworth candy, it was easy to slip in a question about Mr. Crosswaithe. Was he helpful in Maurice's absence? I asked. Oh, yes, Janine assured me, Mr. Crosswaithe was *très gentil,* very nice. Mr. Wesley should not always drive by himself, she confided, and though a true genius, sometimes he did not remember giving money or making promises to unworthy people. Mr. Crosswaithe understood and, like Maurice, he did not shake when Mr. Wesley roared at him in that thundering voice.

"He is *un homme du monde,* worldly, you say," said Janine. "Very European. Not innocent, like the Americans."

Ah, this put handsome Bob in a new light. Perhaps it was my American naiveté that created tension on my part. Perhaps he had this older, European, existentialist view of life, accepting the guilt of whatever it took him to get by.

And perhaps I was full of beans. Nonetheless, Janine made me feel more cheerful than I had in days.

I told her I would return early evening and I left, making my way down through the steep canyon turns back to Westwood and Dellacasa's. I checked in with Mario, who was skewering shrimp while listening to a tape of French irregular verbs. I gave him directions for finding the Wesley residence. He would drive the catering van, taking along the food and our two waitresses, Lupe and Olivia. I planned to go home, shower and dress, and drive my own car back to the party.

I stopped at my office just long enough to return a phone call from Paul Wang. He had been in Westwood earlier, and had hoped to stop by and have lunch. Too bad we missed each other. I agreed. Did he plan to be in the neighborhood again soon? Well, you know police work, he said, you never know. I told him I could understand that, and extended the invitation once more. I asked about Angela.

"She seems to have disappeared," said Paul. "We'd sure like to talk to her. Have you heard anything more from her friends?"

"Nothing," I replied.

"Well, we'll keep in touch," he said. And that was that.

Chapter Eighteen

I t was a lovely party. All the right elements were there: I recognized three high-powered stars; there were other attractive and/or powerful people; a well-stocked bar; Mario's way with a buffet, a deliciously artful arrangement of colors, textures, and tastes, made sumptuous by the heavy, gleaming chafing dishes and trays from the host's collection. The night was so clear, the glittering city lights were like reflections of the stars and crescent moon. Hurricane lamps on the three round dining tables created little islands of illumination that magically seemed to make the patio float untethered above the scattered lights of the black canyon below. Not least, there was the heady scent of success: the movie preview had gone well, there were raves on many of the preview cards the exiting audience filled out. Some of these cards had been passed around during drinks earlier in the living room. Then, during supper, a happy, voluble Ronald Wesley, face flushed on nothing more than a Perrier-and-lime, sat with his editor and thumbed through the critiques again, tapping a finger against a particular comment, making notes.

His guests seemed to accept being ignored. I hadn't seen much of Bob Crosswaithe. Except for a Hollywood-type brush of lips on cheek as he arrived from the screening with some of the guests (he was learning fast), a murmured "Catherine dear, you look lovely," and a few hurried words about serving time, we had not been alone all evening. He was wearing a well-cut navy blazer, grey trousers, and white dress shirt open at the neck. I wondered if they were part of his drab London wardrobe; he looked quite dashing. Apparently, I was not the only one to think so. There were no place cards at supper. (Wesley's theory, I'd been told, was: let 'em find their own level.) Bob, however, seated himself next to the would-be actress with the ripe, kissy lips (silicone, I guessed). She is the daughter of a Detroit industrialist. Rumor has it, Daddy is willing to spend some of his fortune buying into a Hollywood production company (which one to be decided) to help stop the damn Japanese from grabbing yet another beachhead in American industry. If Baby (who managed to make a Scaasi dinner suit look tacky by adding on about five pounds of purple eye makeup) came with the deal, well, so be it.

Anyway, Bob obviously had been assigned to make sure Detroit's daughter enjoyed her evening. (I generously assumed that it was Wesley's plan, not Bob's.) They avoided Wesley's circle and the table where Daddy sat happily next to the sultry-voiced, heavy-breasted beauty starring in Wesley's new film. They chose seats at the far side of the third table, where the light was dimmer. Although Bob did, I observed, join easily in the general table conversation, he saved some special moments for Baby, his golden head almost touching Baby's thick tangle of black curls.

That's all right, I told myself. We're both doing our jobs.

Everyone had been served. Mario was heartily complimented on the goat cheese flan. Several of the men took seconds on the hot apple pie. Along with the two waitresses, I refilled wineglasses and served desserts. Now I stood be-

hind one of the long buffet tables, back to the canyon, real-
izing that the wind had come up and that I was chilly in my
black chiffon dress.

I had a quilted black satin blazer in the trunk of my car; I
decided to slip out for a moment and retrieve it. There was
a service door that opened from the kitchen to a set of steps
that descended to a gravel parking area below and to the
side of the house. A narrow path led to it from the front
driveway, curving down and around to the service area.

Although a dozen or so cars could fit into the lot, it was a
tight squeeze and once the cars were parked, the entry to
the house was through the kitchen. It was usual for a canyon resident to arrange for valet parking when there were
more cars than could fit into a front driveway. I knew there
would be a couple of attendants watching over the expensive cars.

They had not yet arrived when I drove up around seven
in the evening, but now, as I walked down the steps, I could
see two figures lounging against a black Mercedes. One was
smoking a cigarette. They were both large and muscular;
both dressed in what is a standard parking lot uniform:
white shirt, black pants, black bow tie. The parking area
was harshly lit by two spotlights high on the wall of the
main house. Their beams created sharp black-and-white
shadows on the faces of the two men. Somehow, the fea-
tures were familiar. I hesitated on the stairs, my mind running through my card index to see whether I could fit the
faces to any valet parking company I'd encountered. No,
the familiarity had nothing to do with cars. Ohmigosh!
Now I knew them. But what were Cheeks and the Turtle
doing here, parking cars under a constellation of stars as
classy as the neighborhood?

"Hey," said the Turtle, standing up and looking in my
direction, "it's Katie!" He trotted over in my direction, followed closely by Cheeks.

"Are you at the party? It looks like some swell party." He seemed genuinely happy to see me.

"I'm working here," I said. "The company I work for is catering the food."

"D'you suppose you could get us something to eat?" asked Cheeks, patting the belly that was testing the buttons on his white shirt. "We tried the maid but she wasn't too friendly."

"I'll ask her to bring you some sandwiches and dessert. I think the party will go on at least another hour."

"Like Bobby said, you're very friendly!"

Bobby? *What* Bobby? Angela's Bobby?

"Did Bobby get you this job?" I asked.

"He did," answered the Turtle, pulling at the bow tie that appeared to be strangling a neck as solid as a cheese wheel. "We was running out of money. What with the rented car and the motels, we was getting short. But Bobby has connections . . ."

"Bobby *always* has connections . . ." chimed in Cheeks.

". . . so he got us this. And then he's got some other things lined up." The Turtle's smile turned to pain as Cheeks stepped heavily on his foot.

"What did you do that for?" asked the Turtle in indignation.

Cheeks glared at him, muttered "Shut up, sod!" loud enough for me to hear him. The Turtle looked startled, then embarrassed.

"We're okay, Katie," said Cheeks, taking charge. "If you could just find us something to eat, that's a pal."

"Of course," I said. "I just came out to get my jacket." I headed toward my car, took my satin blazer from the trunk, passed them, and smiled on my way back to the kitchen. I knew now who they really were. Tweedledum and Tweedledee. Brought to America direct from the grimier banks of the Thames.

I should have questioned them more, I suppose. It was

just that their presence raised so many questions about Bob Crosswaithe, I didn't want to deal with any of it. I hurried back to the party and served coffee from an immense silver pot almost heavy enough to put my wrist in a sling. As I poured, I could see him exchanging merry glances with Baby, adorable daughter of Detroit.

Chapter Nineteen

After the glitz and surprises at Ronald Wesley's mansion, it was a relief to switch from Blanc de Blancs to apple juice.

I'll admit, one would not list this other weekend party on a résumé when applying to be sous chef at Spago. And, ordinarily, I would not take on a special menu for a children's party this small; it's not cost effective. But Sunday afternoon was for college friend Eva's five-year-old Jason, a slender towheaded boy with spectacles, knobby knees, and allergies. Eva had banned red meat, nitrites, white flour, and refined sugars, so Mario and I planned an allergy-free menu around artichoke-flour spaghetti slathered with lots of kid-pleasing red sauce—and it was with pride in our ingenuity that I placed five candles on the whole wheat flour carrot cake.

After the backyard piñata breaking, after the last scraped knee had been tended to, the last party favors wrapped to take home, and the last child picked up by his mother, I sat and chatted with Eva and Jake. She is small, dark-haired, and competitive, a social worker with lots of drive and few illusions. Jake is a high school English teacher, a lanky older version of little Jason.

I'd given marriage a try and, for now at least, had given up. They seemed to be making it work. They sat together in their small living room, on the homely, child-proof Herculon sofa, holding hands in easy, thirtysomething domesticity. A few years ago, they had borrowed money from Jake's parents for the downpayment on their $180,000 Culver City 1947 fixer-upper. Now they sat with the self-satisfied look of landowners who have seen the value of their house grow to over $300,000 in those few years. Land defines the haves and have-nots in Los Angeles. What was in the house was Spartan and practical. The good life is having enough to make the monthly mortgage payment. And, Jason's doctor bills were high. The fifth birthday party was to celebrate a year of relatively good health.

I hadn't seen Eva and Jake since my divorce, so they approached my current state of emotional health with delicacy.

"I'm happy," I assured them. "I love my work and I'm just back from a fabulous vacation in Europe."

Eva (tactful pause): "Anyone new in your life?"

Me (independence incarnate): "Don't have room for anyone in my life right now."

Jake (smug as only a man who's proved he can make babies can be): "Eva worries about her friends's biological clocks."

Eva (squeezing his hand fondly): "Jake, that's nonsense. It's the old, antifeminist cliché that a woman can't be fulfilled until she has a child!"

Jake (in mock horror): "Did I say all of that?"

Oh, well, Eva at times reminds me of one of those birds that swoops down on you, wings fluttering in panic, as if your lone stroll were threatening its nest. I decided to escape. Olivia had driven away the van with all of our equipment, so I left soon after in my own car. I drove east through the old-fashioned streets lined with palm trees, past rows of rickety bungalows and pastel stucco boxes turned gold mines. I thought about the money I'd splurged on vacation, savings that probably should have gone into my own house-buying fund. I reflected on Gil, home, motherhood, mom's apple pie, the flag, and being single in L.A. in the nervous nineties. Much earlier in the day, I had lunched on a plate of our natural, unadulterated kiddie food and now I realized I was getting hungry. So I stopped at the drive-in window and picked up a Big Mac, large fries, and a Coke. Monday, I took the day off and subsisted on tea, whole grain toast, and organic apple butter. I couldn't get my palate or my mind on an even keel.

It was Bob Crosswaithe mixing me up. If he was also Bobby, he was the man who had written to London, telling the two cockney buddies to come to my apartment. To see Katie, who was undoubtedly Angela, who had been posing as me. *If Bob was also Bobby, he was most likely the man Angela had entertained that first night I'd gone on vacation.* If so, did he know it was my apartment Angela had used? Was it some sort of cosmic coincidence that Crosswaithe and I had finally met? I couldn't figure out any of it.

I suppose I should have been on the phone immediately to Detective Paul Wang. I should have said, Hello, Paul, guess what? Friday night, I saw those jolly guys again. And, you know what else? Their friend is a really gorgeous, sexy man I'm on the verge of getting involved with, but he may be connected—just a teeny bit—to your murder.

Did I call Paul Wang? Let me put it this way. Turkeys, it is well known, are so stupid they will run in the direction of a stranger, bump into each other, and ultimately trample themselves to death. Bob Crosswaithe was a stranger who drew women to him (I remembered Elaine and Baby). I told myself it was safer—if lonely—to stay in my own part of the barnyard.

On the other hand, it was only fair to talk to Bob (aka

Bobby?) before I yelled for the cops. Suppose there was an innocent explanation for his knowing Cheeks and the Turtle. The wrong words from me, and all three of them could be deported. Would I want that on my conscience?

In an ordinary crisis, I would be on the phone to Marcy, my level-headed friend. I'm not sure why I didn't call her. Hold it, that's a cop-out. I do know why I chose not to pick up the phone that weekend. I was afraid of common sense.

Chapter Twenty

He wasn't avoiding me. Next morning, when I arrived at work, there was a message from Bob Crosswaithe. He had called on Monday to say: *I owe you a lunch. How about Wednesday?* More immediate, there was Mario in person, greeting me with an armful of books on Southwest cooking and a request to "Think Apache, *chérie*. Nick says it's up to us. The Indians he knew in Brooklyn were Mohawks, and they liked pizza."

We were doing the invitations-only party after the hundred-dollar-a-ticket benefit movie premiere of *Apache Sunset*. We agreed to meet after I'd returned phone calls. I talked business to a mother-of-the-bride, a linen supply house, and the office manager for a noted brokerage firm who'd opted for a downtrend in the office Christmas party —from a full buffet dinner to, as she put it, some really filling hors d'oeuvres. I was reassuring, agreeable, as can-do as Betty Crocker. Finally, there was the one call left.

"Hello, Bob, it's Catherine."

"Cat! How nice to hear your voice. You were out yesterday?"

"Just took the day off. It was a working weekend."

"Yes, well, you don't have much time for fun, do you? Maybe we can change that."

A bit presumptuous of him, I thought. Of course I had fun. On my own terms. In my own time.

"What do you think?" Bob asked. "Can you squeeze in lunch with me tomorrow? This time I promise it will be just us—no baggage from my past life."

"I'm putting it right down on my crowded calendar."

We chose to meet at one of my favorite small restaurants in Westwood, a place—like Dellacasa's—where the room's sounds are muted. I've never understood the ear-splitting noise levels in some of our more stylish restaurants. There is a theory that the excess noise helps Angelenos cope with the isolation of our lives: I hear, therefore I am. Possibly. But it's hellish on the digestion.

Chumley's is also within walking distance of my office. Perhaps that gave me comfort. If I didn't like what I heard from Bob, I could retreat to home territory in five minutes.

I did like what he was saying now.

"I don't want to wait to pass on this message from Ronald. He was extraordinarily pleased with the way your supper went Friday night. He said to say, thank you, he had a wonderful time at his own party. He meant it, too, Cat. Of course, you realize I took some credit for your great performance."

You were performing rather well yourself, I thought ungratefully, but didn't say.

I said, "Thank you for telling me. I'm glad everything went smoothly."

It did, until my startling encounter in the valet parking lot. But that could wait until tomorrow. I was almost relieved to put down the phone and turn off his voice. There was that hint of amusement that seemed to draw me into some inside joke—life as an inside joke?—no matter how I tried to keep my distance. I resolved to put him out of my head and plunge into Indian Fry Bread and chile peppers and finally, gratefully, I did.

We had a few inside laughs over lunch. Bob had a wicked eye for details, and he took great pleasure in explaining an episode I had guessed at during Friday's supper: a producer, his wife, and his mistress seated together for an intimate game of thrust, parry, and kill.

"It was foolish for Cara to pick on his wife," concluded Bob with a wry shrug. "After all, Marie's been around this track. She was his mistress, she got him to divorce his first wife. You have to look at the bloodlines. Marie's proved she's a champion."

It was almost too easy. What an opening! I said lightly, "This sounds more like a horse race than a triangle."

Pause, while he thought about it. We had been sitting with heads close, as gossipers do. Now he tilted back his chair, crossed his long legs, openly looked me over, then smiled broadly. With his cap of blond curls, he had the aura of an off-duty angel.

"You've found me out," he said. "You've discovered my two favorite pastimes—women and horse racing. No disrespect intended. Not at all. I just find both terribly exciting."

I wondered afterward if he was surprised that I didn't flare my nostrils and paw the ground. Instead I said, quite seriously, "Look, Bob, this is awkward, but I do need to ask you about something that happened Friday night."

He said, "About horses or women? Fire away!"

I told him about going down to the valet parking and finding Cheeks and the Turtle.

"I don't know their names—"

"Sam and Ernie," he supplied, looking interested but not at all alarmed.

"I'd met them before," I continued. "They came to my apartment a few weeks ago. They were looking for a friend —someone named Bobby."

"Ah, Bobby," he said. "The footloose Mr. Buck. That's what this is all about. But why would they come to you?"

I had decided over the weekend to keep the story simple. "One of my neighbors, Angela Cappelli, broke into my apartment while I was on vacation. I've figured out she was using my place to meet her boyfriend. Most likely, it was Bobby."

He sighed and said, "And you want to know how come I hired the chaps to park cars—in other words, how I'm connected to Bobby."

I nodded. It was ridiculous, but I felt defensive: he would sense my mistrust. I told myself I *was* talking about murder.

"Is this so important to you?" he asked.

"Angela may be in trouble with the police. They've asked me if I know her friends."

"Some neighbors you have."

"She's moved."

"Bobby Buck—like in dollars—" he said, staring thoughtfully at the remains of his Souper Sandwich Special. "Let's see, what can I tell you about him?"

He was so open, I felt my resolve wilt like week-old lettuce. But I continued. "How do you know him?"

He shifted comfortably in his chair. "Oh, he's a fellow Brit. Works as a trainer—when he feels like working. We'd have a chat or a drink from time to time at the racecourses near London."

I remembered Marcy prodding me: *Ask him about himself.* Why not? I tried for a look of innocence. "Were you a trainer, too?"

"No, I'm a great racing fan, but rushing to the betting windows is about as strenuous as I get. Why do you ask?"

"Simple curiosity—about a new friend. I can't imagine another job like the one you have with Mr. Wesley."

"My life was rather tame, actually. I worked for a gallery. You know, the kind that mostly sells museum reproductions to artistic young women trying to furnish their first apartments.

"I must have helped half the ingenues in London hang their Degas ballet dancers and Monet water lilies." His eyes were a celestial blue. I imagined the scene: a rainy London afternoon, damp clothing, a renovated attic with chintz curtains, a steaming tea kettle— Damn it, Cat, you're inventing *his* memories!

Perhaps he thought he'd said enough about the mating scene in London. After a silence, he volunteered: "I'd heard Bobby had come to the States, so I wasn't surprised to find him at one of the local pubs. We have our own colony of expatriates here, you know."

"You saw him at the Paddock?" I asked.

He raised a blond eyebrow. "You know about the Paddock? Not your kind of place, I'd imagine. No, I met Bobby down in Santa Monica, at the Crown and Flag." It was a proper pub near the Pacific Ocean; I'd been there myself for authentic fish and chips.

"Every Englishman drifts down there eventually," he continued. "Something within us cries out for warm beer and a game of darts.

"I met Bobby at the Crown and Flag a few weeks ago. We had a couple of pints and talked about London. That's when he told me about Sam and Ernie. Employment is bad at home, you know. Bobby had come here to be assistant trainer at a racing stable near Santa Barbara. He thought he'd lined up jobs for his two pals, too. So he told them to come to California."

Bob shook his head. "Bad luck for all of them. The stable's owner decided to sell out and retire. Bobby will be all right. He's talented, but he never does stay in one place very long." Bob laughed. "We're a pair, we are."

"Would you know how to find him?"

Bob shrugged. "He's lined up something in Maryland. For all I know he's already there.

"Sam and Ernie? Bobby put them in touch with me. I wanted to help out, so I hired them to jockey cars at Ronald's party. They were very grateful. But I paid their wages in cash, and I've had no reason to talk to them since."

Now there was some concern in his voice. "Those two are really on their uppers. I'd hate to make more trouble for them."

I found myself reassuring him. "Oh, I understand. It's just the connection to Bobby—"

"Cat," he said, Why are *you* getting so involved in your neighbor's mess?" He leaned forward, his hand covering mine.

"It's not your place to play policeman. My connection to Bobby is very slight—and yours is less than that. Accidental, that's all, from what you've told me. Besides, Mr. Buck is notorious for loving and leaving. If he ever was involved with this Angela, I doubt if he would take her to Maryland."

It was all plausible, I thought. Bob Crosswaithe was just helping out a fellow Brit: the kiss-and-run Bobby Buck. Why should I be involved—or drag Bob and these acquaintances into a murder investigation? If Angela chose to bet on the wrong horse, let *her* explain it to the police.

Chapter Twenty-One

I still didn't know what to think about Crosswaithe. He kept me off balance; he held out the promise of intimacy like a dangling carrot in front of a treat-hungry mule. Sure, it was a Grade A, fancy carrot, but it didn't nourish. Bob came on with little signals that seemed to say: it's time we got to know each other better. Sometimes it was a hint (but no follow through), or a small, personal confession, or a touch so light it surprised me how it burned. In an earlier life he could have been a matinee idol playing The Sheik, or Rhett Butler—or Mack the Knife. That aura of sexuality—was it conscious? He *must* realize his effect on women.

He called two days after our lunch for the sole purpose of informing me he would have time available for bartending. Ronald Wesley was going to New York for a couple of weeks to check out the Broadway season. Bob would stay behind to work with the decorator and the computer expert who'd be remodeling Wesley's home office. It was not a day-and-night project, he told me. If I could use him, he said earnestly, he was ready to help out.

I felt like a little girl who had dropped her Fudgsicle. Maybe Marcy was right: he's being faithful to a wife left behind in London. Or, maybe he sees me as a chum (I was more than a business contact, I was sure). I still needed a replacement for Philip, who was staying sober and working now as one of my waiters. I sighed to myself and told Bob I could indeed use him if he was available late afternoon on Halloween. We would be setting up a bar followed by a buffet after the Interfacets sales meeting.

"I'll enjoy the shop talk. Ronald has me cataloging everything—his film books, art, whatever—on his new computer system."

I smiled at this boyish eagerness and hired him on for the evening. Then he said, "Cat? Would you be too tired to have late supper or a drink with me afterward?"

Why not? "That would be nice," I said. "I'd like that."

In spite of myself, I was pleased. I'd just about made up my mind that Bob Crosswaithe had no connection whatsoever with Angela. He had explained it so clearly, I was convinced. And, damn it, even if he was married to some tweedy type in London (doubtful), well, here in Los Angeles almost anything is allowed except a U-turn on a major thoroughfare.

I took the stairs down to the restaurant, and poked my head into Mario's cubbyhole, really an alcove off the kitchen. He was dabbing club soda on a speck that marred the stark splendor of his white chef's jacket.

"You're here," he said, looking up, "I was just going to leave you this note."

I'd gone straight from home to Interfacets that morning. "I've made a sketch of the Interfacets lobby outside of their auditorium," I said. "That's where we'll set up the buffet. Can we talk about it?"

"*Certainement,*" said Mario, crumpling up the note. "But there was someone asking for you—and about you— rning."

"A satisfied client?" I asked.

"No," said Mario, a doubtful look on his thin black face. "I thought at first he was a customer. The cashier sent him back here. He asked for you by name. He knew you were the catering manager."

"Did he give his name?"

"I don't think so. I should have asked."

Mario is an inspired chef, but he is not much for business details. I said, "What did he want?"

"He said he was thinking of having a party, and you had been recommended to him. When I told him you weren't here, he asked for a list of some of our satisfied clients. That was easy, it's in our catering brochure. So I gave him one."

"That brochure isn't up to date," I reminded him. "I keep meaning to have it reprinted."

"Funny, that's what he asked. He asked if the client list was recent. I told him it was about a year old."

"Anything else?"

"He wanted to know if I could give him some current references. I told him you'd be here this afternoon, and to call you."

"That was it?"

"Just about," said Mario, "but—I had the feeling he knew when he came in that you wouldn't be here."

"How odd," I said. A thought struck me. "Did he have an English accent?"

"No," said Mario, tapping the desk with long, slender fingers, the way he does when he concentrates. "He was an ordinary guy. Very pleasant. But, you know, our clients don't usually walk in off the street."

"Well," I said dubiously. "He'll probably call later."

"Right."

"If he comes by again when I'm not here, ask his name and phone number, would you?"

"Sure, Cat. What do you think?"

"Nothing," I told Mario, not wanting to worry him. "He's probably trying to choose between us and Pizza Hut."

Angela

We didn't leave that honeymoon suite in San Diego for almost twenty-four hours. I'd never spent that much time alone with him, in bed with him, making love until I was sore all over and he was exhausted. I don't know how he had the strength to drive me back to Jacumba the next day, and then drive himself to Los Angeles. I guess having three hundred thousand dollars in the bank makes you feel extremely sexy. I'll never forget that king-size bed.

He showed me the passbooks from three banks, they were all in his name but I didn't care. They were *ours*, he said, and I believed him. I even let him take me back to Happy Waters—that sewer of a spa—for another few days. He was thinking more about Switzerland, he said, but it would be another few months before he could break away. He was on an important assignment he said (I thought, maybe he really is CIA). He said I'd still have to keep out of sight until he was free to leave. He said he'd been reading the paper every day, and there was nothing more about Mr. Hastings so far.

I made such a scene about staying on in Jacumba that he said, okay, okay, it's probably time to move on anyway. So I stuck it out until Monday. On a few nights, I even waited until all the sickies were gone to bed and then I splashed around in the Jacuzzi. Not bad, I kept wishing Bobby was there with me. Just about the only thing we hadn't tried was doing it under water.

Monday he drove down and I checked out of the spa. I was so happy because he was driving my car, only it had new license plates. A friend of his got them for him. So I had a car again, but he warned me to be super careful not to get stopped by the police, because they'd arrest me for sure. Then we drove to Shelter Island, which is a fancy name for a sandbar in San Diego with lots of hotels and motels.

He found me a motel with a housekeeping room that looked out on the sailboats in the yacht harbor. We went to a little grocery and we stocked up the tiny refrigerator. I felt as if we were married already just going to the grocery together. That night, after we made love (not wild like in San Diego but romantic with the drapes open and the moonlight shining on the water) I fell asleep in his arms. My cheeks were wet with tears of happiness, and he kissed them away.

He had to be back in L.A. first thing Tuesday, so I drove him to the airport for a seven A.M. flight. I sat in the airport restaurant after his plane took off. I looked at the empty runway and it was like a sad movie where the hero goes off to war and maybe to die, only this was real and I knew I'd see him again. He told me he'd come stay with me every Monday. Then I went back to the motel with a travel guide about Switzerland he'd brought from L.A. for me. I was going to read but I fell asleep. I must have slept all day, because when I woke up it was dark.

Chapter Twenty-Two

S
omeday, when I've aged and my hair is like a silvery clump of Brillo, when I'm rocking by the fire with my first edition of Pillsbury Bake-off Winners, watching the flames leap higher than my cholesterol count, maybe then I'll analyze why I was so dumb the day that Detective Paul Wang stopped by for lunch.

I was glad to see him, of course. I'd felt, since that lunch in Chinatown, that here was a kindred soul, someone who would cry hot tears with me over a bowl of cold Szechuan noodles laced with chiles or would blithely split a stir-fried sea slug. I have wonderful friends but they do not follow me off the beaten menu. I'm sure it helped that Paul Wang was ethnic Chinese, but I also detected an enthusiasm that went beyond the comfort factor.

He called me late that morning and asked if he was still invited to lunch. I told him he was in luck, Nick's fine crab raviolis were on today's lunch special, and to rush right over.

He looked like a UCLA graduate student as he waited for me at the restaurant entrance: brown tweed jacket, olive

T-shirt, jeans, and white Reeboks. A spiral-bound pad showed from one tweed pocket. I met him, feeling slightly guilty and hoping my discomfort wouldn't show.

"Business or pleasure?" I asked, leading him to a red leather banquette.

"Business earlier, pleasure now," he said, smoothing his astonishing mustache.

He was in Westwood, he explained, trying to i.d. some of the suspects in last Saturday night's gang killing, a frightening shootout in a parking lot near one of the movie houses. Two gang members dead, one innocent high school kid from the Valley slightly grazed on the shoulder from the crossfire. This is what it's like to live in a war zone, I thought. You cart off the victims, sweep up the broken glass, board up the windows, and open for business again. I shuddered. We are accepting violence too easily. I said as much to Paul.

"I live with it, but I don't accept it," he said. "When I become casual about violent death, that's when I'll get out and go to work in my uncle Henry Wang's grocery." It was a statement with the fervor of a promise, surely one he'd often made to himself.

I saw Nick wave away Joe (born Giovanni), his waiter, also his cousin from Brooklyn. I introduced Paul, then Nick took our order himself, his strong face beaming with paternal good will.

"I'm delighted to meet Catherine's friend. In a big, tough city like this a young woman is lucky to have a detective for a friend. Did you see our blackboard? The ravioli? Excellent, today. Of course, so is our pizza. The pepperoni with double cheese, very thin crust, is famous. How about an order of each?"

Paul succumbed, refusing wine; he was still on duty. I ordered a salad. Nick's sturdy bulk tactfully retreated.

"So," I asked, "how are things going?"

"Do you mean my gang killings?" replied Paul, concentrating on the basket of rolls. "Well, I think I have a positive identification on two suspects from the same gang. They both have records, petty stuff until now. A video store manager and some customers picked them out from mugshots. I checked the scene again this morning. It's a clear view from the store to the street."

"That's fast work."

"Sure," said Paul. "We'll pick them up this afternoon. Someone with a grudge phoned in a tip on them. We know where they are."

A basket of hot garlic bread arrived. Paul finished his roll and tackled the perfumed bread. I sipped my iced tea.

"Not like your ex-neighbor, Angela," he said.

"What do you mean?"

"She's dropped out of sight. Her car is gone, her mother says she hasn't heard from her since she supposedly called from San Francisco. I believe it. Every time I talk to Mrs. Cappelli she goes on a crying jag. I don't think it's faked."

"Did you try that bar?"

"The Paddock? Of course. She hasn't been seen there in weeks. No one in the office hung out with her, and apparently she had no friends—except this phantom boyfriend. She hasn't left a trace."

I found myself reaching for a slab of garlic bread.

"Really?" I said, munching away.

"Let me ask you something."

"So this *is* business."

"No," he said agreeably, "this is the lunch you offered me. I could have phoned. It's about Angela's car. Do you remember it?"

That was easy. "It was a Toyota, I think a Tercel. Not very old. It was grey, like a silver-grey."

"Right. We've checked her registration. Your landlord says your parking space was next to hers. Do you remember anything special about her car?"

"Special, like what?" I asked.

"Oh, anything. Dents, scrapes, a bent bumper. Did she have fuzzy dice hanging from her mirror, or an ELVIS LIVES bumper sticker?"

I smiled and concentrated. "Wait," I said. "I do remember something. One day we left for work just at the same time. She was in a hurry, and when she backed out of her space, she scraped the paint on the white post."

"Great!" said Paul.

"It was just a small scrape, but it left a white streak above her rear wheel. On the passenger side. She never fixed it."

"You see," said Paul, "you never know where you'll get a scrap of information. We're putting out something to the media this week, with her picture. Look for it. You know: 'Angela Cappelli wanted for questioning in the murder of etc., etc.' If she sees it, maybe it'll get her nervous. It's being off balance that causes a person to do dumb things."

"That makes sense," I said.

"If you think of anything else," said Paul, "no matter how insignificant it seems, give me a call."

I hesitated, *almost* said, "Well, something did happen—" Just then the food arrived.

"Ravioli," said Paul. "I believe Marco Polo brought it from China." The cheese on the pizza was bubbling. "Pizza," he said.

"From Brooklyn," I said.

Maybe I'll tell him some other time, I thought.

Dumb. Dumb. Fatally dumb.

Angela

He didn't show up at all on Monday. I didn't start to panic until around noon. I thought he'd drive up, ready with a big smile and a kiss, and I could hardly wait. I'd had such a lonely week. Every day I'd have breakfast in the motel room. I'd go out to a different place every day for lunch, then maybe find a mall and go shopping for new clothes, then I'd pick up some take-out for dinner, and watch TV in the room while I ate. The first night, I'd had dinner in the motel coffee shop, but there were some guys at a convention staying at the motel. One of them—he was chubby with a real red, sunburned face like Midwesterners get because they're not used to being near the ocean—anyway, he came over to my table, leaned close until I could smell the peppermint Certs on his breath, and said he wanted to buy me a drink at the hotel bar across the street. "What's a good-looking blonde like you doing sitting alone?" he said. "I've been watching you, and I think you need some company." I got real scared, I didn't want anybody watching me, besides this guy looked like an overbaked Godzilla compared to

Bobby. So I said I was waiting for my boyfriend who was a bouncer in the hotel bar, and I smiled real casual like, although my heart was beating fast. As soon as he went back to his table I paid my bill, went to my room, and I never ate in the coffee shop again.

By Monday I was feeling crazy just being so alone and waiting for him. I'd bought new white pants and sandals, and a tight white sweater, resort fashions, so I looked like the wives and girlfriends I saw on vacation here, they wore things I never had the nerve to wear around home. Even better, I couldn't wait to undress in front of Bobby, because I also bought a new bra and bikini, with stars and stripes on them like the flag. (I wasn't being unpatriotic, when I saw them in the store I giggled, because I could tell Bobby we were celebrating the Fourth of July early.)

He didn't show up and when I started to call his apartment, all I got was his answering machine and I thought: maybe he's too sick to answer, or he had an accident, or maybe the CIA sent him on a mission and he didn't have time to call. I was so upset I wanted to cry, but I didn't, just in case he did come I didn't want my eyes red and weepy. Finally, around two o'clock the phone rang and I grabbed it like it was a lifeline. It was Bobby and I could tell he was far away. He said, I'm still in Los Angeles, I couldn't get away, I have a lot of responsibilities this week. I understand, I said, although I didn't. I love you, he said, I miss you, and I can't wait to see you next Monday. Please, I said, and I didn't care if I was pleading, can't you come to see me this week? I'm so alone here, I can't stand it. I know, he said, I know. Look, he said, I'll try, if I can I'll fly down tomorrow for a few hours, you can pick me up at the airport, but I'll call first. I waited all Tuesday, I didn't even go out to lunch and by Tuesday night my face and my eyes were swollen from crying, I had to go down the hall and get ice from the motel ice machine to put on my eyes. Around ten o'clock Tuesday night he called and said, this is the first

I could get away, darling, I just can't make it this week, just pretend until next Monday that I'm kissing you and loving you.

After he hung up I sat for a while and looked out at the harbor until the ocean calmed me and I knew what I had to do. I didn't pack any clothes, because I was just going to L.A. for the day. Around midnight I left the motel, but I stopped at a Thrifty Drug Store before I got on the freeway. I hadn't even gone out for dinner, so I bought some snacks to eat on the road. Then I saw this funny Halloween mask on the next aisle. It was one of those rubber ones you pull over your whole head. It looked like a lady vampire, with long black hair and bloodred lips, and even fangs. There was a sign that said: Are you ready for Halloween? I realized it was today and I thought, well, maybe I'll just go to his apartment and say, Boo! when he answers the door. I bought the mask and then I headed for the freeway. It was nearly one A.M. so, for once, there was no traffic and I made great time all the way to L.A.

Chapter Twenty-Three

The newly divorced among my friends fall mostly into two categories: the plungers and the brooders. Plungers lose ten pounds and will date anyone short of a known serial killer. Brooders gain ten pounds and often join self-help groups.

For a while last year, after my marriage broke up, I became the Hamlet of all caterers. I brooded, I worked late; I was feeling—not really pangs, but twinges of remorse at not living up to Gil's expectations. I took up jogging, I lost five pounds of the ten I'd gained. Finally, I took a class in Chinese stir-fry techniques. I'd go home at night and bash things around in a wok. I held the handle of the long scoop so tightly, I sprained my thumb. Inexplicably, the pain cleared my mind. I let Marcy and her longtime friend, Mike, talk me into a date with his stockbroker.

Evan is a genial, former USC jock who devotes his week to the Dow Jones and weekends to tennis. He invited me to a casual Halloween party at his club, Sandpipers, a trim white 1920's relic on the beach at Malibu.

After a while we left the party, kicked off sandals, and

walked down the sand to the edge of the Pacific, watching the dark waves crash, diminish, and turn to foam at our feet. Evan was also newly separated. There we stood, two emotional grotesques with goosebumps, telling sad tales in theffog, as if we had drifted far from the lights and the music. Over the next few months, we had a short-lived but reassuring affair. Since our only common bonds were some temporary feelings of inadequacy, when those went away we stopped seeing each other.

This Halloween was better. Gearing up for the Interfacets party, my spirits were lighter than Mario's hazelnut meringues. I was organized, on top of the details, enjoying the challenge of catering a full day of food, drink, and restrained merriment for 327 computer executives, software designers, regional managers, and star salespeople. They would be hungry and restless after a day of meetings broken only by the Continental breakfasts that Olivia and Phillip had served early in the morning, followed by the box lunches we'd delivered by van at noon.

Starting at 6:30 A.M., I'd dashed back and forth between Dellacasa's and Interfacets, carrying lists and checking details, setting out the croissants, muffins, and bagels at breakfast, moving picnic tables around the patio at lunch, then back to the office to change into my blue chemise and daub on eyeshadow, returning with Mario at 3:30 P.M.

Two weeks had passed since my lunch with Bob Crosswaithe, and except for a couple of phone calls about bartending, we hadn't chatted since. I said a quick hello as he unpacked glasses at one of the bar stations. There was something I wanted to tell him, but I couldn't think what it was.

The cocktail party was set up in the executive dining room; others in my full crew arranged the buffet on long tables in the main lobby. Computer people, I have found, combine innovative minds with prosaic tastes. Our menu was attractive, not too daring: crudités and salads, carved turkey and prime rib, small rolls for sandwiches, bowls of cranberry and horseradish sauces, our notable Thai chicken pizza, salmon terrine, and the accompanying dressings and gravies. As a general rule, Dellacasa's allots a pound of food per person for the main course—some 327 pounds of protein, vegetables, and assorted carbohydrates served that one meal—plus bread, appetizers, side dishes, and desserts, not to mention the Interfacets custom cake in the shape of a computer diskette. For me, the saving grace on such a long day's journey into overload is that food loses most of its appeal. I do my best dieting on our biggest party days.

The thought of a quiet drink with Bob Crosswaithe after the clean-up was more appealing than a whole blushing tray of our glazed strawberry tarts. By 7:30 P.M. we had, on Interfacets's instructions, closed the bar. (L.A. has such stiff penalties for drunk driving, many corporate parties end up sober and early.)

I'd expected that Bob would stay on until I could pack it in, a couple of hours later. Instead, he sought me out.

"Cat," he said, more serious than I'd ever seen him, "I hate to ask for a raincheck on our drink—I don't want you to think it's a habit of mine—but would you mind?"

I remembered now what I'd wanted to tell him.

"It's Baby, isn't it?" I asked. "I heard the news on the car radio when we came back this afternoon."

He nodded. "Terrible accident," he said. "I called the hospital when I heard the broadcast. She's conscious. I'd like to bring her some flowers before visiting hours are over."

"Where's her father?"

"He's in New York looking at plays with Ronald. I imagine Daddy will fly back."

Quite casually I asked, "Have you seen Baby since Mr. Wesley's party?"

He looked at me quickly, as if to measure the depth of my interest.

"Ronald asked me to show her the script of his next movie." He gave a rueful shrug. "He thought there might be a small part in it for her."

"I'm sure she'll recover," I said. "It was a hit-and-run driver, wasn't it?"

He ran his fingers through his curly blond cap of hair. He seemed extraordinarily nervous to me. Perhaps he had been expected to keep her safe in Tinseltown while Daddy was away.

"Her face is badly cut," he said. "She was crossing the street on Dayton, in Beverly Hills. Her private nurse told me Baby's sleeve caught in one of the wheels, and she was dragged a few feet before the car got away."

"How horrible," I said. Bob and I stood in heavy silence for a moment.

"We can have a drink anytime," I said, the soul of generosity and selflessness.

"I knew you'd understand, Cat," he said. He leaned down, held my shoulders, and kissed me gratefully on the cheek.

"I'll call," he said, and rushed off.

I sighed and turned back toward the table where I'd been helping with the coffee service. On the way I passed one of the dessert stations. I looked at the large round tray of miniature eclairs, cream puffs, and chocolate mousse tarts.

"Oh, what the hell," I said. I helped myself to one of each and headed for a corner of the kitchen. What's more, my feet had begun to ache.

Angela

I figured sooner or later, from the description of the car, he would guess it was me. I found the story in the L.A. newspaper I bought, the witness just called it a grey compact, but Bobby would know. I had to giggle, the paper called it a hit-and-run accident. It was probably on TV, too, but I was back in San Diego by then. The headline was cute. It said, VAMPIRE DRAWS BLOOD IN HALLOWEEN HIT-AND-RUN. Well, I suppose I did. I'll bet that witness was the fat woman standing on the curb. She looked like she'd drop dead from fright when she saw me behind the wheel in that spooky mask but I was too busy chasing down the brunette with the big hair to look back. I think I was laughing, though, the way everyone looked so scared and tried to get out of my way. It was rich. Maybe I should have been angry the way that tramp was acting toward Bobby when I saw them in the restaurant. So why was I laughing? Maybe because I knew *I was saving Bobby from temptation*. Yes, that's it. Carnal sin tempts even the strongest men, even when they've made an eternal commitment like Bobby and me.

It started out so innocently. I made it up the 405 in just over two hours, not even going over the speed limit, and got to Bobby's apartment around 3:30 A.M. I parked in the empty space in the carport, ran up the stairs, and rang the bell over and over but he wasn't home. I was disappointed but not alarmed, I knew during the week he'd often sleep over where he worked. I had to admit to myself I hadn't thought it out last night, who knows when he'll be home? So I went to my car and lay down in the backseat to take a nap until morning. That's how I almost missed him, because he parked his car at the curb in front of the building. I woke up when I heard his door slam and then I saw him run down the stairs with a large manila envelope in his hand. He looked fresh, as if he'd just shaved and showered, and he was whistling. I almost called out but then I thought: why not see where he goes, he's so mysterious about everything, not that I don't trust him, I do.

I waited until he drove off, he wasn't in his beat-up old Buick, it was a classy red Mercedes I'd never seen before. I guess it belongs to his boss. That kind of car isn't hard to follow, so I kept a few cars behind and pretty soon he was heading west on Sunset, the rich part where the hedges and the trees are thick enough to hide the big houses. If you landed in a space ship you'd think the only humans who lived there were Mexican gardeners. When he turned into Stone Canyon Road I slowed down; I had a hunch he was going to the Hotel Bel-Air. There was a taxi between Bobby's car and mine, so I hung back until the taxi let out an uptight Japanese businessman with five pieces of real crocodile-skin luggage. Poor crocodile. What with all the fuss about unloading the luggage and paying the cabdriver, I had time to see Bobby turn over his car keys to the valet parking and walk under the canopy. I knew from there he'd follow a path leading to a covered bridge over a stream where some snooty swans paddle around and then, off to the right, he'd come to the lobby. I had been at the

Bel-Air a few times myself, taking notes for Mr. Hastings at some lunch meeting or in a client's suite, so I knew the layout. I was rumpled and messy from sleeping in the car, hair uncombed, no makeup, but I didn't care. I patted my hair down, left my car with the parking attendant, and took my time, hanging back on the far side of the bridge. Bobby didn't enter the lobby. He passed it and turned right, like he knew the way. He was either going to someone's room or to the restaurant.

I was relieved when he stopped at the restaurant—I could keep watch on him there. At the entrance, there's a stack of morning newspapers for the guests to read if they don't want to look at each other. I picked up a paper, opened it, and acted like I was stunned by the weather report. What I really had my eyes on was this brunette cow sitting at the side of the room where the French windows look out to the patio. She was wearing a yellow linen trapeze dress—you knew how expensive it was because it looked so simple—and her hair was messier than mine, the wash/condition/mousse/blow dry/spray/hundred fifty plus tip/messy, but she also looked sleepy and rosy, as if she hadn't got much sleep last night and was glad about it. She got up when Bobby came over to the table, put her arms around him, and shamelessly kissed him on the lips, right in front of the people eating breakfast. I stood there frozen in horror. He gave her a quick kiss back, just being polite, I thought, and he stroked her arm. The hostess came over to me and I could hardly talk, so I pointed to an empty table on the fireplace side of the room. It was perfect because it hid me behind another table with a floral centerpiece about the size of the White House Christmas tree.

It probably didn't matter that I hid. They were facing toward the patio, looking out at the pepper trees and the masses of flowers—purple orchids, pink azaleas, peach and yellow begonias, scarlet bougainvillea. Once, when I was taking notes for Mr. Hastings, I saw a wedding here in the gardens and I was so sad, it seemed like other girls had all the luck.

I ordered something—pancakes, I think—but it could have been sawdust for all I tasted of it. My heart was pounding so hard I thought everyone could hear it but nobody turned my way. Bobby opened the manila envelope and took out what looked like a movie or TV script. He read it out loud, and she interrupted by feeding him strips of bacon. The big fireplace near me sent off heat, but I was freezing cold. I couldn't sit there much longer, like Jane peeking through the bushes at Tarzan. Finally, they left. I threw some money on the table and followed them out. Quiet, very quiet, like I was invisible. She kissed him again, then he headed toward the parking. She went down a leafy path toward the bungalows. I didn't know her name or her room number and I was afraid to follow too close, so I took my newspaper and sat in the lobby where I could see her if she passed by. I didn't care if she saw me, she didn't know me. Nearly an hour passed, and I guess it was time for the Beverly Hills stores to open, because she came down dressed for shopping, in a khaki-colored jump suit that looked as if it was made out of parachute silk, gold bracelets and gold hoop earrings, suede boots the color of Palomino horses, and a creamy suede shoulder bag just big enough to hold some credit cards and a lipstick.

Our cars made a little procession up Sunset to Beverly Hills. I wasn't trembling anymore, I was steaming mad. Mad because I knew all about her type, I'd read about her type in my romance novels: the rich bitch with too much money and too many clothes who thought she could buy love. Well, she'd find out different! Lead him not into temptation. I waited till she left her car in a parking lot and crossed the street. I was parked on the street a few feet back. She never saw me. I had that vampire mask on and got the car racing before she knew I was there. I just plowed into her, I heard the thud and I heard screams but

I kept on going. I didn't stop till I got off the freeway in San Diego. I'd hardly eaten all day and most of yesterday, so I was really hungry. I stopped in a coffee shop in downtown San Diego and I had ham and eggs and home fries and three cups of coffee. Then I drove back to the motel. I wasn't upset or crying anymore. I was just curious, I suppose, to see when he would call.

Chapter Twenty-Four

"Hello, Cat? It's Bob. Sorry about last night, I hated to walk off and leave you."

Crosswaithe was making his apologies the next morning, after the Interfacets Halloween party.

"Oh, just as well," I said. "It took a long time to pack up. I was going to call you later. How's Baby?"

He sounded relieved. "Not too bad, all things considered. A broken wrist, lots of scrapes and bruises, and a gash over her forehead that'll need some plastic surgery. She's still lucky."

"The newspaper story this morning said whoever hit her was wearing a Halloween mask."

"Yes. I want to report to her father later today, so I talked to the desk sergeant at the Beverly Hills police department. They think most likely it was someone—he or she—getting a head start on a Halloween party."

"Did anyone take down a license number?"

"No, the eyewitnesses were so transfixed by the mask—this one lady, the policeman said, kept talking about those

147

bloody fangs—that no one paid much attention to the car. It got clean away."

"What a shame," I said.

"Terrible," said Bob, but he seemed more cheerful than I would have expected. A pause.

"Well," he said, "I seem to owe you a supper this time."

"You don't owe me anything," I assured him, scowling into the phone.

"I put it badly. I fervently desire to take you out to dinner or supper."

My good humor returned. "Want to pick an evening now?"

"Ah," he said apologetically, "it will have to be next week. Wesley's decorator and his computer expert have been at each other's throats since the remodeling started. My life has been a nightmare. But they're finished as of this morning, so I'm taking off for a long weekend."

I restrained myself from asking where to and with whom.

He said, "How about Thursday, a week from today?"

"Fine," I said. "I'll talk to you next week. Have a good time."

"I try, I always do. Do you ever take a weekend off?"

"It's difficult in my business," I said, "but not impossible."

"I'll remember that," he promised.

Angela

He didn't call and he didn't wait until Monday. Friday around noon I heard a car pull into the space next to mine. When I looked out the window, I saw him get out of his old Buick (no red Mercedes this time), walk to my car, crouch down, and carefully run his fingers over the front bumper. Like I said, Bobby is smart.

I opened the door, flashed him a big smile, and said, well, I'm glad you could make it this week after all! He nodded, came in, and closed the door behind him, very quiet. I couldn't read his face at all. He said (no small talk for him!), why did you have to run her down? I could have said, what do you mean? but why bother. He might as well know how I feel. I said, I was waiting in the carport for you to come home when I saw you drive off. I called out but you left too fast (okay, I stretched the truth just a teensy bit), so I followed you. I just wanted us to spend a few hours together. When you got to the restaurant I saw her kiss you. I was so afraid that she was taking you away from me.

149

Good God, Angela! he said, looking kind of dumbstruck, you can't try to kill every woman who talks to me. You could decimate half the population of Los Angeles. I stood up to him, I said, but she put her arms around you and kissed you. He shrugged and answered, this is Hollywood. Everyone in the movie business kisses everyone else, it's simply what one does. I had a thought. I asked him, are you in the movie business, is that what you do? No, he said, you're on the wrong track. Miss Chase, if you read the papers, is the daughter of a very rich man. Her daddy makes cars in Detroit. My employer wants him to invest in a movie. If you were right on my heels, you must have seen I had a script with me. I was showing it to her. She has some influence on her father, at least that's what the man I work for thinks.

I started to ask Bobby another question, but he took my hands, looked straight at me with his dazzling blue eyes, and said, I don't know why I have to explain myself to you, but I'll try. My boss is a wealthy investor who doesn't like to have his name known. He puts projects together with other rich private investors, and they all like to keep a low profile. That's what rich people do, said Bobby. I thought hard about it for a minute, holding tight to his hands, they were so strong. I thought, I wouldn't be surprised if he was CIA after all, he still isn't telling me much about these big private deals. But I didn't push it. There was something else bothering me.

Why *breakfast*? I wailed. It was too early in the morning for you both to look so happy! He started to laugh, a big laugh that rolled out of him. He laughed so hard he started to cough and turn red under his tan. Oh, Angela! he said, and drew me in and hugged me, and I huddled close, feeling his body heat. Angela, dear one, why shouldn't we have looked happy? Having a delicious breakfast on my employer's expense account is a very joyful thing. That's all? I asked. He pulled back so he could look at me, leaving one arm around my shoulder. Haven't you ever heard of power breakfasts? he asked. Breakfast is when the important movie people do business. Miss Chase and I were having a power breakfast. I thought, I believe him. Mr. Hastings had some movie industry clients, and he took *Variety*. I'd read it sometimes on my lunch hour. How the big producers and agents were always making deals over breakfast at the Polo Lounge or Four Seasons or Nate-N-Al's Deli in Beverly Hills. I guess the Bel-Air is in the same league.

Listen, said Bobby, taking my hand in a hard grip, let's sit down and talk about this. He led me over to the bed. The maid hadn't come by yet, so the sheets were all rumpled, but we sat. My eyes half closed, and I could feel myself falling into a rhythm of deep, long breaths. Look at me! he insisted, so I did. He said, you can't come back to Los Angeles just because you feel like it. They're looking for you and your car. Did you see this? He pulled a newspaper article out of his pocket and handed it to me. Under the headline was an old picture of me when I had mousy brown hair. I stared at the picture. No doubt about it, I'm much sexier as a blonde. I thought, I wish those silly bitches at the office could see me now sitting on this bed in a motel with my gorgeous man. See? he said, tapping the article with his finger, it was in the paper this week. The story doesn't say that they've charged you with Hastings's murder, but this proves that they're actively looking for you. If you got stopped now, they'd also find a new dent on your bumper. He frowned, his blond brows coming together like angel wings. He said, it wouldn't take long for them to tie you to this hit-and-run.

Angela, he said sharply, stop daydreaming and listen to me. I sat up and tried to look alert. Angela, he went on, you also can't keep following me around. It's dangerous for you and it makes me feel you don't trust me. I said sincerely, of course I trust you. You have that three hundred thousand dollars sitting in banks in your name. You could have just killed me and taken the money and split. (I thought about this a lot during the past week.)

Bobby nodded. He said, you're right, I could've killed you. I've done many nasty things in my life, in some ways I'm an absolute rotter. And yet, if St. Peter ever calls me to account I can say—at least I've never murdered anyone. He looked proud and added, I suppose it's a character flaw of mine. I thought, was he telling me *I'll* never get into heaven? He still doesn't know, I'd follow him even if I had to get rid of St. Peter. Now his voice was coaxing. Angela, he said, no more stunts like this, please. It isn't necessary, and it gives me the creeps. I asked, so you're not mad at me? Well, he said, Miss Chase will get better and she'll most likely go back to Detroit soon. Just don't imagine things about her. Our three hundred thousand won't last a lifetime, not the way we want to live. So don't be a nuisance when I have a business deal, I can't allow that.

I thought about what he'd just said, and it made me nervous. But then he flashed me this big, heart-stopping grin. Besides, said Bobby, I don't want to stay mad at you, you're such a great lay. I wiggled my toes and said, promise you'll come to see me every week, until we can leave the country. I'll try, said Bobby, I'll certainly try. I'll stay this whole weekend, to begin with. Wait, I said. I got up, went to the door and put out the Do Not Disturb sign. I had my clothes half off before I got back to the bed. Oh, I missed you so, I said, and fell on top of him.

Chapter Twenty-Five

Always after Halloween, my schedule is packed as full as a stuffed potato. Dellacasa's Catering is booked for brunches, parties, afternoon fundraisers, and evening museum receptions.

This year, I found myself calling on Bob Crosswaithe more and more. Ronald Wesley had taken an impulsive detour to London, inviting along a despondent but lovely New York stage actress whose play had just closed after the third night. Crosswaithe was available and agreeable. He had mastered the bartender's pour, that spare and elegant flick of the wrist; a thirsty crowd didn't rattle him, and the ladies loved him.

Was I still beguiled? I could have been, but the situation was like making soup: if you want it to simmer, first you turn up the heat. Looking back at my calendar, I see his name scribbled in that month for a dinner, a lunch, a late supper. No doubt of it, he chose to keep me aware of him, but I wasn't quite sure why. Perhaps (my noble theory) he was faithful to that wife back in Tiddly-on-the-Thames. Or, possibly (my crass conjecture), he was waiting for Baby's wounds to heal so he could pursue her through Movieland, or even back to Detroit. In this scenario, I was the second team, Ms. Kitty Foyle, not rich but cute-as-a-button and close at hand. Baby had left the hospital and was now, Bob told me, at a Mediterranean-style private sanitarium near Santa Barbara. I'd heard of it: celebrities and the merely rich went there to hide after their lifts, tucks, and liposuctions. I'd heard you could see more fancy stitches there than on a Mandarin emperor's robe.

It was also possible that Bob was shy. I laughed my head off at that one and forgot it. I also rejected my last theory (end-of-the-world catastrophic hypothesis) that he didn't find me physically attractive. Impossible—especially after I saw Elaine Stedman, his broad-beamed buddy from Beverly Hills, waiting patiently for him outside the Westside Women's Club. He had presided over the bar at a Sunday-morning brunch for the Friends of the Early California Pioneer Women (whiskey sours, white wine, Perrier, and Diet Pepsi). The bar had closed when the food service began, so he was already packed up and had loaded our van while I still made my rounds between the club's kitchen and dining room. He waved his goodbye and then, through the dining-room window, I saw him walk down the front steps and over to a white Honda parked nearby. In the bright noon-time sun I could see Elaine behind the wheel.

Bob opened the door on the passenger side and slid in. As I watched, fascinated, holding the coffee cup I had been about to refill from the big silver pot, I saw him lean over and they kissed. It seemed to be a long kiss, long enough for the sweet-faced, white-haired lady in the lavender print dress to tug hard at my arm and demand her coffee. As I poured, Elaine and Bob drove off. Well, I thought, he told me he likes women, so why should I be surprised that he sees more than one? Even though she was so *angry* that day. I shrugged.

At about that time, I'd begun to date one Andrew Paisley, solidly Scottish in his pale-blue eyes, sandy hair and eyelashes; his golf swing was so pure it, too, was like an ancestral memory. He was a marketing manager at Interfacets, and I'd met him while planning the menus for their sales meeting. I'd mentioned that I often took Mondays off, so when he called and asked me out for an early-morning round of golf and then breakfast, I thought, well, that's refreshing. As long as he's not another computer-driven man. Not another programmed mind like Gil's. I didn't disgrace myself on the course, and Andy proved to be funny and outgoing. A few nights later, he insisted on picking me up one midnight after a birthday party that Dellacasa's catered in the Hollywood Hills. Andy took me to an after-hours club on Wilshire and, you know? at four A.M., after being blinded by strobe lights and having my ankle kicked on a mobbed dance floor, my feet didn't hurt at all. Andy was the fun I'd been missing.

My aunt Sadie worried. Thanksgiving was approaching, I had a new man, but my ex-husband was invited to her holiday dinner. I'd told her about Andy to keep her from giving Gil too much encouragement. She called me one evening.

"I do apologize, Catherine," she said. "I don't know what to do about Gil."

"What's to do?" I answered, playing it straight. "He's an asset on Thanksgiving. I've always admired the way he carves the turkey."

"Turkey is not the issue," said Sadie reproachfully. "If I hadn't insisted on inviting Gil, you could have asked your nice new friend. At least, I *think* he's nice. You've never brought him around to meet me."

I sighed. "We're hardly at the stage of introducing relatives, Aunt Sadie. What's the hurry? Besides, Andy will be gone over the holiday. He's spending it with his parents in Rhode Island."

It was just as well he'd be out of town. Dellacasa's would

be keeping me busy. I made a mental note to call and reserve Crosswaithe. The UCLA Class of '28 was having a TV tailgate party and fund-raiser near the campus that Saturday afternoon. Sadie broke into my thoughts.

"I suppose it's a relief that your Andy will be away," said my aunt. "Then he won't be upset because he's not invited."

"If he doesn't know he's not invited, why would he be upset?"

"Oh, you know what I mean," she said. "Besides, I sometimes feel there is a hurry. That job of yours, the hours you keep. Don't you think I worry about a young woman coming home alone all hours of the night?"

Although I wouldn't admit it to Sadie, I *did* get edgy leaving the dubious shelter of the carport, well lit as it is, sometimes at two or three in the morning. But I'd have my house keys ready and hurry up the stairs.

Odd thing, though. I never saw anyone lurking around late at night. It was in the morning a few times, as I left for work, that I had the feeling someone was watching for me. Since I never saw anyone, I shook off the uneasiness and, finally, forgot it. "My car's in good condition," I said, to reassure Sadie, "and my neighborhood's pretty safe."

"When you were married to Gil he'd come and get you after one of your parties, or at least he'd wait at the door for you to come up from the carport. I know you love your job, but I wish you'd settle down again."

"I know." I was empathetic. "I'm a *New Woman* kind of woman, I should have it all. Right now I'm not sure what 'all' is, but when I find out, I'll try to have it."

"You're laughing at me, but I promised your mother—"

"And you're doing a wonderful job," I assured her.

"What about Mace?" she asked, in her usual way of skipping along her own thought path.

"Love it in pumpkin pie! Speaking of which, shall I bring the pies again this year?"

"I meant," she said sternly, "that spray, for your purse, to squirt in the mugger's eye."

"*What* has started you on this?" I asked. "We were talking about the holidays."

"Los Angeles is not a safe place for a young woman alone. I feel it in my bones."

"That's your arthritis, Aunt Sadie. Do you want me to get a gun? I'd probably shoot myself in the foot."

"I'd rather you got married again."

"That might be worse than shooting myself in the foot."

"We'll talk about this again."

"Oh, I'm sure we will," I said. "Look, I promise. I'll be careful at night."

"I love you, Catherine," said my aunt Sadie. "Take care."

Thanksgiving was warm and homey, and as traditional as Sadie's lace tablecloth and pressed-glass candlesticks. There were Sadie and *two* of her gentlemen friends, Charles Oppenheim and John Kelsey. Because Sadie was generous and she also liked to even out the table, her best friend, the sweet and birdlike Blanche, was present. Marcy and Mike, Gil and I completed the party.

"White meat, Cat?" asked Gil, presiding over the golden bird.

"I think some white and some dark, thank you, Gil."

"But you've always preferred the white meat."

"People change," I said. "I'm trying to expand my horizons."

"Yes, I see," said Gil, slicing off a generous amount of both.

"Change is good, dear," said Aunt Sadie to Gil.

"Oyster or chestnut dressing?" I asked Gil.

"Don't you remember, Cat?" said Gil, looking hurt. "I never eat oysters."

"Of course," I said. "I should have remembered."

"Gil believes in keeping up the traditions," said Aunt Sadie amiably.

I silently gave thanks for present blessings.

Bob Crosswaithe was not available for Saturday afternoon. Ronald Wesley had returned from London with a full-blown cold and an endless hangover. Bob was to drive him to Palm Springs on the day before Thanksgiving. Wesley would check in at a spa in order to shape up and dry out while Bob, so he told me, would be there to keep Wesley from any bubbly liquid more potent than a Jacuzzi. Thanksgiving Day, Ronald's actor friend had invited them both to the family desert retreat. They would return on the Tuesday after the holiday. I'd almost considered inviting him to our dinner, so I was pleased that Bob had such nice plans. After all, he was a visitor and this would be his first Thanksgiving. He should have a taste of old-fashioned American hospitality.

Angela

I tried to sleep through Thanksgiving, what with nothing to get up for. I had the blues, like the year my old man was killed, and when the holiday came she didn't get dressed all day. I hardly thought she'd miss him so. She used to cook those big, heavy meals for us on Thanksgiving, spaghetti first then turkey and stuffing and everything, red wine so dry it puckered your mouth but he liked it, and three kinds of dessert. He never said much to her he just ate until he had to open his belt and half unzip his fly, but I think the food was the only way she knew how to talk to him. That year he died, finally when I couldn't bear her staring into space like that, after I'd done my laundry and manicured my nails, taken a nap and watched some tear-jerking 1950's movie about women with tight perms and guys with crew cuts having a family reunion, I got into my car, drove over to Kentucky Fried Chicken, and brought home a bucket and all the trimmings. I slapped down the bag in front of her and said, here, happy Thanksgiving, and she cried a little, but she dug in, she never turns down a meal. So we kind of did that KFC scene after that, although one year, when she was really off with her praying somewhere in cuckooland, I just picked up and went to a movie by myself and all I had was popcorn for Thanksgiving dinner.

I should have been together with Bobby for our first Thanksgiving. Maybe we could have bought food and gone to Balboa Park and had a picnic, just us two, like I'd see other couples do. Or we could have gone to a restaurant where they had candles on the table and gold tassels on the menu, and I'd have worn my new jade wool dress that had a high turtleneck and a short skirt that was so tight you'd have to wonder if I had on any underwear. Or, we could have just stayed in the motel and screwed all afternoon, I'd have liked that best. But he'd warned me in advance he'd be away all weekend and through Monday, our usual day, because he was flying up with his boss to a secret investor's meeting in a ski lodge in the Canadian Rockies. I couldn't be mad I was so excited for him, it was like the international conspiracy meeting in some middle-of-the-night movie I'd seen on TV last month. Maybe he was involved in international banking for the CIA, who knows? I think anything's possible nowadays.

I slept until late afternoon, but when I woke up the sun was still shining. I was groggy from too much sleep and I had the beginnings of a headache. So I thought, I'll go out for dinner, it's not as if I'm truly alone, I feel as if he's at my side and next year this time we will celebrate our love together. So I got dressed, something mousy because I didn't want to be noticed being alone when everyone else in the world was with someone they loved. I got in my car and drove and drove, until I remembered the restaurant at the airport. No one would notice me there with all the crowds, and even on the holiday people would be alone because they'd be traveling to or from home. I sat in the restaurant by myself, watching the planes take off and land, and I drank two champagne cocktails—one for me and one for Bobby. It was near dusk and pretty soon the lights began to come on all over the airfield. I had this solemn thought. Right now, I thought, Life is an airport waiting room, and my flight is delayed. But soon they will announce that it's time to board. And, together, Bobby and I will fly into the sun.

Chapter Twenty-Six

Mario powwowed every day by phone with his chef friend in Santa Fe. There were decisions to be made about the party following the movie premiere of *Apache Sunset*. If Mario wanted to be pure about Native American cookery, the menu would be dominated by Indian Fry Bread and Squash Blossom Stew. On the other hand, this would be a crowd whose idea of going native was a do-it-yourself fajitas bar. Eventually, we settled on a Southwest sampler: Indian, Mexican, Spanish, and Contemporary Anglo.

This meant jicama with lime, miniature tacos, chickpea and guacamole spreads; Mario and I stayed on in Dellacasa's kitchen after the restaurant closed to bake blue corn and wild sage breads, to try out fillings for puffy empanada turnovers; I taste-tested green chile enchiladas and cinammon-scented piñon nut tamales. Nick insisted on our trademark, so Mario developed a turkey sausage and cheese pizza. We imported a sopaipilla maker from East Los Angeles. The Santa Fe chef sent his assistant, who arrived with boxes of *ristras,* the strings of hot red dry chiles that I'd requested for decorations. My own office looked like a trading post, what with the *ristras,* the woven baskets of cattails, wreaths of straw and multicolored corn, the piles of saddle blankets to be used as table runners. Caterers are, by nature, hospitable people. I believe we have more fun throwing parties than going to them. Well, our *Apache Sunset* affair would be a first-class production. It would add its own taste of authenticity to that tribal ceremonial, the red-carpet Hollywood premiere.

There was, indeed, a red carpet that night in Century City. It stretched from the curved driveway where the Jaguars, Caddies, Beemers, Mercedes, and hired stretch limos deposited the power brokers and stars. It led to the movie theater where this epic, a sympathetic account of Apache history, would screen. After the movie, the guests would descend by escalator to the private club where Dellacasa's Catering plus the obligatory rock band (*Hark! Bent Feather —what strange-sounding drums are these?*) were encamped for the evening.

By early evening, we were set up, decorations in place, chafing dishes at the ready, our regulars and extra staff looking spiffy in their crisp white shirts, black trousers, and red vests. I'd supplied them—both chefs and servers—with red headbands, each tied in back with a single feather.

The total effect was, I suppose, more New Age California than Apache Nation, but it did help set a party mood. This was important. If the movie proved to be a bust, a good party would help soften the blow to the studio and its investors. If it was a blockbuster, well, nothing is more festive than dreams of Academy Awards and a percentage of gross receipts. Success would rub off on Dellacasa's.

We were on hold until 10:00 P.M. when the movie would end. I was feeling the usual preparty jitters. This is the time when I invent nightmares about the portable pizza ovens malfunctioning (never happened) or the guacamole turning obscenely black (happened once, before we developed a never-fail recipe).

I decided to take the up escalator, stand in the crowd, and gape at the arriving stars. In this illustrious company (how the world turns!) would be Bob Crosswaithe. We seemed to have developed this sometimes master, sometimes servant relationship. It was a bit like alternate side of the street parking. (My friend Marcy once suggested that when it was *my* turn to play master, I could order him home with me. Marcy is pragmatic. She says: when relationships fail, fall back on sex. Oh, gorgeous Bob, if only that was all I wanted.)

It was only a few minutes after I pushed my way into the middle of the fans, photographers, and TV crews that I saw what glorious company he kept. At the head of the red carpet procession was the film's star, the bronzed, cleft-chinned, mighty-muscled, utterly magnificent action hero, Miles Fleming. He walked alone, resplendent in a classic tuxedo, bestowing smiles, no wife or starlet beside him to dim his luster. The local and network news crews shined their loving beams of light on him. Following closely behind was the producer of *Apache Sunset*, a thin, balding man who looked as if he often dined on Mylanta II. He was smiling now, paying attention to the next person in this entourage, that towering bantam, Ronald Wesley. Both were in formal evening dress. Wesley was not the director of tonight's movie; he was signed up with the star and the producer for their next production. Undoubtedly, this was the reason why three Japanese gentlemen, the investors, also smiling, followed close behind. At the end of this small knot of movie moguldom was Bob Crosswaithe, blond, tall, and exquisitely tailored (dinner clothes, I guessed, by Armani—not bad for bartender's wages). I recognized the woman in beaded, décolleté grey taffeta who was gracefully attached to Bob's arm. It was Ronald Wesley's leading lady, the voluptuous Lolly Hart, even more of a knockout than at our supper party. Bob had obviously been pressed into escort service while Ronald looked after business.

I could see, though, that their relationship was one of convenience. Lolly did her star turn, playing to the cameras. Bob, for his part, ducked his head as if the crowd's approval embarrassed him. I wondered if this uncommon reserve was to reassure Ronald Wesley. Although Wesley hardly seemed insecure, Crosswaithe was, after all, a credible hunk.

If Bob planned to keep a low profile, the plan was doomed. As the poet Burns said: the schemes o' mice an' men do indeed gang aft a-gley.

The entourage had almost reached the theater doors when a young man stepped out of the crowd and blocked the path. He was a stocky man with a strong American Indian face. His black, thick hair hung to his shoulders. He was dressed in Southwestern style: plaid flannel shirt, Levi's, turquoise-inlaid silver buckle on his low-slung belt, scuffed brown boots. He carried what seemed to be a six-foot pole.

Although he was half a foot shorter than Miles Fleming, the intruder planted himself toe-to-toe in front of the surprised actor and said, "In the name of the Revolutionary Children of the Mesas, I order you to stop this exploitation of the Native American peoples. I order you to shut down this movie!"

In the first silence, I said to myself, "Hey, publicity stunt!" The TV cameras had swung to cover Fleming. It was only when I saw the security guards rush forward that I thought: this could be real.

The tall pole turned out to be a banner. Before anyone could stop him, the young Indian unfurled the banner, swung it from side to side so that the crowd could read the words: *STOP RACIST HOLLYWOOD!* Just then, the guards reached him. As they struggled to hold him, the protestor flailed around with the banner. It was Miles Fleming's bad luck to be standing in its path. The pole struck the star an audible crack on the shoulder. He clutched his shoulder and fell to his knees on the red carpet. In the ensuing chaos I saw Bob Crosswaithe grab Lolly Hart by the arm and pull her to safety under the theater marquee, but not before the cameras panning across the crowd caught the entire scene. Soon, the stoic-faced man with the long dark hair was hustled away by the guards, off to the side of the theater. Miles Fleming was helped to his feet and waved away further assistance. He moved forward into the theater and the procession continued.

I took a deep breath and rode the escalator down to the calm of a party waiting to happen. The rest of that evening passed smoothly. Just after 10:00 P.M., the chattering guests arrived, parched and hungry after two hours of riding with the Apaches through the high desert. Soon, the open bar and the buffet tables were surrounded. Overseeing the staff and service as I did, I moved at full speed until after midnight. I enjoyed myself: this was an up crowd, self-congratulatory, happy to associate itself with a production that could lead the holiday box office hits.

I chatted briefly with Bob Crosswaithe, who, once inside the club, was his usual jaunty self. Lolly Hart had moved to her rightful place at Ronald Wesley's side. Bob cruised, talking to any number of well-dressed, attractive industry women: wives, actresses and agents, PR execs and producers, the hungry, the bored, and the beautiful. My God! he liked women! He wasn't making future contacts. He was the kid in the Beverly Hills candy store—he tucked away the everyday Hershey chocolate bars in his back pocket and sampled as many as he could of the chocolate truffles and liqueur bonbons. As far as I could tell, he didn't trade business cards or phone numbers but, then, I was busy.

Oh, yes, about our part in the festivities. At our regular Tuesday-morning review of Dellacasa's previous week, we agreed: an A rating for this one. Furthermore, the piñon-nut tamales were a great success; they would be featured in a *Los Angeles* magazine article and enter Mario's permanent repertoire. However, the feathers in my headbands had insisted on twisting to one side or the other so that, by the end of the party, much of our staff looked like a tribe of crazies. This was another of the best-laid schemes that ganged a-gley that night.

Angela

She disgusted me. Those big, heavy boobs like the overripe melons on the day-old stand in the market. Big, heavy boobs pushing out of her dress at any man standing near her. I saw her pushing herself at Bobby, actually brushing his arm, meanwhile her head was turned the other way, toward the crowd, like she didn't know what she was doing. Wanna bet?

I almost didn't see them. I was in bed at the motel reading this romance about Miranda who inherited a crummy old plantation that had a curse only the mysterious stranger with the birthmark on his cheek could break, but you couldn't tell at first whether he would turn out to be her true love. I wanted to keep reading, but I thought, if I get too keyed up I won't sleep well, what with being so alone here, so I turned on the eleven o'clock news.

It was the usual crap: Russians marching in the streets about more food, farm workers near the Mexican border in Chula Vista marching for better wages (doesn't anyone stay indoors anymore?), and the boring San Diego weather—low clouds in the morning, sun in the afternoon—so I was

getting sleepy when, it was the last story, they showed the
fight that broke out at this movie premiere. I sat up straight
because Miles Fleming is—next to Bobby—the sexiest man
in the world. At first I was just watching the celebrities arrive and then, all of a sudden, there was Bobby on the TV
screen. Even though he was six or seven people behind
Miles I picked him out right away—his blond curls and
height and the broad shoulders and narrow hips, oh, I
know those hips. I was so shocked I screamed, I had to clap
my hands over my mouth so the couple from Wisconsin in
the next room wouldn't think I was being murdered.
They're harmless, I say hello, I told them my husband is in
the U.S. Navy and away on maneuvers—some maneuvers,
I could hardly believe what I was seeing on TV. I kept
trying to keep him in sight and then it dawned on me that
there was this sleazy tramp hanging on his arm—Lolly
Whatshername, she's in the movies but that doesn't make
her less of a tramp, maybe more. The Japanese guys walking in front of him were short so I could see that she was
holding on to him, not vice versa. Then the camera, all of a
sudden, showed this Indian guy coming out of nowhere
and hitting Miles, and everything went crazy. I saw Bobby
grab the tramp and pull her under the theater marquee, I
saw her put her arms around him and push those boobs up
against his chest. The camera was jerking from side to side
like it didn't know where to look, then it cut to Miles and
the Indian and I got frantic because I couldn't see Bobby
anymore.

I lay there in bed and I was trembling. I mean, seeing
Bobby in such danger from another scheming woman. Oh,
I could tell she wanted to get him alone later. She wasn't his
type, practically falling out of the tight dress with the crystal
beading and I bet she wore some musky perfume you could
smell as far as Arizona. I wondered, what was he doing
there? Did his boss, the big investor—the degenerate—ex-

pect him to be an escort service for every horny broad in
L.A. County? It wasn't fair to Bobby, no, it wasn't.

Too many women, too many women. I got chills and
then I began to sweat, even though it was cool I kept sweating until my nightie was soaked. I sat up in bed staring at
nothing until, toward morning, I dropped into a sleep so
heavy it felt like death. I woke up groggy but I knew what I
had to do. I couldn't wait until Monday for Bobby to come
to me. Maybe I was being a silly thing, but I wanted to tell
him we had to move up our plans and get out of town *now*.
Before his boss threw him in the path of more conniving
women. Like this Lolly Whatshername. Was he meeting *her*
for one of those power breakfasts? And who was this boss,
anyway? During the night I figured that the man must
have been at the premiere. Maybe it was time to look him
up and tell him how he was really getting me pissed off.

Sometime before dawn I'd made up my mind to drive up
to L.A. for the day, just for a teeny weeny visit. First,
though, I'd find a hairdresser, I'd been in hiding so long
my roots were beginning to show. Maybe I'd change the
color again, a dark red this time. I was getting good at
being anyone but me. I'd buy the L.A. newspapers to read
at the hairdresser, see what the papers had to say about the
premiere.

I thought, maybe Bobby will be mad at me at first, but
when I point out how Hollywood is trying to corrupt him,
he'll understand. I'll wear my peach silk push-up bra and
bikini, just in case he has time for a quick one—so I can
show him I'm the only woman he needs. Then I'll go back
to San Diego and wait. Soon, maybe as soon as this week,
I'll hear that knock on the door. I'll open the door, and
he'll be there, his blue eyes crinkling at the corners as he
smiles at me. He'll be holding a suitcase full of our money
and I'll know that this is it, we're on our way. Slowly, I'll
open my robe and let it drop to the floor. Then I'll fling
myself, naked, into his yearning arms.

Chapter Twenty-Seven

I'd just taken a big bite of my Tofu Cheddar Cheese Alternative on a pumpernickel bagel when I saw the headline and picture, and I nearly choked. She was dead, murdered by person or persons unknown, savagely beaten on the head with a weapon that could be a wrench. The security guard found her body near the front entrance of the bank parking structure when he made his 7:00 A.M. rounds yesterday. She'd been dead a short time, the body was still warm; the guard had missed the killer or killers maybe by minutes. Robbery did not seem to be a motive; her purse was near her body, wallet and credit cards intact. She wore a gold watch, a jade-and-diamond ring.

There was no doubt about it in my mind: the name and the blonde in the newspaper picture matched. It was Elaine Stedman who'd been beaten to death early on a bright December morning, the same Elaine Stedman who had raged at Bob Crosswaithe in a Beverly Hills gourmet shop. Son of a gun.

Perhaps the murder had been on the TV news the night

171

before, but I'd worked late at the first office Christmas
party of the season. We had served up a Mexican fiesta for
125 employees of a citywide carpet cleaning firm. The
party was at the owner's home, a cantilevered, severe architectural cube that seemed to teeter over nothingness high
in the Holmby Hills. Saturday morning, as I prepared a
late breakfast, I hummed a ballad of love and longing that
had been sung at least five times last night by Pedro's Stroll-
ing Mariachi Players. Romantic love, eternal love. I added a
dash of wistfulness as I measured and ground my French
Roast/Antigua blend. Soon the fresh, rich coffee aroma
blotted out the scent memory of too many trays of fajitas,
too many pans of jalapeño-strewn Mexican pizza. I men-
tally gave myself a star for my nutritionally sound low-fat
and dark-grain breakfast. All was right with my orderly
world until I unfolded the morning paper.

Ordinarily, a run-of-the-mill bludgeoning in Los Angeles
would make the second—the Metro—section for local
news. Elaine Stedman's demise, however, was on the front
page. I'd never thought to ask Crosswaithe how his sometime friend earned her living, although I'd assumed she
was a working woman.

She was, I read now, Operations Officer at the main
branch of California Patriot Bank (in greedier days, California Patriot Savings and Loan). Although other S&L's
were tainted by the nationwide scandal, Cal Patriot was
mired in muck of its own. There was talk that some loan
customers couldn't have passed a credit check at Ralph's
Supermarket; that the majority shareholders had gained
control illegally during the laissez-faire eighties; that the
bank had connections to South American drug money. Recently, Washington regulators had stretched and yawned
after their long sleep and ordered investigations. Only last
month, Cal Patriot's Vice President for Lending had committed suicide. The Stedman story had recapped the bank
history, noting that their VP cashed himself in by firing a

pistol down his own throat. Yeechh. I sipped my coffee and read on.

Although the Stedman investigation was in its early stages, detectives did not rule out the possibility that her murder was connected to the bank scandal. According to Homicide Detective Paul Wang of Wilshire Division, reported the *Times*, "We are looking at both Ms. Stedman's personal and business relationships." Paul Wang. Of course. The main branch of Cal Patriot was located on Third, not ten blocks from my apartment. It would be in Paul's jurisdiction. I groaned.

I still felt guilty that I hadn't contacted Paul Wang after I'd seen Cheeks and the Turtle parking cars at the Wesley party. Bob Crosswaithe had convinced me that I could make trouble both for him and his down-and-out buddies with the Immigration people. I'd gone along with him both out of fairness and, yes, my own vexing attraction to him. I had no proof that Bob knew the possibly murderous Angela. And yet, here was gorgeous Bob with perhaps some tenuous connection—perhaps, definitely perhaps—to another killing. Coincidence, to be sure. How could he possibly be involved in Elaine Stedman's death? He and Ronald Wesley were out of town. A few weeks before, I'd offered him the bartending job at last night's party—he always seemed so eager to earn a few extra dollars—but he'd had to refuse. Ronald, he'd told me, was scheduled to be an honored guest at a three day film noir symposium that weekend at UC Santa Barbara. It was to begin with breakfast on Friday. Bob would drive them up early; they'd stay in Santa Barbara for the banquet on Saturday night and return on Sunday. It was a major film event for the industry and the fans; I'd seen the write-up in the L.A. paper under the week's Best Bets.

Undoubtedly, Bob Crosswaithe was gone from the scene when Elaine Stedman was murdered. He'd have a solid alibi. *Now what made me think he'd need an alibi?* And yet, the guilt worked on me.

Suppose I called Paul Wang and told him I'd met up with Cheeks and the Turtle again. I wouldn't even have to mention Bob Crosswaithe, if it didn't seem comfortable. Just say that I'd seen my two visitors again in an unexpected place, and thought he should know. Why didn't I mention them before? Well, Paul, I've been busy. It's the party season, you know.

On the other hand, Bob Crosswaithe had been involved with Elaine Stedman. Not that she'd seemed angry with him anymore. Last time I saw them together, as they sat in her car, she was clinging to him like frosting to a cake. Thinking of cake made me remember the leftover butter cookies I'd brought home after last night's party. I helped myself to a few of them, poured a third cup of coffee, and thought: I do have to tell Paul Wang. I don't feel right holding back my tidbit any longer. I'd hate to get Bob into trouble, but, as my aunt Sadie says about life in general, *qué será, será*. It helps her cope with the inexplicable. I didn't know if detectives worked over the weekend, and I suppose I didn't feel pressed to find out. I'll call Paul on Monday, I decided.

At that time, I did not see a shape to the events that disturbed me. It still seemed likely (I told myself) that Elaine Stedman either was involved with the seamy doings at her bank, or she was another victim of the haphazard violence that roams L.A.'s freeways, lurks in shopping mall parking lots, and makes you afraid to hand a dollar to a shabby homeless man. Yet, there *was* a shape emerging from the urban violence, a dark shape still undefined, that hovered in the shadows along my street and searched for a familiar face.

I'd taken the day off on Monday. This was leisure earned after an engagement party in Beverly Hills on Saturday night (second wedding for him, third for her; artichoke-size diamond ring; buffet of lamb chops, lobster ravioli, salmon; Perrier-Jouet champagne) and Sunday afternoon's Bel-Air lawn party in support of Juvenile Rheumatoid Arthritis research (plucky kids and parents; hungry scientists; benevolent donors; Yule logs, fruitcakes, tortes, tarts, other seasonal sugarplums; punch and coffee).

I woke early, made a few trips to the communal laundry room, threw out the milk that had soured, the lettuce that looked like green slime; I'd lived on take-out food and left-overs the harried past week. Finally, when I could avoid it no longer, I picked up the telephone and called Paul Wang at the Wilshire precinct. He answered his phone on the first ring.

"Detective Wang."

"Paul? Hi, this is Catherine Deean."

Pause, then "Hello, how've you been?" So restrained. This would not, for some reason, be an easy confession.

"Um, busy. You know, my business—catering—it's the busy season."

"I'm sure." Another pause. "I'm glad you called. I've just been talking about you this morning."

I was so preoccupied with my prepared speech, I hardly listened to him. I said, "Paul, something slipped my mind that I want to tell you about. Not important, no, I'm sure it's not important, but you said to call if I remembered any little thing at all—"

"Cat," he said, his tone grim, "I have a man coming to see me in about half an hour, someone I'd like you to meet. I was about to call you. Can you be here soon?" It wasn't a question, or a request. He was polite but no-nonsense: this was assuredly an order.

What man? Why? I had phoned *first*, but it didn't seem to matter.

"Why, yes," I said, "it's my day off. I'm home. I'll just get dressed and leave, shouldn't take me long." I realized I was babbling. Was my one sin of omission that serious? Paul gave me the precinct address and I promised again to rush right along.

Shower? Already taken. Breakfast? Eaten. Clothing? What *did* one wear to the police station? I settled on corduroy pants, a turtleneck, my Levi's jacket. Comfort clothes.

For once, traffic was light going south on La Brea past body shop row: stucco buildings like squat, pastel temples offering L.A. believers the hope of scrapes, dents, and total wreckage transformed into automotive rebirth. I turned east on Venice Boulevard and found the precinct station. It was built low and fortresslike, of red brick and concrete. The facade was so blank it looked incomplete in the glaring noonday sun, as if the city architect had left early the day it was designed.

At the desk, I was pointed toward Detectives. I put my head inside the door; an unsmiling Paul Wang saw me and came over.

"Cat," he said, pointing toward a windowless cubbyhole, "let's go in here." The room was brightly lit from overhead. No frills. Inside was a small, scuffed desk with a metal chair behind it. Two more chairs were crammed in on the other side of the desk. A man sat in one of the chairs. He looked about forty, average height, brown hair, pleasant face, a lumpy nose that might once have been broken. He wore tan slacks and matching socks, a tan open-collar knit shirt, brown gabardine sports jacket, brown suede shoes. A neat dresser. He rose and smiled as I stood in the doorway.

"Catherine," said Paul, "I'd like you to meet Benny Ellis. Benny is the private detective who's been following you."

"How do you do?" said Benny Ellis. I had been around Nick long enough that I recognized Brooklyn in Benny's accent.

"I surmise from your look," he said, "that you've never seen me before. Which is the way it should be. That's why I'm a success as a detective."

Angela

I didn't mean to spoil it for us. Everything just went haywire, nothing came off right. Temper, temper, I suppose I'll have to learn to curb my temper. And then, the Monday after, he acted so strange. He behaved like I had *planned* what happened in L.A.—although I told him over and over again that I'd just lost my temper, why couldn't he understand?

I never want another day like that Monday. For whatever reason, he couldn't do it at all, no matter how I tried. It was awful. Then I made it worse when I sat up in bed and said, I thought it only happened to men when they got older. He gave me such a murderous look I got up, went to the kitchenette and drank a glass of water, giving him time to calm down. He had half covered himself with the sheet and he lay there on his back with this gloomy Gus look on his face. But how was I supposed to know? I'm certainly not what you'd call promiscuous. Bobby is my one and only.

Anyway, his visit started bad and ended worse. I'd spent the morning pacing off my motel room—eighteen steps from the door to the round Formica table and two chairs, eight steps from the table to the queen-size bed, seven steps from the bed to the fake French Provincial white-and-gold dresser—when he knocked on the door. Real sharp knocks. I could tell when I opened the door that he wasn't bringing champagne and airline tickets. No kisses, no fun.

Right at the door he demanded, where were you Friday morning?

I'd already decided to try to keep it light. I tossed my head airily (the way Miranda did when Jacques Beaudry demanded the deed to the plantation). Where were *you*, I replied saucily, on Thursday night?

What the hell are you talking about? said Bobby, but his eyes shifted away from me for a second, like I'd caught him in a fib.

You know, I said (no airs this time), you know where you spent Thursday night.

Then you did kill her, said Bobby, kind of shocked, you killed Elaine. It wasn't connected to the bank, it was you.

I'd had my answers ready, just in case. I said (I was calm but righteous), she forced me to do it, she made you betray me. I'm learning that you're weak sometimes when it comes to women, Bobby, you know you are.

He didn't look convinced, so I reached up and put my arms on his chest. I pressed myself tight against him and said, looking up into his eyes: what would you do if I wasn't there to protect you—protect us? Nobody else has what we have, sweetheart.

He kind of squirmed as if he was, well, uncomfortable, and that scared me more than if he'd knocked me across the room. We'd always laughed together, no matter what he said or I did, but now he was, oh, God! nervous around me.

Carefully, very carefully, he put his hands over mine, lowered them from his chest, and stepped back. He said, she was a nice woman, at one time she was very kind to me.

We'd been standing near the door during this. I figured,

if I get him over to the bed, I can make him forget Elaine. I
said, I think we both need a drink. He didn't say anything,
just kind of stared at me, so I turned and walked slowly to
the kitchenette, swaying my hips like it was Saturday night
on Sunset Boulevard. I was wearing a purple low-cut tank
top and black tights, guaranteed sexy. I found the bottle of
Beefeater gin I always kept for Bobby. I took out glasses
and ice, poured a good shot of gin into each glass, and
handed him one. I said, you look tired, dear, let's sit down
and have a drink. I took his hand and he followed me (I
have to say, almost grudgingly) to the edge of the bed and
sat down next to me.

Here, I said, let's drink up! and even though I've never
been a drinker, I tossed down that gin as if it was Pepsi. My
eyes started to tear and I coughed a little, but it was okay. I
felt a nice burn starting in my throat and going down.

He stared into his glass and told me how he'd met Elaine,
on the plane coming to L.A. He said, she took me home
with her, she put me up the first month I was here. He ran
his fingers through his blond curls and, very solemn, told
me—but it wasn't like he was talking to me, it was more like
he was talking to the room delivering a eulogy for Elaine
Stedman, remembering only the good things like people
do in church—he told me, she'd even lent him the money
to buy his car. He tossed down his drink.

I said, let's have another round. I got the gin bottle, this
time I took it with me and after I poured I set it on the floor
next to the bed. Bobby looked down at the bottle and then
at me and—he couldn't help himself—he started to smile,
just like the old Bobby. He said, I do believe you're trying
to get me drunk.

We each had another couple of drinks, hardly talking,
barely touching, and then I got up my nerve and said, why?
aren't I enough for you?

You mean Elaine? he said, and her name came out a little
slurred as if the drinks were getting to him (they should

have been, I was pouring *his* double-strength). He kept rubbing his fingers over his beautiful mouth in a nervous way, then he said, God! I've had a rough week.

Well, I said, truthfully, I didn't intend to make it worse.

He asked, how did you find us? When did you know about Elaine? I told him, I didn't. I told him about seeing him on TV with that Lolly Whatsherface—Oh, yes, dear Lolly, he said, grinning and settling back, making himself comfortable propped up on the pillows. I hated the way he'd grinned, but I felt he was, finally, loosening up. He said—and it was like he was ordering me—give me the whole story. So I said, I saw you with Lolly and I decided to come to L.A. for a teeny visit because you were looking so handsome on TV I realized how much I was missing you. Then I told myself, Angela, don't say any more, *anything* could piss him off today.

He was eyeing me like he was puzzled, then he said, surprised, you're a redhead.

The roots were coming out, I told him, so I thought I'd try something different, do you like it?

Not bad, he said, raising an eyebrow and looking me over, if you pulled it into spikes and wore black leather, you'd look like a biker. Y'know, skinny and scary—I think you're definitely the black leather type.

I thought he was being a teeny weeny nasty, but I decided to act like it was a compliment. Would you like that? I asked, should I buy something in black leather?

Bobby groaned and said, don't, Angela, no more surprises, you'd probably add a whip and chains. (I thought to myself, if that's what it takes to keep love alive, I'll do it.) He was saying: Angela, I'm still trying to deal with the way you keep following me. I want to know what happened.

I started to say, I wouldn't follow you if we were together all the time—but I didn't. Instead I went on: well, I got to L.A. late, because of the hairdresser, you know, and I thought I'd wait at your apartment until you got home from work, and then I'd stay for a few hours, just a wee little visit. (I didn't tell him about my other plan—to look for Ronald Wesley if Bobby didn't show up at the apartment. I had a hunch that this big-time director was Bobby's boss. There was a picture in the *Times* of Wesley and Lolly together at a party after the premiere. I figured that Bobby was taking her off his boss's hands before the movie. The caption said she was his "longtime friend"—although that didn't mean she shouldn't be watched, the tramp, or that Wesley wasn't pimping for her. Hollywood people have no *morals!* I'd thought: I could break into the Screen Director's Guild office. There'd be a directory, and I'd get Wesley's address, because I'd already checked the phone book and he was unlisted. But I didn't have to.)

I said, when I got to your apartment, *she*—this Elaine woman—was waiting for you at the top of the stairs, the way I used to. I could see her from the street. So I parked a few doors down and, when her head was turned, I slipped into an empty carport—it's dark in December, she didn't see me waiting in the shadows.

Bobby didn't say anything, he just listened. No expression on his face, I couldn't tell what he was thinking. But I hurried on. I said, she had a couple of bags of groceries sitting on the landing, and I knew she wanted to cook for you—before she got you in bed. The thought of it—the two of you—I felt sick.

Bobby said, for the record, I didn't expect her, I'd gone home to pack, I was driving up the coast with my boss next morning.

I saw her kiss you, I said—I couldn't help it, my voice was accusing—and you didn't push her away. Bobby reached for the gin and poured us each another round. He laughed, but he didn't sound happy. Would you turn down a steak dinner and a quick bang? he asked.

It wasn't quick, I said fiercely, she stayed all night.

So true, he said, sipping his gin, but—as the Bard says—

never a borrower or a lender be. I demanded, what does *that* mean? He drummed his fingers against the white and gold headboard.

It means, said Bobby, that I owed her money—for the car and a few other things—and she was taking it out in trade.

I thought about this, and asked, couldn't you just have paid her back? Bobby said, very matter-of-fact, she didn't want to be paid back, she wanted to get banged, regularly.

The lousy nerve of her, I thought, but all I said was: how could you say she was a nice woman? She was, said Bobby, after all, she could have gone to the police.

You owed her *that* much? I was shocked. Shhhh! said Bobby, some things I'd rather not talk about. But I knew he'd never blab even this much if he was sober.

What you mean is, I said, Elaine Stedman was blackmailing you. I refilled his glass as he considered this, I had stopped pouring drinks for me a few rounds back.

As if he was reading my mind, Bobby said, y'know, I don't like to drink like this, don't ever like to lose control. But I'm tired, been doing a lot of driving all over this bloody state—and then this news about Elaine.

Listen to me, Bobby, I said. I was saving you in more ways than I knew. That woman not only seduced you, she blackmailed you. I got you out of a nasty situation, don't you see that, my dearest?

Possibly, said Bobby, I'll have to think about it when my head is clearer. What did you do, follow her to work?

I followed her home first, I said, she stopped at her place and changed her clothes. I was surprised, it was so early.

Bobby said, I told you, I was leaving town, she had to get out. Since she was up, he said, she told me she'd get an early start at the bank. Poor Elaine, he said, shaking his head, if she'd just waited until later, with more people around, she'd have been safe from you.

He was wrong. I told myself, I'd have waited. After all, I

had my old man's tool kit in my trunk—hammers, wrenches, pliers—for an emergency on the road. Well, this was it. The emergency. Sooner or later, that morning, that night, next day—I'd get her alone. But why tell him?

Like Dear Abby says, I explained, it's a problem in communication. He said, it is? I said, in a soothing way, if I'd known she was so kind, maybe I wouldn't have lost my temper.

You do have a rotten temper, Angela, he said, I don't know what to do about you. Perhaps the police won't get on to you. Perhaps they'll simply keep on looking for international bank criminals.

Just love me, Bobby, I said, that's all I want. Here, I said, let me make you comfortable. I unbuttoned his shirt and I began to lick his bare chest—quick little licks like a cat lapping up milk. He shuddered and he said, oh, what the hell. Then he helped me take off the rest of his clothes. I undressed so fast I just about ripped my clothes, pulling at them like they were burning my skin, then I slid into bed with him.

I thought we'd kiss and make up, but it didn't work out that way. I even tried in the middle of the night, after the drinks should have worn off, but nothing helped. Who'd ever dream that men are so sensitive?

Chapter Twenty-Eight

I t could have been a low-budget, made-for-TV mystery movie: cramped room, blank walls, stark overhead light. There was this trio, the cop and the private eye working together (male bonding), grilling the suspect. (Beautiful, tough, defiant me. Kathleen Turner. Cher. Turner or Cher?—It was *my* fantasy—I upped the talent budget.) My mind floated above the scene—

Fade to what I'd rather have avoided—hard reality—as Paul Wang said, "Cat, did you hear me? What do you know about this Bob Crosswaithe?"

I hedged. "Not very much. What's this about?"

"A woman named Elaine Stedman was murdered Friday morning. Mr. Ellis here has volunteered information that a visiting Englishman, Bob Crosswaithe, may be involved."

Why connect me to Elaine Stedman? "I only met her once, for a few minutes. I was with Bob. He introduced us so I know her name, but that's all I know. Of course, I read in the weekend papers that she worked for the bank that's in trouble."

Paul rephrased it patiently, "What I'm looking for is

more background on Crosswaithe. For reasons that I'll explain, I'm not ready yet to question him directly." He
turned to the private detective. "Ellis, why don't you tell
Miss Deean why you've been following her."

"It's my pleasure," said Benny Ellis with a courteous
nod. "You see, back in October Miss Stedman hired me to
shadow you."

I remembered the inquiries to my landlord and to Mario. More than once, the feeling I'd had of being observed.
I could only stare at Benny Ellis and note that the tan
blandness of his wardrobe could not hide sharp, intelligent
grey eyes.

He held up a hand, as if to field my questions, but I was
speechless.

"Oh, she didn't have any beef with you—especially when
I confirmed you were a mere business acquaintance—but it
was through you I tracked him down."

"She gave him money—about ten thousand dollars and a
car. She'd met him on the plane from London, took him
home with her, like a souvenir, like an ashtray with a picture of the Tower of London—" He made a clucking sound
like a dismayed rooster.

"I'll never understand," said Ellis, "why a smart woman
like Elaine Stedman—a bank officer and, by the way, I
think she was clean in the bank scam, she was a local girl
who worked her way up at that branch—why she'd invite
Crosswaithe home just because he did a funny impression
of Prince Charles somewhere over the Atlantic."

He appealed to Paul Wang. "Do you understand it?"

"Well, I've seen bright women lose it over men you
wouldn't trust to deliver a chop suey dinner," said Paul.
"But then, I'm a cop. I've seen everything."

"I own this terrific mutt named Grizzly," said Benny Ellis, "and I know more about his vet than she did about this
guy."

"It wasn't a misunderstanding? About the money, I

mean." To me, Bob wore his chronic lack of money like a proud badge.

"He disappeared one day," said Ellis. "They'd been living together about a month. She came home, he was gone, so was the car. I'll say this: it wasn't robbery, he wasn't interested in her jewelry or the VCR. He just kept what she'd offered him."

I felt the need to stand up for a friend. "So where's the crime? She gave him gifts. Were there strings attached? Did he sign any loan papers?"

Paul shook his head. "No," he said, "the only thing he signed was this farewell note." Paul held up a note-size sheet of lined yellow paper, ragged at the top, as if hastily torn from a pad. "Benny here got this from Elaine. It says, 'Didn't we have fun! You're a love. Cheers, Bob.' "

A cheerful way to end a love affair. Quick. Painless. No chance for tears or recriminations. But my first thought was: Bob Crosswaithe didn't meet Ronald Wesley fresh off the plane, as he'd told me. He'd been in Los Angeles at least a month. He'd been with Elaine Stedman, until he'd dumped her.

"Was she in love with him?"

"Love? Oh, I don't know," Benny mused. "She was angry at him when she hired me. Maybe she was feeling—you know—like a women scorned."

"Maybe," said Paul with a wry shrug, "she wanted a better return on her investment."

"I wouldn't be surprised," said Benny, turning to him. "She was good at making deals. First time I worked for her —a little bank matter—she negotiated my fee, and then she wouldn't hire me until she checked every reference. She was a woman who liked being right, and she liked winning."

"So she thought she bought him," said Paul, "and he left without giving her a refund. I'll bet she didn't take it kindly."

I'd listened quietly, but I had to disagree. "You're both being unfair," I said. "Women are attracted to him, he's an extremely attractive man. But he's also a man who works hard, I know. Why treat him like merchandise? That's not Bob at all."

I had their attention now, and I could feel my face becoming hot. I don't blush, but this was close. I changed topics.

I said to Benny Ellis, "I still don't understand what you wanted from me."

"Nothing personal," said the private detective. "After Miss Stedman spotted the two of you—when you left the store, Miss Deean—Crosswaithe poured on so much charm he could've flooded Bedford Drive. He gave her some alibi about being out of town on a big business deal, that he'd just gotten back and he'd meant to call her, etc., etc." Benny's hand made slow circles in the air, like a well-worn tape going round and round. "Well, she didn't believe it, but she wanted to keep track of him—"

Paul Wang interrupted. "Did she say why? Anything specific."

Benny shook his head sadly. "Just that the car was in her name, and she worried about the insurance. But that wasn't the real reason. She just wanted him back. Like I said, who can figure it?"

Indeed. I couldn't imagine being rejected as if I were a soggy waffle and then coming back for more. Poor Elaine. So pathetic. At that point, I was directing my scorn at the betrayed rather than the betrayer. How we do fool ourselves. Amazing.

Benny turned to me. "Miss Deean, I only followed you to get a lead on Crosswaithe. He wouldn't give Miss Stedman his telephone number. But he'd introduced you by name, and when I checked with the store manager, he knew you and that you were with Dellacasa's. Crosswaithe had told my client you were a business acquaintance, and I thought possibly you were. I had a hunch you had too much taste to get involved with a guy like that any other way."

He beamed at me and then at Paul, who beamed back. I tried a tasteful smile, but it didn't have much conviction.

"Anyway," Benny continued, tipping back his chair as if he were on some front porch spinning yarns, "the manager said you were helping this Crosswaithe pick out wines, but the guy didn't buy them that day. The manager had never seen Crosswaithe before, but he remembered this tall blond fellow with the two women, and that he left the shopping cart with the wines. Then the next day he came back, picked out the same wines again, and paid cash. My guess is, he didn't want his name on anything that Miss Stedman could trace. But Benny Ellis outsmarted him!

"I found you right away, Miss Deean. Not only did I know where you worked, but your home address is in the phone book." He looked at me reproachfully. "You shouldn't make yourself such an easy mark."

Memo to myself: call the phone company and delete my address from the next directory. Who knows who else might come tap, tap, tapping at my door?

"Anyway," said Benny Ellis, "it was a quick assignment—the first time. I called Miss Stedman, told her I had traced *you* so far, told her that you were a legit caterer and that Crosswaithe possibly was one of your clients. She seemed excited, wanted your home and work address, then she said maybe that was all the information she needed, and to just send her a bill.

"I think, though, she'd been annoyed when I told her how easy it was to find you. Like I hadn't earned my fee. She'd probably have been happier if I'd told her I'd chased you around the UCLA campus waving a .45, but padding a bill isn't my mode of operation."

He rocked back and forth in his LAPD-issue chair, saying, "Yet this tough money manager handed over ten thou-

sand to her new boyfriend, just so he'd feel welcome in
America. Go figure."

I, too, had jumped at Crosswaithe's touch, felt his heat.
Would I have been as susceptible as Elaine Stedman if he'd
made the right moves? It was the Double Jeopardy question.

Benny Ellis was saying, "I had the definite impression
she still felt you were Crosswaithe's girlfriend and she was
planning to do a little detective work herself."

"Good heavens," I said, appalled, "Elaine Stedman followed me, too? You mean I had two of you lurking around
my apartment house?"

"Well, not *together*," said PI Benny Ellis.

Paul Wang had been silent. I demanded of him, "Is that
legal?"

"Mr. Ellis has a license, Miss Stedman didn't—but she
wasn't harassing you. And, remember, she ended up as the
victim."

Was that a rebuke? I studied him: thick black hair
sleeked back, bright almond-shaped eyes carefully hiding
any expression, long, square jaw. A face that would be severe if not for the mustache; I noticed that it had shrunk
somewhat.

"You trimmed your mustache," I said.

"My superior's orders," he explained. "He thinks the
LAPD doesn't need a new Charlie Chan."

He had lost part of his ready-made persona. "Never
mind," I said, "you can always sleep in your raincoat and
be Columbo."

Benny Ellis looked puzzled, but I needed time out to
deal with his story. I felt my blood curdling like an over-
cooked custard. How dare these people out of a penny-
dreadful novel come skulking in my backyard?

"Tell her the rest, Benny," said Paul (they had become
first-name buddies by now), "I want to get to the good
part."

"Okay," said Benny, "what happened next was, a couple of weeks later I get another call from Miss Stedman. She'd flunked out as a private eye—even if she didn't say it in so many words. Either she got tired of hanging around your place to see if Crosswaithe came around, or a neighbor saw her and scared her off.

"Now she wanted me to keep on with it, find Crosswaithe, don't worry about the expense. Miss Stedman had been very firm about not contacting you directly, she wanted this handled discreetly. So my assignment was to get Crosswaithe's address or telephone number for her, and then stop. That's when I began to follow you for real, Miss Deean, which was *no problema,* as our Latino friends say. Even though I was chasing you and your catering trucks all over the Westside, you lead a very regular life. By the way, you belong to a nice gym, you should go more often, get more oxygen in your lungs, you won't look so tired after a long day."

Inwardly, I sighed. Mr. Benny Ellis, ace investigator, was turning out to be my aunt Sadie in brown suede loafers.

"Halloween," he said, "I finally hit the jackpot. I knew what Crosswaithe looked like, Miss Stedman had given me his picture. Do you have it, Paul?"

Paul opened the file folder he had in front of him, drew out a snapshot, and handed it to me. It was Bob Crosswaithe, all right, standing on the deck of a sailboat. I recognized the channel at Marina del Rey in the background. He was smiling into the camera, sun changing his blond curls into gold, breezes flattening his white tee and khaki shorts against his body. He had one hand loosely on the mast; Elaine Stedman was welded to his side, clutching his other arm. She was more attractive in the long red tee and white pants than she had been in clinging jersey; she also looked happier, her face turned up to Bob with an expression that mixed pride and possession. For the first time, I felt some pity for her. I handed back the picture.

"That was taken on her bank's department outing," said Benny Ellis. "The boat belonged to her manager, but, according to Miss Stedman, he depended on Crosswaithe to help him crew. To hear her tell it, her chap was Admiral Nelson running the British Navy."

"He does seem," I said, perversely amused by this masculine reaction to Elaine Stedman's golden boy, "to do many things quite well."

"More than you think," said Paul, cloaking himself in Oriental inscrutability. "Go on, Benny."

"Oh, well, on Halloween, you were running back and forth, Miss Deean, to that computer company. I was just about figuring this was no way to find Crosswaithe, when he drove up in Miss Stedman's Buick and parked it at the curb. He looked like he was dressed for work, white shirt with black pants and bow tie, so I waited a while. When I looked through the glass front doors at Interfacets, I could see there was a swell party going on. I decided to join the guests and see what Crosswaithe was up to. I slipped in so quietly you'd never know it—in fact, I'm an expert at becoming invisible."

At this point, Detective Wang, LAPD, gnawed his lower lip, and Benny opened his palms toward Paul as if to say, big deal, so I crashed a party. He continued. "I saw Crosswaithe tending bar, which, I will admit, surprised me, I didn't know until then he was working for you. Then, excuse me, Miss Deean, I helped myself to a delicious prime rib sandwich. I shot the breeze with a few engineers about the Rams' season, kept out of your way—you certainly move fast—and watched Crosswaithe pour drinks. When I left, I hunkered down in my car across the street and waited.

"I figured it would be a long wait, but about 8:00 P.M. he left and went for his car, kind of in a rush. So I tailed him to this hospital in Beverly Hills. It turned out he was visiting a young woman who had been run over that day by a hit-

and-run driver. A Miss Caroline Chase. In the next day's papers, they mentioned she was from a wealthy Detroit family."

No surprise. It was the night he had gone to see Baby.

"When he left the hospital, I tailed him to an old Colonial-style apartment house on Hollywood Boulevard near La Brea. Not far from the place where Janice Joplin bought it—you know, high rents for not much living space, but no leases and the manager not too curious about references.

"I watched him go up the outside stairs, and I waited until his lights went out. Next morning, I came back early, I picked up a breakfast burrito and coffee at the Weinerschnitzel and went back to his place. His car was still in the carport so I sat and finished my breakfast before he came downstairs.

"Tailing him was easy until we got to Benedict Canyon, then I had to hang back and use my finest skills because there wasn't much traffic. Finally, he parked in the driveway of this big mansion—"

"Ronald Wesley's house," I said.

"Right. Midmorning, he drove off and I rang the bell, told the French maid I was with the Department of Water and Power and needed to know—because of the drought and water rationing—how many residents there were now compared to last year."

Paul Wang squirmed in his chair and coughed. Benny said, apologetically, "I didn't even go into the house. I did find out that Mees-ur Crosswaithe has a room there but keeps his own apartment for days off. Don't worry about the water, I told the maid, a part-time resident won't show up much on the water meter.

"Then I got away before Crosswaithe came back, wrote up my report for Miss Stedman, and submitted it to her that night. Needless to say, she was delighted with my efficient and discreet handling of her case, and that was the last I saw of her."

"Did she indicate what she intended to do with your report?" asked Paul.

"No," said the private detective, "but I'd say she looked happy. She was surprised that he worked for a big shot like Ronald Wesley, in fact she laughed while she was reading that part of the report. Maybe she figured it was a job he wouldn't want to lose."

The small room had become stuffy. Paul stood up and opened the door; my back was to the bullpen, but I became aware of other voices: conversations, inquiries, detectives talking into phones in flat voices that offered neither judgment nor hope. I wanted to leave, be alone to absorb what I'd heard. But it was my turn to show and tell. Almost my turn. I hadn't heard the final shocker.

Chapter Twenty-Nine

" She paid my bill," said Benny Ellis, "the case was closed and filed away. Then I opened the paper Saturday and read about Miss Stedman's murder. Well, of course, I called Detective Wang here first thing this morning and told him about the little inquiry I had handled recently for Miss Stedman involving you— innocently to be sure—and this Crosswaithe."

It was Paul's turn. He told me: "Benny, although he didn't know it, had a vital piece of information. He made the connection between Crosswaithe and the hit-and-run assault on Caroline Chase."

"Oh, come now," I scoffed, "you can't believe that Bob Crosswaithe ran down Baby—Miss Chase. There's no close relationship, as far as I know. Her father is a friend of Ronald Wesley, that's all."

"No," said Paul slowly, "we're not after *him* for felony hit-and-run, or murder. Not at this point. What intrigues us about Mr. Crosswaithe is that he's possibly involved with an old acquaintance of yours.

"Think back about the attack on Miss Chase. We asked

194

the media to report we were trying to i.d. the vehicle. All the witnesses could remember was that the driver wore a Halloween mask, and that the car was a grey compact. No one came forward then, but we think we finally have a break.

"When Miss Stedman was killed, the security guard was on the scene probably minutes after it happened. What we kept out of the newspapers was that before he found the body—it was hidden by her car—he saw a car screeching toward the garage exit. It made a wrong turn and passed near him. He didn't get a close look at the driver, she had on large sunglasses, but he thinks it was a woman with short red hair. He did notice—" Paul paused for emphasis, "she was driving a grey compact with a white streak over the rear wheel."

"My God," I breathed. "Angela!"

Paul nodded. "Thanks to Benny, we can tie Crosswaithe to both Chase and Stedman. "I was hoping," he said, "that you could make another connection for us. You said you had something to tell me."

It was time to spill the beans. About Cheeks and the Turtle. About Crosswaithe hiring them for the Wesley party. About Crosswaithe meeting that fellow Brit: the elusive Bobby Buck. About travelin' Bobby as Angela's possible lover. Not only was it the right time to spill the beans; I'd have to fry and refry them, and serve them up with a big helping of humility. Could I be arrested just for being stupid?

I returned home and it was still early afternoon, but I felt as if I'd been on a long trip to the edge of chaos. I double locked my front door and checked the window bolts. I'd never felt so vulnerable. There were two messages on my answering machine: Aunt Sadie said, "Please call me, dear, it's urgent"; Andrew Paisley had called from the Hyatt in

Manhattan, sounding disappointed that I wasn't home and saying he'd call back later.

I called Aunt Sadie. "Oh, I'm so glad to hear from you," she said. "Were you out shopping?"

"No, just errands. Is everything all right?"

"It will be as soon as I finalize our Christmas Day dinner. Do you realize it's only two weeks off?"

"Well, I'll be there," I said wearily.

"I know that, Catherine, but is there a special man I should invite for you? Gil is taking a Christmas week tour to Rio. You said that Andrew—when *will* I meet him?—is going east for the holidays. I've had a thought. How about that good-looking Bob I saw on the TV news when you did your premiere party? The one who works for Ronald Wesley? You've talked about him more than once."

"I have? Well, he may not be in town. Mr. Wesley depends on Bob to drive him everywhere."

"Too bad. You know, my friend Blanche has a bachelor nephew who owns a drugstore in Laguna. Suppose I ask her to invite him."

"Does the table have to balance, Auntie? Will there be less joy if there are an unequal number of males and females?"

Pause on the other end of the phone. "I can tell you're in a mood, dear. I'll just do the best I can."

"I'm sure you will," I said and I sincerely meant it.

Ten minutes later, the phone rang. It was Andrew.

"I've just got back to my empty hotel room, and I'm thinking about you. A lot."

"How's New York?"

"It may snow, all night and tomorrow. I may never get out of this hotel again. Would you miss me?"

"Sure. Get a shovel and dig."

"Want to get on a plane and meet me here for the holidays?"

"Can't. I'm working up to the last minute before Christmas."

"There's a book title, something about life being too short to stuff a mushroom."

"I don't stuff 'em myself, I just make sure they get stuffed."

"Doesn't sound too exciting."

"You'd be surprised," I said.

"Want to go skiing in January?"

"You're on."

"Great. I'm leaving for a Christmas party now, my client invited me. I'll call you tomorrow night."

"Make a list of the kinds of hors d'oeuvres at the party."

"Seriously? I'll try."

"I like you, I definitely do."

Andrew smooched into the phone and hung up. I felt carefree and happy. At least for a while.

Angela

After Bobby drove off early Tuesday morning, I killed time by shopping for his Christmas gift. I was nervous and restless, and hitting the malls gave me something to do.

He'd been warm enough when he left, a big kiss and hug and he told me he was probably catching a cold, that's why he was under the weather (he didn't say *undersexed*, but we both knew what he meant). I'd asked him about being together on Christmas Day and he'd said, sure, sure, whatever you want, love. So I should have been happy, but I don't know. I had that sinking feeling like that Christmas a long time ago when I begged the old lady for a Barbie doll in a pink gown with sequins and all she said was, Angela, don't whine I have a wonderful gift for you. But Christmas morning I knew the package was the wrong shape, too flat and too small, and I was almost too angry to open it. Then she said, don't you want to see what it is after your father and I went to all that expense? So I unwrapped it, and it was a child's picture book of the Life of Jesus. I threw a tantrum, I cried so hard I couldn't breathe. The old man took the book away from me and said to her, I told you so, get the girl something she wants. She told him she would but she never did, and I guess he never asked.

But why was I feeling now that I'd get stuck again this Christmas with the wrong package? It was hard to stay awake, I wanted to go back to bed and sleep all day, but I shook it off, finished the breakfast coffee, and turned on the shower full blast, letting the water pound sense into me. Angela, I told myself, this is your first Christmas with the man you will love and cherish unto death. It's up to *you* to make it beautiful for him.

It took me two full days to find the perfect timepiece for his gift. (I could tell from the ads that any watch costing over a hundred dollars becomes a timepiece.) I shopped almost every jewelry store from Coronado to La Jolla, until I found it in Mission Valley: Swiss Made, Goldplated, Quartz Accurate, Water Resistant to ninety feet. I had it engraved on the back: *Bobby. Our First Christmas. Always, Your Angela.* I'd never spent twelve hundred dollars on anything smaller than a Toyota, but I'd give my all to keep Bobby happy. My money was beginning to run a little low, what with the meals out, and movies and new clothes and things, and this twelve hundred dollars really made a dent, but I wasn't too worried. Bobby had been paying my motel bill every month—in cash—and I knew there was plenty more left of the three hundred thousand in our accounts, so why worry?

Thursday night, after I'd had the timepiece engraved and picked it up, I got back to the motel and I was so excited, I had to call him. He'd said, don't call, the motel may keep a record, but I needed to hear his voice and tell him how much I loved him.

Well, he had a surprise for me. I called his apartment and his phone was disconnected. I tried again, I couldn't believe it, and again I got that recording: *The number you have called is no longer in service!*

I was frantic, I called the Los Angeles operator and she tried Bobby's number then she told me, yes, it was disconnected and there was no new number.

I hung up the phone and I screamed, then I covered my mouth tight with a pillow and I screamed again until my head started to hurt and I was gulping for air. My nails were dug so hard into the palms of my hands that the palms started to bleed, and the blood blended with the color of my fingernails and all I could see was red, bloody red covering my hands.

Then the miracle happened. The phone rang and it was Bobby. My heart flipflopped: it was another sign of our perfect communion, he could feel my anguish hundreds of miles away. We were bonded for eternity whether he knew it or not.

Hello, Angela, he said, it's Bobby. I took a deep breath to the bottom of my lungs, and he said, are you there?

I'm here.

Everything all right, love?

Fine, Bobby, just fine.

Well, I'm sorry, I'll have to disappoint you on Monday. My boss has me scheduled to drive him to a couple of meetings.

Then when will I see you?

I'll call as soon as I know I can take the day off. He's keeping me busy doing his gift shopping. I'm St. Nick in designer sunglasses, that's who I am.

Bobby?

Yes, my love?

I called you just a few minutes ago. Your phone is disconnected.

Pause. Oh, yes, that, he said. Well, in view of circumstances I don't believe we should discuss on the phone, I thought it advisable to give up my apartment. Just in case anyone, y'know, official, decided to see how well I knew, um, Miss S.

I said, how will I get in touch with you?

I'll call you, he said. I'll call you Monday, around this time. Well, have to run. Have a good weekend.

I love you, Bobby. Eternally.

You're my very own Angela. 'Bye for now!

He hung up, and I sat by the phone, thinking hard. In spite of his phone call, I didn't like this development, not one bit. Well, Bobby didn't know I'd guessed who he worked for. Or that I'd read in the L.A. paper how Ronald Wesley's new movie was screening tomorrow, for a benefit to help broken-down directors or something, and that he was introducing it. I could be there and if Bobby was driving Wesley, why couldn't I follow them home? If I was wrong about Wesley, I'd go back to the motel and try to keep my skin on.

Bobby, please don't try to walk out on me. I had your Christmas gift engraved, and it says: *Always*.

Chapter Thirty

I drove along wide, palm-lined streets past an Italian-ate villa, a couple of Spanish Mission revivals, one neo-Colonial mansion and a Frank Lloyd Wright clone. It was a neighborhood of stately homes in mid-Wilshire; it was totally L.A.: handsome, eccentric, an enclave with more streets of dreams than a movie studio back lot.

The Weber manse was a three-story Tudor of mellow red brick overgrown with ivy. It sat back from the sidewalk on a grassy knoll; a large, aged bloodhound on a heavy chain lolled in front of the arched brick entryway. The dog raised itself as I parked in the circular driveway, loped over, and panted welcoming *huh huh huh*s at me. Nice doggy, I said, as I rang the bell, hearing ethereal chimes sound within. A tall, greying houseman in black sack jacket and pants opened the door and addressed us.

"Miss Deean? Mrs. Weber is expecting you. Ashley? Have you welcomed Miss Deean? Would you come in, please."

An unleashed Ashley stepped in with me, our footsteps and paws sounding tattoos on the entranceway parquet. I looked around. We had entered the great hall of the mansion, two stories of oak-paneled grandeur with a wide, curved staircase leading to a railed gallery on the upper story.

The thick oak front door had hidden the sounds of activity, but now I saw a frenzy of florists at work throughout the hall. There were other distant sounds of hammers from an unseen room. A tall and splendid green Christmas tree stood to one side of an arched doorway, surrounded by boxes of silver bells and red velvet bows. Three besmocked young assistants bustled around the tree, while others bent over the railings of the stairway and gallery, fastening silvery wreaths topped by lavish red velvet bows.

I stood enjoying the Dickensian cheer, while Ashley placed a massive paw on my foot and began to lick my ankle.

"Ashley, what are you doing?" Sally Ruth Weber strode toward me. No fragile blonde in chiffon today. She was tailored efficiency in an emerald-green silk shirt and pants. Her feet opted for comfort in fluffy pink scuffs. She seemed frazzled.

"Hello, Mrs. Weber—"

"Sally Ruth, please!"

"—Sally Ruth. We were testing recipes for eggnog at the office. I think Ashley's wiping up a spill."

"Ashley, you nut," said Sally Ruth as she eyed the hall. "It looks so *naive*." She sighed. "Don't you think so?"

I thought, as Ashley yawned and trotted off to the kitchen.

"Walter and I just returned from Paris. The chestnut trees around the Etoile are hung with streamers of gold foil. The branches *shimmer* at night. I knew right away it's the ambiance we should have here." She looked dejected. "But it's too late. We'll have to get by with silver this year."

She frowned, and then broke into a radiant smile.

"Don't I sound spoiled rotten?" said Sally Ruth Weber.

"Sometimes I have to remind myself I wasn't born rich. Come on, Cat, let's talk in the kitchen. I have my decorator hanging pictures in the living room and the library. We came back from Paris with a small Picasso, a Duchamp sculpture, and an Oldenburg so big we have to redo an entire wall."

She walked off briskly to the left of the main hall and I followed. I'd read about the Picasso self-portrait. The Webers had purchased it as an intended gift for the L.A. County Museum of Art. I'd have given up my Victorian stuffing spoon to see the new acquisitions, and the rest of the Weber's renowned collection. Just a few artworks were in the great hall; the family's living quarters would be off limits for the party.

We were expecting five hundred guests Saturday evening, between 5:30 and 8:00, at the Weber Open House. Dellacasa's would provide and serve hot and cold hors d'oeuvres, nonalcoholic eggnog, a Wassail bowl, champagne, coffee, seasonal desserts and fruits. Thanks to the Webers' generosity, an eclectic range of Los Angeles movers and shakers were to be feted for their charitable good works: Skid Row's Para Los Niños mingling with the Assistance League, Fashion Group's sleek professionals sharing toasts with the Salvation Army, and so on. The reception would end in time for guests to make their own dinner plans. Early enough for my augmented staff to clean up, leave, and get some rest before Sally Ruth's Downtown League party for the homeless the following night.

We sat under racks of copper pots in the sunny blue-and-white kitchen, checking last-minute notes at a butcher block table large enough to lay out a banquet for Henry VIII. I'd already worked out the menu for Saturday night with Sally Ruth's secretary while the Webers were traveling; Mario had visited and given his nod of approval to the kitchen. Today, I'd do a walk-through with Sally Ruth to fix the positions of our tables and the bar: my staff would serve hors d'oeuvres from the kitchen, with the buffet tables holding desserts and the beverage service. We'd have a separate bar for champagne. As a courtesy to a good client, Nick would be on hand to help supervise.

Sunday's affair was more problematic. I'd confirmed the menu with the vice president of the Downtown League. I'd enlisted the major downtown missions, trying to guess at the number of homeless we'd be serving. Estimates ranged from two hundred to a thousand. Mario, Nick, and I had visited the party site: the baroque lobby of a landmark Hearst newspaper building about a mile west of Skid Row. The *Herald Examiner* closed in 1989 for lack of love and advertisers. The building was available for rentals, and had been a setting for films and TV shows, its dilapidated City Room now an echoing space inhabited only by the dustballs on the scuffed vinyl floors. We were the first private party to take over the huge downstairs lobby.

I spent a productive hour with Sally Ruth; we made our tour of the kitchen facilities, the service entrance, the great hall. When I left with my new buddy, Ashley the bloodhound, seeing me to the door, I felt the stirrings of the holiday spirit. All is calm, all is bright, all is under control. If only I knew what to do about Bob Crosswaithe.

It seemed to me that, from the beginning, I never quite knew what to do about Crosswaithe. Now I was more unsettled than ever. My instruction from Paul Wang was: business as usual.

Weeks ago, I'd booked Bob Crosswaithe for two out of three large holiday parties. He'd pleaded duty with Ronald Wesley the evening of the brokerage party on the eighteenth. He was available, though, for the Weber reception on the twenty-second and the party for the homeless on the twenty-third.

"Don't change any plans," said Paul Wang the day after our meeting at the police station. Paul had stopped by Del-

lacasa's for a cup of cappuccino and some brief orders for
me. "We don't want to alarm him, we're not questioning
him—yet. We've got teams surveilling him, day and night."
   I raised my eyebrows.
   "Look," said Paul, "we believe Angela's out of control.
We also believe Crosswaithe's in touch with her. At this
point, we're not even calling him an accessory in the Hastings and Stedman murders and the Chase attack. Most
likely, she acted alone.
   "We've put out an APB on her, and that includes San
Diego up to Santa Barbara. If she isn't hiding in L.A., she's
somewhere close, but she moves fast. We call her the Road-
runner. But we'll get her through him.
   "We'd faxed our information and Stedman's snapshot of
him to Scotland Yard. This morning we got an answer."
Paul looked at me closely. "Will it bother you to know that
his middle name is Buck? Robert Buck Crosswaithe. I
doubt if there's another Bobby Buck."
   "I suppose," I said, "that I'm not surprised." What was
W.S. Gilbert's rhyme?

   Things are seldom what they seem,
   Skim milk masquerades as cream.

   "I also suppose he's the man Angela brought to my
apartment. I don't know what to think about that."
   "Don't worry about it now," said Paul. "Let's concentrate
on getting Angela before she attacks again."
   "Do you think she will?"
   "It gets easier each time," said Paul. "Besides," he added,
"Crosswaithe seems fairly harmless. At one time he ran car-
nie games. He spent six months in a British pokey for par-
ticipating in some boiler room operation selling love po-
tions to elderly women, but that was a few years ago.
Nothing else on him, so it's possible he's been clean since.
   "He's also refined his style, I'd imagine," Paul added,

sipping his coffee appreciatively. "Angela's a case, but Elaine Stedman was nobody's fool."

I'd put out a plate of chocolate almond biscotti for Paul. After he left, I helped myself to the rest of them—only two or three, I think—settling into gloom as I dunked the cookies in my coffee and wondered: Was I taken in, too? Cat, I told myself, I believe you were. I don't understand it yet, but it feels lousy.

I'm not a good liar. So it bothered me immensely that he could look into my eyes—so sincere, such dazzling blue eyes—and tell whoppers without a blink or a blush.

I kept thinking about Crosswaithe in *my* apartment with Angela. Somebody—call him Goldilocks—sleeping in *my* bed. There was something else I wanted to look at about that episode, but I couldn't quite get it into focus. Angela at the Paddock? The strange phone calls? What? My stomach felt like the leftover slush in a marguerita.

So, the question is, how do I act toward Robert Buck Crosswaithe? How will I get through two festive evenings in his company? And what does he really want from Cat—the essential woman, the big-time caterer? It couldn't be as simple as copying our technique for carving radish roses.

Angela

The house had no roof or walls or floor. It was a skeleton, a bare wood frame, so high up on the hill it overlooked Ronald Wesley's big ugly mansion.

It was like a treehouse, I suppose some stockbroker or movie tycoon ran out of money before he could get it finished. When I spent the night up there, that Friday, the moon was so bright it shone down like a spotlight on the mansion. I kept watching the upstairs dormer windows, wondering which one belonged to Bobby's bedroom, imagining me there in bed with him, until one by one the lights went out and there was nothing but the moonlight.

I wasn't scared, even though the trees were just outlines, dark shapes, and I could hear scurrying noises around me. I could also hear coyotes racing above me on the ridge, they were howling. They made me shiver, but not from fear or the cold, I felt like they were blood brothers, I wanted to run with them, they sounded so wild and free.

I sat on a small platform on the top level of the frame, holding on to a post, my legs dangling down into black space, half dreaming about the house Bobby and I would build in Argentina, it would be open to the sun, and there'd be a green pasture where our thoroughbreds ran loose. And that's how I got through the night.

I'd left the motel in Shelter Island early that morning, with my suitcase packed and in the car. Bobby had the right idea, it was safer to move.

I was headed up to L.A. to track down Bobby's boss but first I had to do something about the car. The bank guard had seen me in the grey Toyota and even though the papers didn't mention it, I wasn't taking any chances. I drove south to Chula Vista, about ten miles from the border crossing to Tijuana. You don't have to look too hard to find auto upholstery shops, body shops, and places to get a cheap paint job. No questions asked, and you pay cash.

I cruised slowly through a neighborhood where the grocery signs pushed carnitas and menudo, until I heard banging and the hiss of a blowtorch coming from a garage in back of a run-down pink cottage. I went up the driveway and parked. The banging stopped and two scared-looking guys in grease-covered overalls stepped out. I gave my best smile and opened my hands to show them: no badge, no gun, no cop from Immigration. They were puzzled, I was white bread in tortilla land. I reached into my purse—I had to giggle, they were ready to bolt—and came up with two hundred dollars. I held up the cash with one hand and asked, you speak English? They both shook their heads no, so I pointed at the Toyota, swished my hand as if I was slapping the paint with a brush, and said, you make car *negro*, sí? They understood. I said, now, *ahora*, sí? Sí! They found me a chair, and a beer—at seven A.M.—the old lady would have crossed herself ten times, and in an hour I was on my way, sticky black paint job and all.

I stopped in Oceanside, had breakfast, and found a mall with a beauty supply store where they sold wigs. This time I

went for a full head of curly black hair, like the style I saw
on Carolyn Chase. All that wild hair made me look like a
homeless poodle but my idea was: people would remember
the hair, not my face.

The rest was easy. After I got to L.A., I wasted a few
hours at a movie in the Century City mall. There were lots
of holiday shoppers, I wouldn't be noticed, so I had coffee
and window-shopped, like the lonely old days before I
killed Hastings and my life changed for the better. Later,
around six, when it was early enough to get a good parking
space, I headed for the screening.

It was at a movie house on Wilshire, in Beverly Hills. I
parked on the next block near the corner, close enough to
see the guests arrive. Right on schedule, along came Bobby
driving the red Mercedes, with Ronald Wesley and Lolly
Whatsherface in back. I'd guessed right! He let the valet
parking take the car then went in after them. He made
Wesley look like a midget, he was so handsome in the navy
pinstripe suit with the Italian silk tie I'd bought for him. I
wondered if he'd sit next to Lolly and play kneesies. How
could she let Wesley touch her—with a real man like Bobby
around? And who knew what to expect from a woman like
that?

I'd stopped at Jack-in-the-Box for a Double Whopper
and large fries, so I scrunched down in the car, keeping my
head low, and ate and napped until the movie was over and
everyone came out.

Parking in Beverly Hills makes me mad, they could fi-
nance a war against L.A. with what they make on parking
tickets. I was worried about keeping up with the Mercedes
if I had to park near a restaurant, but I was lucky. They
were having an early evening. Bobby headed west on Wilshire and pulled into the driveway of one of those hi-rise
condos that cost about a million and you still have to buy
your own washer and dryer. I thought this was the last
stop, and I didn't know how I'd get past the doorman, but

only Lolly got out. I wrote down the address. She smiled and waved goodbye to the Mercedes, then she brushed past the doorman like he wasn't alive. In general, actresses suck.

Bobby drove north to Sunset, then east. I was careful, I hung behind a tan Chrysler coupe that was acting suspicious; it turned onto Sunset when the Mercedes did, and I would have thought it was following them, only Bobby made a left toward the hills and the Chrysler kept going on Sunset. Pretty soon we were climbing one of those winding roads, one lane in each direction. I kept as far back as I could, finally I turned off my headlights which was scary, but no other car came by. I saw the Mercedes pull up in the driveway of this mansion, and I just kept going, driving up, up into the hills until I saw the skeleton of the house. There was nothing else around, so I parked and climbed up to the top story and that's where I stayed all night, watching over Bobby.

Saturday morning, I knew why they'd been home so early. Around eight, Bobby came out the side entrance where the Mercedes was parked. He drove it around to the front. Wesley came out and a butler followed with a couple of matched suitcases and a garment bag. I saw Bobby hand Wesley an envelope, it could have been airline tickets. Bobby took the wheel and off they went down the hill. For a minute I was scared that he was going with Wesley, but it didn't look as if he'd taken his luggage. I figured he was driving Wesley to the airport.

It was noon when Bobby came back carrying a plastic dry cleaners bag, and I didn't see him the rest of the afternoon. I was hungry, but I didn't dare leave, what if he went off for the whole night? What if Lolly called him as soon as Wesley left town?

About four o'clock he came out the side entrance. He was carrying his old black nylon overnight bag. I could feel my heart beating fast. He didn't take the Mercedes or the Jaguar, he put the suitcase into the trunk of his own Buick.

This time I followed him, keeping far back because he wouldn't be turning until he reached Sunset. What surprised me was that a tan Chrysler coupe pulled out of a side road a little above Sunset, as if it was waiting for him.

Bobby turned up Sunset, the Chrysler followed him, and I followed the Chrysler. You'd think we were all going out for a good time on Saturday night.

Chapter Thirty-One

So how open was this Open House? The stocky fellow in a dark suit checking invitations at the door was the private guard hired by the Webers for large parties. Another guard, uniformed, was on duty where a side alley led to the service entrance. The Webers had hired carolers to arrive halfway through the party, and they all had invitations. The pale young lady who'd be playing the harp had an invitation. My own staff carried Dellacasa i.d. cards to get them in at the service door.

I'd had to tell Nick and Mario what was up, persuade them that I wasn't in danger. Sweet-natured Mario vowed to keep a lookout from his kitchen command post. I saw Nick prowling the vast room, quietly alert behind the professional smile. Although the Webers didn't know it, Detective David Velasquez was my newest temporary employee, decked out in a red vest and bow tie and conscientiously manning the coffee urn. Bob Crosswaithe, in his red vest, was tall and dapper behind the trays of champagne glasses. He waved to me across the gleaming expanse of parquet floor. I waved back, feeling as phony as a lentil burger at a barbecue. I couldn't believe that Angela would try to crash this party, but whither Crosswaithe went, so went the police. I'd been told there were other detectives parked on the street to keep Crosswaithe under surveillance after he left work.

By a quarter past five we were at our places, as if waiting for the curtain to rise on this grand holiday pageant. The room sparkled; we had all contributed our magic. Sally Weber stood near the doorway, diamonds flashing, bright in a fitted red velvet jacket and red chiffon skirt, as animated as if she'd been touched by the sorcerer's wand. Walter Weber, a glass of Scotch in hand, was calm and dignified in a navy suit enlivened by a tie of tiny silver trees embroidered on red silk.

I'd followed my usual policy of not competing with the hostess. My silk suit was light grey and softly tailored, my pearls were the good ones Gil had given me two Christmases past, I wore my grey-and-black Chanel slingbacks, with a pair of emergency flat heels waiting offstage in the kitchen. Let the revels begin!

The guests arrived, first a trickle then a surge. By six o'clock the lovely harp music was drowned by a few hundred conversations happening at once. I was helping Mario reload serving trays in the kitchen, avoiding the eyes of Ashley the bloodhound who watched with yearning as the trays passed over his head. I wiped off yucky cheese trays; I shlepped empty silver bowls through the crowd for refills of eggnog; I lost track of time.

When the carolers arrived in their mufflers, greatcoats, and other Pickwickian finery, I was surprised at the hour; my watch said seven o'clock. The carolers began with "God Rest Ye . . ." as they climbed the curving staircase and formed into a group behind the gallery rail. Movement and sound dwindled as the guests looked up. My staff memo last week had instructed everyone to stop service, at the Webers' request, during the half hour of entertainment. It was a good time for me to switch to flats after hours of tottering around in my designer knockoff heels.

I pushed at the swinging door that led into the kitchen, then held it back for Olivia and Phillip who were hurrying out with covered trays of pastries. Otherwise the kitchen was empty.

"I'm taking a break," I told them.

"We're going to drop these off," said Olivia, "then listen to the carolers, like everyone else." She rushed away.

"Mario's looking for Nick," said Phillip. "He doesn't know why Nick ordered that." He nodded at the butcher block table and left.

I gaped. Rising above the trays of party foods on the table was an immense pyramidal shape. It was the largest *croquembouche* I'd ever seen. It rose about two and a half feet high, a conical tower built of tiny cream puffs, row upon row. It glistened with threads of spun caramel that spiraled round and round up to a peak crowned with a tiny porcelain ballerina in a red tulle tutu. Red and green maraschino cherries and shiny green leaves were tucked aesthetically around the cream puffs. It was a triumph of the pastry maker's art, but where *did* it come from?

Suddenly, the door at the far end of the kitchen swung open. It was the service door; it led to a small porch and past that to the side entrance. I found myself staring at Bob Crosswaithe. He looked as startled as I was, and although he moved quickly to block my view of the service porch, I could see he wasn't alone. Behind him was that dumbfounding duo: Cheeks and the Turtle. Both wore starched white chef's jackets. Cheeks gripped a huge, empty pink cardboard bakery box in knockwurst-size fingers. The box was large enough to hold—a *croquembouche?*

I was disoriented. Bob's chums were in the pastry business?

"Cripes!" said the Turtle. "It's Katie. She's seen us!"

Crosswaithe kept his eyes on me, saying over his shoulder, "You chaps get going. I'll worry about her."

"Right, Bobby! We'll see you at the gate." And they were gone. I could hear them clattering down the wooden steps.

"What does this mean?" I asked, sounding melodramatic even to my own ears.

Crosswaithe moved forward and took a firm hold on my wrist. His smile was warm and reassuring. "Let's go into the pantry," he said. "We'll talk there."

"I don't want—"

He clamped a strong, hard hand over my mouth.

"I'm not going to hurt you, Cat. Just move—fast."

He opened a door adjacent to the service porch and briskly shoved me into the walk-in pantry. He closed the door and we were in almost complete darkness, except for a sliver of light that came in at the doorsill.

I was pushed up against a wall of shelves, a row of cans cradling my head, Crosswaithe's body pressed against me, his hand still covering my mouth. I was too startled to be afraid: how could a nice girl like me end up in a pantry like this?

"Let's see, I'll have to switch on the light for a sec, I need something I can use to tie you up."

I tried to say, *Let me go, you sonofabitch*, but it came out *mphmphmph*. The light came on and Crosswaithe stepped back, rapidly checking the shelves.

"Aha! Drawstring trash bags. Just the thing." He tried to pull the string from the top of a bag, but it wasn't a one-handed task.

"Listen, Cat, I've got to tie you up and get away from here, but I'll free your mouth if you promise not to scream."

I nodded and he took away his hand. Just in case, he had me blocked with his body while he pulled the drawstrings from four bags, then turned off the light.

Ah, Crosswaithe and I, alone in the dark, bodies pressed

together. What did I feel? Indignation. Anger. Curiosity.
No spark of desire, no rising flame—not even a pilot light.
He was using two of the ties to double bind my hands be-
hind my back.

"You and Angela," I said. "You planned this together."
Whatever this was.

"Oh, no, love, Angela has nothing to do with tonight."
He was busy making knots. Cheerfully he said, "Angela has
her murders, I have my thefts. We're a two-career couple."

"Thefts. Of course. You're robbing the Webers. And I
trusted you! What—?"

"That swinging door facing the pantry leads to the dining room. The dining room is connected to the living
room. There's a nice little Picasso on the living-room wall.
Actually, there *was* a Picasso there. Cubist period, 1912.
About eighteen inches by twenty-five inches. Just the right
size to fit in the false bottom of a very large bakery box."

"The *croquembouche!*"

"Rather a nice touch, I thought. Everyone loves cream
puffs. Who'd want to stop two blokes carrying a load of
cream puffs? Took me a week to find a French baker who'd
make a thing that big. I hope it's still tasty. We had to pick it
up yesterday to fit out the box."

He was feeling chatty. Good. If I kept him talking long
enough, someone would return to the kitchen and rescue
me.

"How did you get those two in here, past the guard?"

I heard a soft chuckle.

"You trusted me too much. I've been bartending for you
for months. I managed to keep two of those Dellacasa's i.d.
cards."

I groaned. I'd ignored my usual policy. I hadn't cleared
him—no references, no bonding company. I rationalized:
"You worked for Ronald Wesley. I thought he'd checked
you out."

"Ronald was drunk when he hired me. I could have been

Jack the Ripper. He's a lucky man, I never took advantage. Actually, he was my fallback position, he owns some nice stuff. But small cheese compared to the Webers. That Picasso cost them a shocking amount of millions. On the black market? I expect about a million two from a very private party who's got pockets stuffed with cash."

What would the crime do to Nick—and Dellacasa's? I could see the headline: "CATERER SERVES UP MIL-LION-DOLLAR ART THEFT."

"You planned this very well," I said with some bitterness.

"Thank you, love. The museum gift has been in the news for months. I didn't expect a Picasso at first, I would have settled for a Braque or a Rouault. When the Webers flew to Paris and chose the Picasso, I broke out the champagne. They'd make the gift before the tax year ends. I took a chance that they wouldn't bother having it wired to an alarm—and I was right. The challenge wasn't how to grab it, it was how to get it out."

"But how did you—?"

"Know the layout of the house? Easier than you think, you Americans are so trusting. A trip to the library for a back issue of *House and Garden*—lovely color spread on how the Webers hang their art collection. Then, a bit of luck. I found a tour. In October I bought a ticket to a charity tour because the Weber house was on it. Did you know this house was built in 1926 by a sausage tycoon from Wisconsin? Farmer Olaf."

There was an implied sneer at the industrious Olaf, who'd made his fortune in trade. I wondered if there was a higher good in robbing inherited titles. I regretted I'd never asked Crosswaithe why he left England. It isn't an L.A. question: we're apt to shed our pasts along with our overcoats.

"During the tour," he continued as he threaded two more handle ties through the bonds on my wrists, "I saw that the door from the dining room to the family living room has a lock I could slice with a butter knife. Actually, I used a small chisel tonight, I nipped in when the carolers started—your staff memo helped with my timing, bless you for being so organized.

"I've replaced the Picasso with a rather crude copy. Not that it will fool anyone—but it might give me another few minutes of grace before they send out the hounds."

"How did you know—?"

"Sorry, Cat, you'll have to sit down. I need to tie your ankles." He pushed on my shoulders and I sat. Crosswaithe bent over my legs and rapidly went to work at my ankles. My eyes were becoming adjusted to the dimness. In the light from the doorsill I could see him well enough. No shakes, no stress, no sweat. The self-assurance that comes from doing a job well. I told myself to match his calm, to stay watchful, but it was an effort. I hate feeling helpless.

"How did you know I'd hire you for tonight?"

He gave a final tug at the ties around my ankles.

"I must finish this up and go. I wanted Sam and Ernie to get completely clear of here before I left."

As Crosswaithe stood, I heard voices from the kitchen. What a relief! Mario and Phillip had entered.

"Bloody hell!" muttered Crosswaithe. His bartender's towel was still tucked into his belt. Quickly, he pulled out the towel, twisted it and tied it into a gag, fastening the ends at the back of my head. I tried to struggle but I was trussed like my aunt Sadie's Christmas goose. Gloomily, I imagined the conversation when Marcy phoned after her skiing holiday in Banff.

Hi, Cat. How was *your* holiday?

Oh, I was tied up right until Christmas Day.

Did you have fun?

Sure. I sat in a pantry and watched my career disappear.

My wrists were beginning to numb. I tried to push against the strings but he'd tied them well. I was sitting with my back against the shelves, legs together and straight out like a doll in a curio cabinet.

In the kitchen, the two men were talking cream puffs.

"Nick didn't place the order," said Mario. "I was in the kitchen with that Crosswaithe guy when the thing arrived. Both of us heard the delivery men say it was Nick. And I can't find Cat."

"She was in here about ten minutes ago."

"Well, let's set it out on a table. Otherwise, the party will be over and we'll be stuck with it."

"On a tray?"

"No, I don't want to move the monster off the cardboard base. Let's take some holly sprigs and spread them around the base."

Crosswaithe was listening. He shrugged, sat down next to me, whispered into my ear.

"I'll leave after they do. Meantime, I imagine I owe you some answers. I'll make them fast."

His soft breath came in puffs. Damn it, I thought, this man knows what to do with an ear. My plight reminded me of an old Chinese curse: *May your fondest wish come true.*

"My being here, working for you tonight," said Crosswaithe. "It was never in doubt. You'd begun to depend on me. I'd planned it that way—ever since I spent the night in your apartment. Nice place, by the way. Too bad I never was invited back."

I felt like a developmentally disabled chick pecking slowly through its eggshell. It had taken me a long time to see the light. Crosswaithe didn't really have to tell me. I knew what had happened that night.

"Your briefcase was there. And your planner." As Crosswaithe had said many times, I was so organized.

"Angela had picked me up in the Paddock and taken me home—to what she said was her home. She was terribly proud of being caterer to the celebrities. She kept waving around that book—your planner—and showing me all the fancy houses she'd be visiting. When I saw the Weber name for December, I knew this was the girl to take home to mum."

But Angela was a fake, I wanted to tell him. And she's crazy.

"Even though Angela was faking it," affirmed Crosswaithe, "she has other fine attributes." Again, there was that little chuckle in the dark. "Although I'm afraid I'll have to leave her behind. She's become, um, rather possessive. Spoils the fun, you know." He seemed to brood for a moment.

"Did you think it was simply accident that you were hired to cater Ronald's supper? I suggested Dellacasa's and he went along with it. If he hadn't I would have applied directly to you for a part-time job."

He had conned me from the beginning. At least I hadn't been so dazzled that I'd hopped into bed with him. Score one for me and self-respect.

"Not that I'm not fond of you, Cat. We could have had some good times together. I like that unruly black hair of yours, the way your eyes change color from hazel to something deep and unreadable. It makes me think there's something wild and adventurous about you that you won't permit anyone to see."

Oh, God, here we go again! Is this man a total romantic, or a complete cynic? And why am I listening. Why, Cat? Because you're tied up and can't move, that's why. I felt reassured.

"Unfortunately," sighed Crosswaithe in my ear, "you were too important to me as access to the Webers. I couldn't take a chance on lovers's spats and breakups. Oh, well, one should settle for the possible. And a million or so tax-free dollars is possible."

The voices in the kitchen were retreating.

"Keep it steady." That was Mario.

"You just back through the door, I'm holding on to it."

The silence of the *croquembouche*.

"There, now," said Crosswaithe. "It's time for me to leave. I'll just walk out the back door and vanish. I've tried to keep the ties loose enough so they won't cut you. Someone should be along soon.

"I'm sorry," he said, sounding truly regretful, "I had to gag you. Can't have you screaming your head off."

He tested the gag. He'd already tied the bonds on my wrist to a shelf post so it was impossible to move toward the door.

"Goodbye, Cat," he said, with a feather-light pat on my shoulder. "I'd like to kiss you, but what with your hands tied, it goes against my code of honor—such as it is."

I saw a slip of light as he opened the door and looked around. Then he was gone.

I wriggled and pushed and sawed and strained, but not one of my efforts freed me. Crosswaithe, Sam, and Ernie were off and running with a million-dollar painting, and I couldn't stop them. It might take another hour—after the party ended—before any real search for me began.

My muscles were screaming so loudly, I hardly heard the soft scratching at the pantry door.

Scratch. Scratch. Scratch. Then a familiar *huh huh huh*. A solid shape blocked some of the light that came under the doorsill. It was Ashley come to visit. Ashley inquiring politely why I didn't come out to scratch behind his ears. Hmmmn.

Desperation lit my way. I had seen, before Crosswaithe switched off the light, the shelves of the well-stocked Weber pantry. My mind raced along the shelves. Whole bean coffee. Fortnum & Mason tea canisters. Bitter Orange marmalade, Oregon jams. Canned veggies. At least five kinds of pasta. I smiled in satisfaction (as much as I could, considering the stifling gag). The dog food was on the bottom shelf; there were, if I remembered, cans of food and boxes of biscuits over to my right. Let's see. I squirmed as far to the right as I could, fumbled behind me, pulled out whatever I could touch with my numbing, tied hands. A small avalanche of cans landed close to my side. I leaned over.

Aha! Not only dog food, but the pricey, individual cans of dog food, the ingenious, energy-saving, quick-serving, no-can-opener-needed, pop-top cans! Each serving would be no more than an appetizer for a hound as large as Ashley, but ah, the heart has its reasons, and the Webers obviously loved Ashley.

I got to work. Should you ever find yourself in a similar bind, here is my suggested technique.

First, with hands in crossover position behind your back, grab can firmly in left hand.

Grasp pop-top ring with index finger of right hand. Yank hard.

Scrunch body to the right, bringing arms and legs together as closely as possible.

Bat open can of premium dog food from hands to tip of shoes. (Don't be discouraged; practice helps.)

Grasp can with shoes; straighten legs.

Propel can forward, hockey-puck style, until it hits door.

Repeat until dog reaches meaningful anxiety level.

I kept batting open cans toward Ashley; I managed five or six of them. H-e-r-e comes Cat! comely caterer to pampered canines!

Poor Ashley. He lowered his head and I could see the wet black nose sniffing at the doorsill. He tried to push two big, furry paws under the door. At last, Ashley had had it with the big tease. No more snuffling. No more scrabbling. Ashley sat back and let loose with a bloodcurdling howl.

The Saturday night before Christmas. Trying to make time to L.A. International Airport. Trying an alternate route. Everybody has one. Your hairdresser. Your dentist. The newsboy. Even your worst enemy takes pity and offers you a faster way to LAX. Detectives Velasquez and Wang were debating routes in monotone grunts: *left, go here, turn back.* I sat in the rear seat of the unmarked police car; I rubbed my chafed wrists and watched the lights streak past as we zigzagged across the dark landscape.

La Brea to the 10. Gridlock: an injury accident. Off at La Cienega. Past the dinosaur shapes of oil rigs trapped in the gathering fog. To La Tijera, right to Aviation, left to Century, and down the wide boulevard under streetlights haloed by fog. The police radio crackled out the latest on what had become a slow-motion chase. Crosswaithe's trail was picked up as he left the Weber house, by the detectives assigned to the Angela Cappelli murders. The suspect had driven leisurely down Wilshire to La Cienega, stopping first on Wilshire at a neon-lit drive-in. He'd ordered a double burger, fries, and a Coke, eaten them slowly in his car, in the darkest part of the parking lot. He'd used the men's restroom, entering with a red vest balled up in his hand, emerging without it.

At about the time Crosswaithe arrived at the drive-in, I was discovered by the Webers' houseman, who rushed into the kitchen as Ashley's howls threatened to drown out the carolers. Unbound—just a bit unglued—I'd called for Velasquez and, after some hurried words of apology to the Webers and an explanation to Nick, I'd left with the detective. The guests remained unaware of the theft, and the party went merrily on—minus one bartender/thief, one waiter/cop and one caterer/fool.

The police decision was to keep Crosswaithe under surveillance and follow him to his meeting. "See you at the gate," the Turtle had said, and that likely meant a flight out of L.A. with the stolen painting. But which airline? What flight? As the only person who had seen Cheeks and the Turtle firsthand, I went along for the ride. Would the trio meet up with Angela? Crosswaithe said he was leaving her behind, but Angela had popped out of more places than the filling in a jelly donut.

Velasquez and I had stopped at the Venice Boulevard precinct to pick up Paul Wang, who waited with copies of mug shots of Cheeks and the Turtle. The pictures were in from London; they'd arrived late that afternoon. It had taken time: all that the L.A. police could supply as information were my descriptions and an approximate date of entry into the U.S. There they were: Samuel and Ernest Hotchkiss, cousins and partners in petty theft, graduating to fur theft and art theft. A last bumbled effort—a Degas sketch—landed them in an English prison for two years. But the picture was never recovered. It was assumed that a partner planned the London gallery heist. A person unknown. I could guess who.

We'd left the station as word came that Crosswaithe was now headed toward the airport. The local law enforcement were joining us: three squad cars and airport security would be waiting.

"How did you let that SOB get away with it?" Paul snapped at his partner. "What happened to Oaks and Tamido?"

"Okay, so sue us," said Velasquez. "We were watching for a skinny murder suspect, not an art theft. He didn't get away clean. Oaks and Tamido are still tailing him."

"Sorry," said Paul. "You're right. It's just—I was hoping he'd lead us straight to Angela. I almost hate to pick him up."

"You'll love it when we get a commendation and promotions for grabbing these jokers." Velasquez frowned at the traffic building up on each side of us.

"It's going to be a bitch," he said. "That airport will be more crowded than an all-you-can-eat, dollar ninety-nine buffet."

"It's not that bad," said Paul Wang. "We don't have to

chase around the whole airport. He'll go to one terminal, and we'll be tailing him. I don't care if this is the busiest night of the year, he can't lose himself in the crowd."

"He's leaving on a late flight, wherever he's going. I wish we'd had time to stop and eat." Velasquez called over his shoulder, "Too bad you didn't bring along some of those little hot beef-and-peppers sandwiches. I'd forget my cholesterol for one night for a plate of those."

Paul Wang looked back at me. "Are you all right, Cat? You said he didn't hurt you."

I considered the question from all sides. "Just my dignity. If we get the painting back, I'll be fine."

"We'll get it. And Crosswaithe . . ." He looked at me and his smile was questioning. "You do want him caught?"

"Of course I do," I told him. "I know this isn't a caper movie. All charm and excitement—and no pain. It isn't like that in real life."

"Welcome to the wonderful world of the LAPD," said Paul, turning to the endless stream of taillights ahead.

There was an update on the police radio: the suspect had parked at the Delta terminal at LAX. He'd opened the car trunk and donned a brown suede jacket; he'd added a black Stetson pulled down low over his blond hair. He carried a black overnight bag.

At 9:05 P.M. he sauntered into the terminal, took the escalator up to the departure-gate level, and purchased a newspaper. Presently, Crosswaithe was at a back table in the cocktail lounge drinking Scotch on the rocks, the paper half hiding his face. No sign of a red-headed woman. Or the Hotchkiss boys. Per instructions, Crosswaithe was being kept under surveillance and not approached.

Deftly, Velasquez moved from Century into the flight-departure lanes. He inched the car through the bumper-to-bumper, horn-blasting holiday traffic, sliding up to a NO PARKING strip at the curb. Two plainclothes airport security police, two Westchester detectives, and two additional squad cars with uniformed police were waiting. Paul Wang distributed the mug shots.

The detectives filled us in. Every airline reservation computer had been checked. No reservations out tonight in the name of Crosswaithe, or Buck, or the two Hotchkisses. It was to be expected; Santa wasn't bringing us this gift.

The lawmen looked at me. I knew the Hotchkiss boys, it was my assignment: Identify them. And, while you're at it: save Dellacasa's reputation; stop Cat from offering her resignation.

I didn't look like a heroine. Before we'd left the Webers, Velasquez had asked whether I had a change of clothes, a disguise. We'd stopped at my car and I'd grabbed my earthquake outfit from the trunk. Talk about life's absurdities!

Earthquake clothing is what you carry in your car in case the Big One hits while you're away from home. I'd assembled a worn pair of Reeboks, a Dodger baseball cap (for summer's tremors), a moth-eaten ski sweater with reindeer and snowflakes for survival in a tent city. Standing at the curb, I donned the sweater and cap, added dark glasses, and decided that, when tonight was over, I'd give more thought to survival chic. Why face the postquake world looking this hopeless? We set off through the crowds.

Was I an avenging and steely—if makeshift—terminator? Not for a minute. The hundreds of bodies hurrying along, burdened with overcoats for colder climates, toting sleepy babies or carryalls bulging with souvenirs and holiday gifts, had made me mildly claustrophobic. I was sweating in the reindeer sweater, which was strange, because my hands were clammy. I do admire the new breed of fictional female PI's. The ones who'll survive a throttling, a kidnapping, a punch in the kidneys from a Mafia goon and then wind up the evening making love to a helicopter pilot. In the helicopter. I think I need more time at the gym.

I was having the adventure of my life but there was no rush of adrenaline. I was somewhere in limbo watching myself: this oddly dressed woman peering through dark glasses, dodging through the crowds, covertly eyeing the passengers lined up at each gate and sitting in every waiting area. Detectives Wang and Velasquez walked with me, one per elbow. We looked like a drill team.

Finding Sam and Ernie Hotchkiss was anticlimactic. The cousins weren't hiding, they were buying San Francisco sourdough bread in one of the airport kiosks that allow travelers to make their final contributions to the Golden State's economy before boarding. Cheeks (Sam) wore an hibiscus-patterned Hawaiian shirt. Ernie The Turtle had acquired a new T-shirt. It read: VISIT L.A. . . . IT'S A RIOT. Both wore their straw fedoras. Incredibly, I had a moment of wanting to protect them, but the two detectives also had spotted the Hotchkisses. And their package. Ernie carried, tucked under his arm, a loosely wrapped painting. There was just one width of brown wrapping paper around its middle. A single piece of twine held the wrapping together.

The paper didn't hide the classic pose of a bullfighter twirling his scarlet cape, the crude, bold strokes on a field of black velvet. The painting was a Tijuana special, beloved momento of the day trip over the border into exotic Mehhee-co! My hunch was: there's more to the bullfighter than sideburns and tight pants. Very likely my future credibility was there, in another painting concealed under the black velvet.

Within seconds, Velasquez had summoned his backup, and the kiosk was surrounded. I watched from a distance as the accomplices were confronted, read their rights, handcuffed, and quickly walked away. There was no fuss; I saw only surprise and resignation. The other shoppers stopped and stared, but the arrest had gone fast. Crosswaithe's months of planning had ended in less than five minutes, without a bang or a whimper. One plainclothes detective tenderly carried the bullfighter; Cheeks managed to tuck his sourdough loaf under his arm as he was led away.

"There's no reason now to wait," said Paul Wang to his partner and the other detective. "Let's get Crosswaithe."

I hung back as the three policemen hastened along the corridor to the cocktail lounge. As they entered, I could see him lounging in his chair, drink in hand, idly watching a blonde in a pink jersey dress who sat alone at the bar. Under the circumstances, I doubt if he was considering a pickup; it was simply an appreciation.

Quickly, the three detectives surrounded Crosswaithe. Velasquez spoke to him, he looked up, seemed amazed, then stood. There was another brief conversation, a pair of handcuffs and it was all over. Conversation in the bar stopped for a moment; the blonde looked around then returned to her marguerita; then the men left, two of the detectives silently locking arms with Crosswaithe as if they were off, shoulder-to-shoulder, on a holiday jaunt. I retreated to the side and watched the black Stetson move along, following Crosswaithe's departure until the broad shoulders and slim hips were blocked by the ceaseless crowd. He hadn't seen me at all.

Paul Wang turned and came back for me. "Well, it's done," he said. "Nice, clean pinch."

"Congratulations. I suppose it could have been messy with all these people around."

"Not much risk. These guys weren't packing guns. Nothing in their files says they ever did. Thieves, they're all optimists, you know. They never think they'll get caught." Paul hesitated. "You don't have to see him. We'll send Crosswaithe and his buddies along to the station in a squad car. Wait five minutes, Dave and I will be at the curb and we'll take you home."

"That's very considerate. Thank you."

"I asked him about Angela," said Paul. "He said he hasn't seen her in weeks. We'll get into it with him at the station."

He strode off, and I began to walk slowly toward the down escalator. I passed a shop, its display window filled with glittering last-minute gift ideas for tourists who hadn't splurged it all at Disneyland and the Farmer's Market. I stopped to look more closely at a gold necklace that might be nice for Aunt Sadie. I'd barely started my Christmas shopping.

I sensed that another window-shopper had come up close behind me, almost touching. I looked past my reflection in the glass and saw a thin-faced woman with a pouty crimson mouth, a great mop of tangled black hair. She seemed to be staring at my back, but I assumed I was blocking her view of the display. When I turned to leave, she'd vanished.

I felt spooked, but no wonder. It had been one damn thing after another all evening. The crowds were thinning out as the late-night flights began to board. I reached the escalator and let the moving steps carry me down toward the night and the fog.

Next morning, I woke earlier than I'd planned. I opened the freezer and liberated the fourteen-dollar-a-pound Blue Jamaican coffee beans. My little treat to myself—positive, constructive, noncaloried—after the stress of the night before. I deserved it. After all, I'd acquitted myself well. I'd helped recover the painting, I'd fingered the crooks, I'd left Dellacasa's reputation unsullied. So what if I couldn't face Crosswaithe at the airport?

I heated two Sara Lee croissants and spread them with butter and sugar-free jam. Why this sense of loss? Was it his deception that hurt so? Or, was it my fear of being less than perfect? Cat does *everything* well. No project too big, no detail too small. Well, Crosswaithe had looked me over and found a vulnerable spot. Oh, I wasn't crazy, like Angela, or needy, like Elaine Stedman, but I did let down my guard in front of his naked approval.

I tore a croissant into buttery chunks and ate. Perhaps I was suffering from a deficiency of romance in my life, somewhat like a lack of salt that makes you weak on a hot day. Not sex alone. After all, Crosswaithe wasn't my lover. He was Angela's lover. And Elaine's lover. Probably Baby's lover. He slept around, in a time when that had become unfashionable and unsafe. He was a liar and a thief. So what was I mourning?

I suppose I always recognized the outlaw in him, and that was as powerful an attraction as sex. Until I divorced Gil, I had never been rebellious. Crosswaithe offered a touch of deviltry. He shared the kick he got from taking risks—and it was seductive. From the safety of my carefully arranged life, I responded. Should I blame myself too much?

The telephone rang, breaking into a soliloquy that could have meandered on and wasted the morning. It was Paul Wang.

"Hi, Cat. Did I wake you?"

"No, I'm having coffee and thinking over last night."

"Want me to drive you to the Webers to pick up your car?"

I was grateful. Half an hour later he drove up in his own car, a restored red Mustang convertible. He opened the passenger door for me, saying, "I didn't get the chance last night to thank you."

"What for?"

"You picked up on Ernie Hotchkiss talking about the gate. That meant they were meeting at the airport. We'd have stopped Crosswaithe without your help. But his two buddies could have seen us, avoided contact, and flown off with the painting."

I fastened my seatbelt, feeling okay. "Where were they going?"

"We found three tickets for Miami. The 10:55 flight."

"Why Miami, do you think?"

"We're thinking drug money. You said he told you he had a buyer with cash in his pockets. That sounds like some drug dealers trying to launder a million or so by buying a negotiable asset."

"I'm not sure I understand. There's been so much publicity about that particular Picasso—you know, the Webers' gift—who'd buy it?"

Paul explained: "We'll probably never know. Whoever bought it from Crosswaithe could fence it to any number of private collectors—maybe in South America or the Middle East—and have the check deposited into a nice private bank account in the Caymans or in Switzerland. Very neat."

"I wouldn't think Bob would have such contacts."

"Oh, he's a pro. At least he's getting better. This job was slicker than the London one. Next time—if he doesn't complicate his life with women—he might even pull it off."

I drew a shocked breath. *"Next* time?" I demanded. "You think there'll be a *next* time?"

"Sure. I said he's a pro, it's a career with him. He's probably planning his next job already. I didn't tell you," said Paul Wang, "the Webers have decided not to prosecute. They don't want any more publicity. They want the painting quietly turned over to the museum, and we forget the incident."

The fresh December wind stung my cheeks as we drove along in the open car.

"Then what will happen to Bob—and Sam and Ernie?"

"We could get the Hotchkiss boys on something as dumb as working—you said they were parking cars—without a green card. Then we'll deport 'em back to England and let Scotland Yard worry about their futures."

"And Bob—Crosswaithe—what about him?"

"Well, he's a different scenario. We searched him at the precinct. He had a money belt tied to his middle, with about two hundred eighty thousand dollars in it."

Not bad for someone tending bar for a few bucks to sharpen up his wardrobe.

"He says he made it on the horses. We think it has something to do with Angela and Hastings's murder. The way we've figured it, she was robbing her employer's office safe. Hastings found her and she picked up a bookend and cracked his head. What was in the safe? Some bonds and jewelry, we know, but we haven't been able to pin down how much. Hastings's client is too senile to help much."

"So what do you do now?"

"We're checking banks and brokerage houses, to see if there are any accounts in Crosswaithe's name. We may find them, maybe not. We don't know if he and Angela conspired to kill Hastings, we don't think so. It wasn't premeditated. But he could have helped her plan the robbery, then hid her somewhere until he could score last night at the Webers.

"Angela's the key to a lot of this. Oh, we can get Crosswaithe for the assault on you last night, although the Webers wouldn't be happy. We can get him for working for Ronald Wesley without a green card, and turn him over to Immigration for deportation. Or, we can try to get him on income tax evasion for not reporting two hundred eighty thousand in track winnings."

I watched the streets change from sedate old apartment houses to big lawns and beautiful homes.

"Have you told him all of this?"

Paul sighed. "Funny thing is, he almost lit up like Tinkerbell when I laid all of this on him. He said: 'A few years in a well-run American prison and then deportation? That's not too bad. Although I'd be happy to settle for just deportation.'

"So then I asked Crosswaithe, you're not upset? He said, 'Well, Angela's become a bit of a problem. I shouldn't mind getting her off my trail for a while. Being under the protection of the U.S. authorities would do it, don't you think?' "

Said Paul, "I was flabbergasted."

"I don't blame you. What about finding Angela?"

"Crosswaithe's admitted she was tucked away in a motel in San Diego. But she checked out Friday, and the trail is cold."

Paul hesitated and then said somberly, "Listen, Cat, at this point, you're about our only link to Crosswaithe and Angela."

Me? Angela hovering near me? The thought was as distasteful to me as eating Twinkies for breakfast.

I said as much to Paul.

"I know," he said. "Maybe she's miles away by now, but just to be on the safe side, we're going to keep watch on you for the next few days and see what comes down. Are you still doing your meals for the homeless at the *Examiner* this evening?"

I told him I was. He said, "We're going to have a couple of plainclothesmen, Detectives Oaks and Tamido, drive you downtown. They'll wait and bring you home again. Curb-to-curb service for the next few days. And we'll have a car parked outside overnight."

We drove up to my car; it sat like a patiently waiting friend at the curb near the Weber house. We arranged for the detectives to pick me up at three o'clock.

"Meantime," said Paul, "this afternoon, keep your door double locked and don't open it unless you're sure of who it is. I'll call you Monday and get your schedule for the rest of the week."

"Sure, Paul. Thanks."

"Don't worry, Cat. She'll make a mistake and we'll nab her."

"I won't worry."

What's to worry? Just about your everyday neighborhood maniac, who's already broken into your apartment once.

Angela

The old woman looked like a pile of rags, red and blue and green and grey, like Joseph's coat-of-many-colors. Everything was grubby and she smelled. I'd nearly stepped over her, I didn't know there was a person inside until she gave this sharp little snore. I stepped back and looked at her, she was crouched against this rusty iron fence on a dark side street off Main. She had this black knit seaman's cap pulled down around her ears. She probably had lice under it, but I didn't care. I needed her clothes.

I poked her with my foot. Old lady, I said, I want to buy your coat and hat. She moved a little and mumbled, but she didn't wake up. I poked her a little harder. Whatever she was dreaming, it was too good to give up, she just gave another snore. I thought, I'll pull the clothes off her and leave some money. I was getting frantic. I had to get Catherine alone and find out what the police had done with Bobby.

I'd watched the whole horrible scene at the airport. They'd put him in handcuffs and taken him away! *Taken him away!* Oh, I know he was planning to leave town, but I could've handled that. I could've rushed up at the last minute and bought a ticket as soon as they called his flight. I guess he was still mad at me about Elaine, and I don't blame him. I was out of line. But I'm dead certain I could have won him back, we belong together, I'm nothing without him.

And that Catherine, the stuck-up bitch. She wasn't in the police car following Bobby when he left that fancy mansion, but she showed up at the airport. I saw her standing at the side when they handcuffed him, so she could be the one who got him arrested. I wouldn't be surprised. Or, maybe this was a put-up job. Maybe he'd testified against his boss, and now he was in a witness protection program. They'd give him a new identity and he and Catherine would go off together and lose themselves in another state. It wasn't crazy; there was a Steve Martin movie like that, the cops hid him in a suburb. I'll get it out of her, she won't destroy the one good thing in my life.

I didn't dare go to her apartment; the neighbors know me. So I waited in my car down the street. I didn't follow her when that cop I saw last night picked her up, and later she came home in her own car. Then that same tan Chrysler that had been tailing Bobby drove up and she got inside, so I knew she was playing along with the cops again. I followed them, which wasn't easy when they got on the freeway, but I'm pretty good at this by now.

She parked at this closed-up newspaper building, in the parking lot at the side with a chain-link fence around it and a security guard at the entrance. I saw a couple of Dellacasa's catering trucks already in the lot and I knew she was working. She works in the goddamndest places. I cruised around the block, then I saw, on Broadway, lines of people waiting outside the building.

They gave me the creeps. It looked like every loser from here to hell and back was lined up on Broadway. I pulled over to the curb and yelled, what's going on? Christmas dinner, some of them yelled back. It's free, if you're hungry, get on line.

I was hungry but not for food. It struck me, what with the mob there, it was a good place to get hold of Catherine. Even with the cops protecting her, I could lose myself in the crowd, until I had my chance. I parked on a side street where a couple of trash cans had dying fires in them. Nobody was there to get warm, they'd gone for the free meals. It was cold, but I didn't feel it. I was halfway down the block when I realized I couldn't pass for homeless in my Shelter Island powder-blue sweater and pants. It was then I nearly stepped on the old woman. It was like a sign from heaven.

So when she didn't wake up I kicked her a few times. Then I started to grab her greasy cap and I tried to pull her out of her coat. Her hair was dirty grey, in thin wisps, and I could see she was bony. She woke up and started to struggle with me. We were like two dancers holding each other close in a tango. Her breath stank of alcohol and I almost got sick from the smell, but I grabbed harder at her coat. Suddenly, she started to yell, real loud and scared. The street was still deserted, but I couldn't take a chance. I had my daddy's long mechanic's screwdriver in my purse, just in case I needed it for Catherine. I pulled it out and stuck it, hard, into the old biddy's chest. What else could I do? There was nothing about Bobby in this morning's paper. Nothing about him on the news last night. I could see him slipping away from me and I'd be lost forever.

The old woman gave a gurgling sound, like she was drowning. Then she sunk down to the pavement and she didn't move anymore. I took her coat and her hat and I put them on, pulling up the torn collar of the coat to hide my face. I could hardly stand the smell—her sweat and booze and dirt—but I made myself think about fresh lilacs. I pulled out the screwdriver and wiped her blood off on her skirt. Then I walked down the dark, empty street to meet Catherine.

Chapter Thirty-Two

The *Herald Examiner* Building on Eleventh and Broadway stands out like a wedding cake abandoned in a slum. Back in 1912, William Randolph Hearst had it designed in an exuberant Mission Revival style: Moorish blue tiled roofs, arched openings, and gold-touched domes. Its main lobby changes mood and becomes a baroque extravaganza, with sweeping staircases, a marble floor, and gilded cherubs floating near the ceiling.

Upstairs, the editorial floor has the shabby grit of what used to be called the newspaper game. But Marion Davies once kept an apartment on the top floor and, rumor is, her ghost still glides along the balconies adorning the facade.

The building's only nearby competition for architectural *chutzpah* is a restored movie palace with the facade of a Mayan temple. There are some dusty bargain outlets, a Mexican restaurant, a fast-food Chinese, a Job Corps school, an insurance company's cautious headquarters building. A couple of blocks to the east is a small wholesale garment industry that would look at home in the back alleys of Hong Kong. Beyond that, Skid Row encroaches and, at night, spills over into the deserted streets.

The night of our party, a cold winter fog surrounded the streetlights and by five o'clock, with the lines of the shabby homeless waiting patiently for food, it felt as if the only cheer left in the world was in our pathetic little island of light and warmth inside the *Examiner* lobby. Between the hours of five and eight, we offered the temporary joy of a full belly.

I knew the building well. I'd placed "Help Wanted" ads at the lobby-level Classified department. Other times, I'd visited with the food editors upstairs, swapping recipes and gossip as Los Angeles achieved stardom in the culinary universe. I'd even dated a sports columnist, but I couldn't take all that fresh air on Sunday afternoons.

I liked seeing the place busy again. We'd set up serving tables cafeteria-style around the lobby. As our guests entered, they'd be directed, counterclockwise, to their dinners. First table, appetizer slices of cheese pizza. From there to a spread of tossed salad, cranberry sauce, trays of bread and butter. Next, the steam table, with turkey, stuffing, green beans, and candied yams. Completing the circuit were desserts: fruit cocktail, pumpkin and mince pies, paper cups of mixed nuts. Leaving the hands of Dellacasa's professionals, L.A.'s hungry would move along to the good ladies of the Downtown League.

The volunteers had taken over the large room, formerly sales offices, to the left of the entrance. They'd filled it with rented picnic tables and chairs. Now, as the street people sat down with their dinners, the ladies, dressed in Christmas aprons and wreathed in smiles, bustled along the tables offering juice and coffee. Mostly, the diners were mute and watchful, huddled in their frayed coats, eating steadily. If they liked the change from the drab earnestness of the missions and shelters, few showed it. Some quiet smiles to the energetic ladies of the Downtown League. A scarf loosened, a sweater opened. The poor have their own smell, compounded of unwashed clothes, bad digestion, and hopelessness. When the room became warm, and their body heat wafted up and mingled with the blithe fragrances of affluent women, I was nearly overwhelmed; I wanted to rush out into the clean night air.

I suppose I was reacting to last night's events. I was shaky. I was feeling as wary as the people who shuffled past me tonight. They took the food but rejected the gesture; they knew that the goodwill was transitory, that once the last fancy nut was finished, they'd be asked to rise and go back to the bone-chilling streets.

We were, in fact, feeding them in shifts. A quick, shivery walk outside confirmed that the line was still reaching to the end of the block. We'd planned to serve six hundred people, and it was a question now whether we'd have to stretch our supplies to feed more.

I'd seen and talked with Sally Weber earlier in the evening. We'd hugged and recounted what I viewed as my fall from grace and redemption last night (she was more generous to me than I was able, at that point, to accept). It would be another embarrassment for Dellacasa's to run out of food while nourishing the homeless—even worse, in front of the Downtown ladies, as I called Sally's peers.

I tried to do a quick mental count of the pizzas we'd warmed and served from our portable ovens, and those still stacked in one of our vans. I lost track. Better to do a real tally than trust my somewhat flawed judgment. Visions of hot cheese pizzas danced in my head as I started down the long corridor that led to the building's side entrance and the parking lot.

I remember first of all the fetid smell, then the sharp jab in my side.

"Hello, Catherine." Her mouth was against my left ear.

"Don't bother turning around. I don't think you'll recognize me. I've changed a lot."

I knew who it was. But I'd never had a conversation with her beyond a neighborly hello. So why did her voice sound familiar? It was puzzling.

"Don't try to scream," she said, jabbing me lightly with whatever she'd held at my side. "I don't want to hurt you."

For pity's sake, I told myself. This is the same conversation I'd had with Crosswaithe. Was it last year? Last night? And why were these swinish people so concerned with not hurting me?

"There's a door over here to the left," said Angela. "Let's just walk through it."

It occurred to me why her voice sounded familiar. It had the same swooping, girlish trill as a Disney Snow White. Angela, it dawned on me, was a cartoon ingenue gone bad. An insight that did not help my current predicament. I walked through the door, feeling that cold metal jab in my side.

The clatter of feet on the lobby's marble floor, the chatter, the amiable fuss of dinner being served were receding. We'd entered a stairwell. My brain went on red alert. There is something about the danger of imminent death that shakes you out of your doldrums. Don't show fear, I told myself.

I turned my head to see the pinched face, the filthy black cap, the overcoat that was a living history of stains.

"Some outfit you're wearing, Angela," I said. "And you used to dress so well."

"Hah, hah," she said, straight-faced. "I have to talk to you. This was the only way I could get near, since you have those cops baby-sitting you."

Those cops. Where were the stalwart Oaks and Tamido? If they still sat out in the parking lot they were missing all the fun.

"You could have telephoned," I said reasonably. "I'm in the book."

"Hah, hah," she repeated. "Don't make me laugh so hard. I'll bet you always know what to say, don't you?"

"Why don't you ask your questions and we'll see. Then let's both get out of here. I've got work to do, and I don't think you want to hang around." Stay calm.

"Not here, someone could walk by. Let's go upstairs." Again, the prod of metal. I didn't know whether it was a gun or a knife, but I was sure it would make a mess. I started up the stairs. At the top was the silent editorial floor, devoid of reporters, desks, phones, computer terminals, fast-food debris: the intense, twenty-four-hour life of a newspaper.

I could see moonlight hitting the balconies outside the French doors, gleaming on the echoing, empty floor on which we walked, Indian file. We stopped near a door and I turned my head back. In the moon's pale light, Angela's face was ashen, her eyes deeply recessed. I thought in surprise: she's suffering.

"It's hard to talk this way," I said. "Why don't I turn around?"

The jab told me it wasn't a good idea.

"Why was Bobby arrested?"

"He stole a valuable painting from the house where we were doing a party."

"Did you call the cops on him?"

"No, I didn't." So I lied a little. "They were following him anyway, hoping he'd lead them to you."

She thought this over. "I knew they were tailing him, I was following *them*."

Angela seemed calm enough, almost reasonable. I was relieved.

"There, now you know. Why don't we go downstairs? My friends, the cops, will be looking for me. My staff, too."

"No one saw you leave, I looked around. Sorry, Catherine, but I'm going to have to kill you now." Not one change in her voice, she was still the cartoon ingenue. I expected the Seven Dwarfs and a chorus of "Whistle While You Work."

Keep her talking while I figure this out.

"Why? I've never hurt you."

"You think I don't know you want Bobby all to yourself. Well, he's mine. And as long as you're alive, I'll have to worry." Jab.

"Angela, I swear to you, I'm not interested in Bobby at all."

"Why should I trust you?" Jab, sharper this time. "Either the FBI will help the two of you disappear—or they'll put him in jail and you'll be able to visit him, but I won't."

The FBI? I tried to edge closer to one of the French doors. Perhaps it was only latched, not locked. From the sharpness of her weapon, I'd decided it wasn't a gun. She'd used it forcefully, like a blunt weapon, but it had gone through my blouse and punctured my side. I could feel blood, warm and sticky, trickling down. My heart thumped so loudly I thought the sound was booming around the room, careening against the bare walls, rebounding and filling my ears with my own fear. I had the wild idea that if I got on the balcony I could shut her out, then I'd lean over and scream down to the hundreds of people on line below. It was probably a lousy idea, but better than dying without a fight. Here goes.

I swiveled my head, looking back toward the staircase.

"Bobby," I called into the gloom, trying to get some ecstasy into my voice. "Bobby, it's you! Come rescue me!"

She whirled around. "Where—?"

In that moment I flung myself at the French doors, my hand grabbing for the latch. I twisted it and the door gave.

Angela screamed, a sound so furious it was as if hell had opened up. She lunged for me; I pushed at the door, but before it shut her hand stabbed down and the long gleaming metal shaft pierced my left arm. I yelled in pain. She crashed through the door after me, her hands scrabbling at the screwdriver, pulling it free. We struggled; my left arm was bleeding, but I used my right hand to try to stop that searching, stabbing weapon. Her black cap fell off, and in the moonlight I could see matted red hair above a face wild with rage.

"You can't have him!" she screamed. "He'll always be mine."

I don't know what would have happened, my strength was almost used up, but then I heard this fierce shout.

"Drop it, Angela, or I'll shoot!" It was the magnificent six-foot-two bulk of Detective Oaks, standing in the corridor. In spite of my relief, I said to myself: he can't shoot now, he'll hit me.

Angela had me pinned against the balcony wall, her arm still raised. She slipped in back of me and we both looked at Oaks who stood, gun in hand, aiming at us. I could feel the tautness in her body, her chest rising and falling. Then she giggled, a pure little-girl giggle that made the hairs on the back of my neck stand up.

"Well, then," she said to me—or to no one in particular, "I won't go to jail, so I guess it's over. I'm not surprised, deep down I knew good things don't last."

She released me and, before I realized it, she had dropped her weapon and scrambled over the low wrought-iron balcony railing. For a moment her feet and hands clung to the railing. I stood frozen.

"I'll always love you, Bobby," she called into the wind, and flung herself down two stories, just missing the heads of the homeless still waiting for a free hot meal.

I was drifting along bright corridors; they were crowded and noisy. The two pizza delivery men, one on each side, kept moving me along. I heard the short one say, Don't let her sleep unless the doc says it's okay. I wasn't sleepy, I just wanted to know if we had enough food. After all, we were feeding the hungry. And the homeless. And the riot victims who'd seen everything go up in smoke. When did the violence blot out the bright blue skies? Not only do we eat on the run, now our deaths are as mass-produced as fast-food burgers. When did L.A. become take-out city? I was annoyed. Where were my pizzas? I had to feed the hungry . . .

It was five in the morning before I was released from County-USC Medical Center. Even with Paul Wang to hurry things up, I'd had to wait my turn in the Emergency Room, behind the cases brought in from car crashes, gang shootings, domestic stabbings; the addicts who'd overdosed, the drunks who'd had too much holiday too soon. Paul had rushed to my sore side as soon as Oaks and Tamido tracked him down at a cousin's wedding in Chinatown. The hospital gave us a cubbyhole; I dozed then struggled back to awareness as the sturdy Oaks and the slender, meticulous Tamido took my statement, which I repeated when Paul arrived. I was aching; I had temporary first-aid bandages on my side and around my arm; luckily, Angela had missed the bone.

After I'd assured him, with false bravery, that my hide was as tough as a thirty-minute egg, he filled me in. The police looking for Angela's car had found a street person, a woman, who'd been stabbed and her coat and hat taken. She would recover and she'd been able to describe Angela. The newly black Toyota was found nearby. Angela's suitcase contained about two thousand dollars; it also held, wrapped in a sweater, some of the jewelry that Hastings had taken from his client for safekeeping. There was a scrapbook with newspaper clippings about Hastings, the Stedman murder, and the Chase assault. She'd also pasted in several stories about Ronald Wesley and Lolly Hart. On one of these, with a picture of Lolly Hart, Angela had crossed out the actress's face with a red crayon and written over it, "Don't you dare!"

"Except for what else was taken from Hastings's safe—probably what Crosswaithe had in his money belt, but go prove it!—the case is closed."

I asked, "What will happen to Crosswaithe now, after tonight?"

Paul yawned and stretched. "With Angela dead, probably very little. We'll talk to the D.A. on Monday, but I have a hunch, since there's no one to testify against him—even as an accessory after the fact—we'll insist that he pay his estimated income tax and then we'll ship him home."

"Does he know Angela is dead?"

"Not yet. We'll break the news to him tomorrow. I think he'll be sorry he talked as much as he did—we could, after all, hold him as an accessory, he did hide her after Hastings's murder. So we'll let him sweat a little. Although he certainly has a Teflon hide—charges seem to slide off him."

I sipped my atrocious black coffee in a gummy paper cup. I'd called Nick—for the second night in a row—and reassured him that I was safe. Mario had phoned me at the hospital to say that one more death near Skid Row didn't seem to stop anyone; they'd served meals until eight o'clock and managed to have enough to feed everyone. I restrained Nick and Mario from coming to the hospital; the police, I told them, were taking excellent care of me. I didn't even want to think about what to tell Aunt Sadie.

Finally, it was my turn to get looked over and patched up. It wasn't too bad. A harassed resident gave me a tetanus shot, a new plaster on my side, and a better bandage on my arm. He patted my shoulder, told me I was a lucky girl, gave me some pills for pain with orders to see my own doctor on Monday.

Paul had promised to see me home. We walked slowly out of the Emergency entrance to see the first light make streaks on the winter sky. Sometime during the night I'd sat next to a stabbing case; we'd listened to the weather report on his boom box.

It was warming up in Los Angeles. Today, a mild Santa Ana condition would raise the temperature and sweep away the smog. The extended forecast promised more of the same for the holiday.

Christmas was in two days.

I'd be with the nearest and dearest in my life. I'd be fussed over and waited on; we'd sit around the table and take snapshots of the goose and the guests for Aunt Sadie's album; I'd get the choicest slice of pecan pie.

In January I'd go skiing with Andy and see what developed.

I said to Paul, "I'm almost afraid to take a vacation. Look what's happened to me since the last time."

"Yeh, the crazies and the hustlers. I don't know which is worse."

"Oh, the crazies. Loving someone to obsession." I was almost apologetic. "When I was fourteen and read *Wuthering Heights* I thought, how romantic to die for love. Tonight changed my mind."

"You did all right," said Paul. "You had me worried the past few weeks, but, basically, your head is on straight."

We'd reached his red Mustang; thankfully, the top was up. I was feeling many things in the predawn, but breezy wasn't one of them.

"I'm getting hungry," said Paul. "I missed a terrific wedding banquet last night. How about you? Want to stop and eat?"

I realized I hadn't had even a crust of bread since noon the day before.

"I have an aunt," said Paul, "who has this great coffee shop in Monterey Park. She's always there early for the breakfast crowd. She'll be glad to see us, even at this hour. Say, have you ever tasted Chinese porridge?"

"Why, no, I don't believe I have."

"Hers is the best."

"Then let's go."

We dodged an ambulance that was clanging up to the Emergency entrance and drove off. I leaned back and, as my eyes closed, I thought about plump, sizzling dragon-fried dumplings. Noodles are so comforting; I wondered what kinds his aunt served for breakfast.

Then I slept.